Princess of Broken Dreams

The Guardians of Light Saga

II

by Mia Herald Hill

A Mightier Than the Sword UK Publication

©2023

Princess of Broken Dreams

The Guardians of Light Saga

By Mia Herald Hill

A Mightier Than the Sword UK Publication

Paperback Edition

ISBN Paperback 978-1-99-117191-7

ISBN Hardback 978-1-99-117118-4

ISBN Kindle 978-1-99-117115-3

Copyright © Mia Herald Hill 2023

For
Scattergood, Payne, Seaton & Warner

AUTHOR'S NOTE

What follows is the account of the fall of Her Royal Highness, Queen Kasnata, Anaguran & Queterian Queen and Queen of the united peoples of Celadmore. The language of the Order is highlighted by the use of a different font in the paperback copies and in bold in the electronic format. The other languages of Celadmore are also displayed in different fonts in the paperback and digital copies, but because of e-reader formatting, it may not display properly.

THE CHARACTERS

Queen Kasnata	Queen of the Order & Nosfa kingdom. Wife of Mercia
King Mercia Nosfa VI	King of Nosfa kingdom. Husband of Kasnata
General Lord Rathe Bird	General of Nosfa
Phoenix General Marissa	General of Kasnata's Phoenix division
Kestrel General Amalia	General of Kasnata's Kestrel division
Hawk General Kia	General of Kasnata's Hawk division
Eagle General Hesla	General of Kasnata's Eagle division
Condor General Samara	General of Kasnata's Condor division
Vulture General Quisla	General of Kasnata's Vulture division
Raven General Misna	General of Kasnata's Infiltration division
Horsemistress Cara	Horse mistress of the Order
Swordmistress Anna	Sword mistress of the Order
Bowmistress Serra	Bow mistress of the Order
Horsemaster Horace	Horse master of the Order
Swordmaster Oswin	Sword master of the Order
Bowmaster Wist	Bow master of the Order
Benaiah	Master of the Forge
Cassandra	Warrior, mercenary, pirate and spy. Guardian of the Wilds
The Abbott	Warrior, mercenary, priest and spy. Guardian of the Spire
Hermia Nosfa	Former Queen of Nosfa
Tola	Hero of the war of the east, Rathe's second in

	command
Lord Haston Bird	Lord of Mercia Nosfa's court
Shaul	A Queterian, also known as Tam
Methanlan	A Queterian, also known as Sidney
Rosla Nosfa	Former King of Nosfa
Lady Marcia Bird	A lady, deceased
Lady Mia Bird	Forced consort to King Mercia Nosfa.
Jephthah	Shield of Hermia. A bodyguard
Haman	Leader of the Gibborim
Mathias	Assassin
Neesa	Assassin, Bodyguard of Mercia. A Valian
General Avner	General of Kasnata's Order of the Hound
General Shamgar	General of Kasnata's Order of the Bear
General Yoav	General of Kasnata's Order of the Wolf
The Baron of Fintry	Mercia's steward and dogsbody
Jack	A soldier of Nosfa
Harry	A soldier of Nosfa
Duke Kelmar DeLacey	Regent of Delma, a nobleman
Joab	Shadow of Hermia. A bodyguard
Layla	Shadow of Hermia. A bodyguard
King Baruch Delich	King of Delma
Queen Adina Delich	Queen of Delma
Helez	Shield of the Gibborim
Asahel	Shield of the Gibborim
Leinad	Prince of Nosfa & the Order
Kasna	Princess of Nosfa & the Order

Kia	Princess of Nosfa & the Order
Payne	Healer of the Order
Scattergood	Leader of the Eight
Merinda	One of the Eight
Lucinda	One of the Eight
Warner	One of the Eight
Resha	One of the Eight
Colm	One of the Eight
Vaike	One of the Eight
Adino	One of the Eight
Jericho	Brother of Scattergood
General Seaton	General of Nosfa

PROLOGUE

Magic has all but disappeared from Celadmore. Many civilisations have graced the face of these lands. Empires have risen and fallen like the sun. Each people had a magic they cultivated, magic they could summon and control, all within the gift of the goddess.

But when each civilisation fell, the secrets of their magic disappeared with them. Scrolls and parchments contain secrets of magics that have long passed out of usage, some magics that no longer have any power.

Only one type of magic still exists on Celadmore: blood magic. Tied to the blood of the goddess, not all those born of the blood can wield it. Those of the Order have all but ceased using the craft, but the Valians have kept it alive.

The Valians, a sect of the Order that split from them when their civilisation was still young. Valia, Queen of the Anaguras, had caused a civil war. She had been a practitioner of blood magic, and it had driven her mad. Granddaughter of Anagura and Queteria, daughter of Brigid and Allamonto, the power of their blood was also their weakness; their bodies too weak to survive the power of the goddess that coursed through their veins.

Queteria and Allamonto lived to see the madness of Valia. Her mind so clouded by paranoia, she believed her own sisters coveted her throne. In the city of Queteria, the father of their people ruled, his son-in-law holding power in the city that was named for him.

As Valia's madness became more apparent, her sisters, Landra and Mala went to their father and grandfather for help. Their brothers were with their father. They left their two youngest sisters behind. When they returned, Landra and Mala led an army with their kin beside them.

Valia had prepared and as the army approached, demanding that she lay down her weapons and submit the throne to her grandfather. Valia's mind had become so warped that she no longer possessed any form of morality. Her belief in her sovereign rights was absolute; she no longer believed that any law could govern her, or any man.

She ordered her youngest sister, Ina, to be brought to the battlements. Ina was barely four years old. In a single stroke, Valia severed Ina's head from her body.

Dana, the last of the five daughters of Brigid, was so stricken with rage and grief at seeing her youngest sister murdered that she attacked. She was eight years old. Valia's royal guard impaled Dana on their spears, Valia laughing cruelly at how pathetic her sisters were.

When the army arrived at the city, Valia ordered the bodies of Ina and Dana to be catapulted over the battlements onto those that stood below.

Thus began the civil war. It was bloody and brief. Valia had many that were loyal to her, but the sheer number of those in the combined armies of Allamonto and Queteria overwhelmed the Valian forces.

Though Valia was defeated, the war was not without casualties. Mala, the last daughter of the Order, was made queen. Those that had fought for Valia were asked to swear allegiance to the new queen. Those that refused were exiled.

They formed the Valian Order and swore to one day retake the throne for the descendants of Valia, the true ruler of the Order, marked for greatness by her mastery of blood magic.

My lady was a woman of honour. She fought for the lives of her people, and her actions were a tribute to our lineage. Her daughters were a shining reflection of their mother in their dedication to their training and the teachings of the Order. Her reign was marred by war and scandal that she stood strong in spite of, her strength of character was something that all our people should aspire to emulate. There is no one that has ever walked this realm that I would more gladly or willingly follow.

Condor General Samara

Aide to Queen Kasnata

Chapter 1

2431GL 93RD Spregan

"The battlefield; a place where heroes are made, legends thrive, myths enthral and lives are broken,"

A sword plunged into the barren, dusty ground. The wind whipped ash and dust in tiny cyclones around the shining silver metal of the blade. Deep, distant eyes gazed out at the ruins that lay before them. The light was fast bleeding into dark, but the eyes did not struggle to see.

All things had changed, not one element of what had been now remained for her. Kia, youngest daughter of Queen Kasnata and King Mercia Nosfa VI, shook her hair and listened to the sound of the bones tied to her warrior braids chink together and echo across the barren land.

She had once been a prisoner, living under the threatening veil of her father's tyranny, separated from her mother and denied the freedom to even leave the palace. Her older sister, Kasna, and their older brother, Leinad, had been held as hostages to force their mother and her army to march against their father's enemies.

Kia and Kasna had escaped, but Leinad was still held hostage. He was being held in the capital, under the watchful gaze of their father's most loyal lap dogs; the princesses had been sent away to one of the most remote corners of the kingdom and kept under house arrest, valuable not as heirs but as bargaining chips.

That had been until Duke Kelmar DeLacey, Regent of the nation of Delma, had come to call on them. In one night he and his men had eliminated the guards, maids, tutors and other members of the household staff, all to kidnap the princesses.

But he had failed. He had failed all because of Neesa, an assassin and mistress of King Mercia. She had killed the men that had accompanied Kelmar to the castle but had missed those that were waiting further out, at his camp. Neesa had forced Kelmar to retreat, and then disappeared, leaving the princesses to their own devices.

The girls had fled to the wilds and had been found by Mathias, and it was because of him they were still free. Mathias, his cousin, Tola, and General Renta of their mother's army had all ensured that they were kept safe and from the hands of Kelmar.

Renta had been captured, had given her life so that the princesses could escape from Kelmar's grasp.

They had found refuge in the village of Tulna and now trained with their warriors to hone their skills, avenge the death of Renta and re-join their mother as an asset, not as burdens.

"Such needless destruction," Kia muttered as Mathias approached. He had taken the princess out on patrol with the small group of warriors from Tulna. The warriors often spent days out patrolling the wilds around the village.

"War breeds such things," Mathias shrugged as he stopped next to the young princess.

"War brings nothing but sadness and pain; there is little honour in it," Kia sighed as she repeated the words she had heard Kania utter. Mathias laughed.

"War is sometimes the only option, though it should be a last resort."

Kia looked at the older warrior. She had very little training and no guidance in matters of war, save for the things she gleaned from listening to her mother argue with her father when she was barely old enough to understand the language, let alone grasp the complicated politics that governed the alliances between the nine kingdoms.

To her, Mathias seemed to know all there was to know about war. He had fought in many battles, survived through the ambling alliances and the conflicts that had resulted. His opinions had been formed from experience, not studying history or plotting to see the war turned to his own advantage.

He did not see war as simply as Kasna did. Kia's older sister saw only fighting to win and destroying the enemy that stood against her, though Kelmar was the only enemy she had ever faced and in none of their encounters with the Duke had they come out the victors.

But neither had Kelmar won, the princesses had remained out

of reach and would for as long as they remained in the Oasis of Tulna.

"Then why are we at war now?" Kia asked, turning expectant eyes towards the horizon.

"For the reason that most wars are fought; the greed of those that rule," Mathias shrugged. He knew that the princess wanted more of an explanation than he was willing to provide and that more questions would follow, but there was little time for that now, as Mathias had been sent to fetch the young girl.

"There is time to meditate on such philosophical questions after I have taken you back to Kania. She has prepared the feast for the festival that you cannot miss the start of, no matter how much you would prefer to gaze at the horizon," He smiled down at the daughter of Kasnata, who nodded and followed the Roencian back to Tulna.

Tulna was not a large place; to call it a village was generous, though it was far more important to the realm of Celadmore than most of the large cities, even though very few knew of its existence.

Tulna was one of the Free Cities of Celadmore, one of the few places within the land of Nosfa that did not fall under the control and rule of King Mercia Nosfa VI. It was led by Kania and Nodarto, an older couple that served their people as though the village occupants were their masters.

It had seemed strange to Kia, but Kasna had found their style of leadership fascinating. The older princess had barely left Kania's side since they had arrived in Tulna. Kia could see her sister was desperate to learn from the village matriarch in the same way that Kia had wanted to learn from her mother for as long as she could remember.

Both girls knew that they would be expected to lead the people of the Order upon their mother's death; or at least hoped they would. Leinad, though first in line for the throne, would be king of Nosfa and could not rule both kingdoms under the law of the Order, nor would the will of the people of the Order allow such a thing.

It was a law that had been created after the tyranny of Valia. Valia had been named Queen of the Order; however, she had desired power, and through this desire for dominance had come paranoia.

It had led to the murder of the youngest of the royal line and the only civil war to have been fought amongst members of the Order. It was why Kasnata's husband was king of his own land, but held no such title amongst those of the Order.

As Kia walked back into the village with Mathias, she felt the air around her change. There was a reverent stillness that had descended on the place that seemed to steal her voice from her throat. There was something about it that made her want to weep.

Mathias smiled as he saw the emotion welling up in her eyes and tried to remember what it was like to experience the atmosphere of the festival for the first time.

He steered the young girl to the village square where the entire population of the village was gathered. All were sat in silence upon the ground, in rapt silence, barely daring to breathe.

Kania and Nodarto sat with the Abbott, Tola and Kasna in front of a long wooden altar that had three large candles stood upon it. Kia was steered to the same place and sat, waiting for the last of the light to fade.

There were no lights shining anywhere in the village so that, as the last of the light bled from the sky, the gathered villagers and guests were plunged into darkness.

Kania's voice drifted out from the darkness, her voice soft and quiet, yet as clear as the tone of ringing silver bells.

"Night has come to these lands that we call home, all light has been turned into dark. Though our eyes cannot see you, our hearts, they are close to you and we know that you will bring back the light,"

Her voice hung in the air, almost like a shroud over those that were seated when the drums began. The first beat caused Kasna and Kia to jump and squeal as it broke through the reverence of the moment. It was like a hammer shattering glass as it pounded, reverberating off the buildings of the village. It echoed and died, the silence replacing it again, but the atmosphere had changed.

Instead of reverence and overwhelming emotion there was now a sense of excitement that was brewing amongst the residents of Tulna. Another drum beat sounded, followed by another and another, building as more drums joined in until the air was full of noise. Kia felt a smile spread across her face that she couldn't explain as the drums reached a climax and light burst from the torches that stood around the festival square.

The villagers all cheered and music began to play as dancing broke out so that the square was filled with joy and colour. Kania smiled in a warm, motherly fashion as she sat down beside Nodarto.

Tola was sat with a sour expression upon his face; he had not smiled since Renta had died. The weight of his grief had caused dark circles to form around his eyes and the princesses had heard him wandering the halls of the main house during the night, his mind and heart so full of hate that he was unable to lay down and rest.

Nodarto clapped along to the music, his happiness at seeing the villagers expressing their joy clear in every contour of his ancient face. Mathias stood behind the giant drums, beating them with wild abandon but still managing to keep perfect time.

Kasna looked at her sister and smiled as she took her by the hand and dragged her out into the throng of the villagers so that they could both dance.

"Do you even know what you are doing?" Kia asked her older sister with exasperation.

"No, but does it matter? It looks like fun!" Kasna replied with a grin.

"You have never wanted to have fun before, you always wanted to practice with our weapons and avoid the guards and servants," Kia laughed as she watched her sister attempt to copy the dance that some of the other women were doing.

"But we weren't safe then, right now, right now we are!" Kasna looked completely different to her sister, she was almost carefree as she tripped over her own feet and struggled to keep time, the idea of relaxing being completely alien to both daughters of Kasnata.

Kania was glad to see the two princesses feeling so comfortable as they moved amongst the celebrating villagers, though Tola's mood worried her, as did the fact that she had heard nothing from Cassandra.

It had been weeks now since the Guardian of the Wilds and the assassin Joab had ridden out of Tulna into the night, trying to find Lady Mia Bird. The daughter of Lord Bird of Afdanic had been rescued by Joab from the clutches of King Mercia Nosfa VI, but when they had reached Tulna, the king's lover and assassin, Neesa, had been waiting and had kidnapped Mia when the young lady had retired to her room for the night.

Kania was not worried for Cassandra; there was little reason to worry herself when her daughter had honed her skills over centuries of studying warfare. It was Joab that she worried for.

Joab had been brought to Tulna by a woman named Layla. He had been found in wilds, cold and alone with no memory of who he had been before Layla had found him. He had been brought to Kania and Nodarto, as Layla had seen a spark in him that she felt would make him a suitable candidate for undergoing the training of a Shadow.

When Mia had been born, Nodarto had seen her future, had seen the pain and heartbreak she was to endure at the hands of Mercia, and that pain was something that they could prevent as part of their wider duty to the realm.

So Joab had been trained for months and years for one task, to be the Shadow of Lady Mia Bird, to rescue her from the hands of Mercia and protect her from the pain that she would have otherwise endured. What neither had foreseen was how the relationship between Joab and Mia had developed.

There was an unspoken understanding that the relationships that formed between Shadows, Shields and their protectees would not involve fraternisation and though it was clear that Joab had observed those rules, thus far, there was something more in his heart for her and something more in the Lady Mia's heart for Joab.

Watching him take off into the night in such a reckless fashion after her had told Kania that there was cause to worry for him, and her mind would not be put to rest until they were both safely back in Tulna.

Tola had been forced to attend the festival by Nodarto, the older man refusing to allow him to fume in peace. Since Renta had been killed by Duke Kelmar DeLacey, the Roencian had plotted his revenge, dreamed of how he would make DeLacey suffer for every drop of her blood that the Duke had spilled.

Kelmar sat brooding. So far he had failed in his mission to capture the two princesses of Nosfa and the Order, and had become so frustrated with his own failure, he had ordered his own men to attack and kill the young girls.

He knew that had he returned to Delma with the blood of the daughters of Kasnata on his hands, then there would have been no force on Celadmore that would have kept him from suffering at the hands of the Queen of the Order.

Then there was Renta to consider. He had taken no pleasure in killing Kasnata's general, especially in the way he had chosen to inflict torture upon her, leaving her to bleed instead of offering her a noble warrior's death. She had stolen his victory from him in securing the princesses' safety and he had hated her for that. His anger had been so all-consuming that he had wanted to inflict pain and suffering on the general for denying him his victory.

Renta had managed to kill two of his men and render three of others unfit for duty and the Duke wasn't entirely convinced that they would ever be able to fight again.

Renta had been careful not to kill all those that had assaulted her, but instead, had delayed DeLacey's forces for long enough so that Mathias had been able to lead the party to Tulna, where they were now out of his reach. Kelmar had taken his frustrations out on the Condor General of the Order in a manner that he considered beneath him.

"I'm sorry, Renta," Kelmar said softly to himself and shook his head. There were many things in his life that he regretted and how he had chosen to murder Renta, the satisfaction he felt and the words he had said to the woman he would have once called friend, would haunt him for the rest of his life. He had left men behind in order to prepare her body to be sent back to Kasnata. The three men would deliver it and then return home to report to the king and queen. He at least hoped that they would be allowed to return to Delma after.

He knew that Kasnata was a woman of honour, who would not harm his men for the actions that Kelmar had taken, however, the other members of the Order, especially those that served under the Condor General, might not be so understanding.

From where he sat, Kelmar could see the oasis of Tulna on the horizon, or at least he could see the lights in the largest building in which the princesses were now safe. There were plenty of old wives' tales about the oasis and those who lived there, but Kelmar had not expected to meet with a warrior as strong as the woman that had single-handedly caused his men to retreat. There had been something in her eyes that made him wonder whether the rumours of immortals residing there had more truth to them than most realised. But whether Tulna held immortals or not, he had to retrieve the princesses.

"Rider approaching," a lookout shouted, breaking into Kelmar's train of thought. "Messenger."

Kelmar stood and moved his gaze from Tulna to where the lookout was indicating the messenger's approach. The messenger seemed to be in no hurry to arrive, his horse was walking at a sedate gait, not even a hint of swear or foam on its coat. The messenger wore a hood that obscured his face; even when he was less than a stone's throw away from the Duke DeLacey, and a thick cloak that seemed to be rather unnecessary given the warmer temperature of the desert, even in the depths of Wentrus.

"You have news for me?" Kelmar asked with irritation as the messenger finally reach him and dismounted.

"Impatient as always," the deep voice that greeted Kelmar from inside the hood caused the Duke to drop to his knees.

"Your majesty," he stammered.

"Get up," King Baruch Delich said in a bored voice, "I have

travelled a long way to talk with you and do not need to waste time on ceremony out here."

The Duke rose to his feet and looked at the king. It had been a long time since Kelmar had seen him, but not long enough for all the changes that the Duke could see in the king's appearance to have occurred.

As he lowered the hood, Kelmar could see that the king had aged at least ten years since their last meeting and there was a distracted look in his eyes, one of focusing on thoughts and problems of far away, rather than on the here and now.

"The princesses are in Tulna," Kelmar announced.

"And you are not," the king said disdain. "What happened to all the men that were with you? There is but a fraction of them here now. You were supposed to acquire the princesses in the Palace of Abergorlech."

Kelmar bowed his head in shame. He had not yet sent a report to Delma on their progress and he knew that he king riding out to find them was a sign of how displeased he was but the lack of results.

"Neesa was waiting for us. We dispatched the household but the whore of the king killed the men that I took with me to the fortress. The princesses escaped and were met by Mathias of Roenca, he kept them out of my reach. There was one occasion where we had them cornered but General Renta of the Order and Tola of Roenca stopped us," Kelmar explained, trying not to turn his description of events into an excuse for failing in his duty.

"Where are they all now?" the king growled.

"Tola and Mathias are with the princesses in Tulna. Renta is dead," the Duke confirmed.

"Good, then at least the barbarian bitch will know what it is to lose someone she cares about," the king snarled.

"Sire?" Kelmar asked in confusion.

"Prince Jayden is dead. He was murdered by the bitch Queen when the prince and our armies came across her and a small portion of her army," the king spat on the floor.

"My apologies, sire. My prayers – " Kelmar began, but the king cut him off by raising his hand.

"Save your fawning, you disgraceful worm. You will get those princesses out of that place and return them to Delma, even if it kills you. And if extracting both of them is too taxing for you, then I will settle for one of them," the king snapped and remounted.

"Sire, won't you stay in our camp tonight, then tomorrow I can send some men with you as an escort to ensure you return to Delma safely," Kelmar offered. The king looked down at the Duke from astride his horse and scoffed.

"There is no protection your men can offer me, DeLacey."

CHAPTER 2

2431GL 93RD SPREGAN

Methanlan rolled over and yawned. The sun was weakly rising over the camp of the combined forces of Nosfa and the Order. The camp fire, which sat in the middle of the ring of thin tents that the soldiers of Nosfa used, had gone out in the night, dowsed by the freshly fallen snow.

He shivered as he rose and started to dig out the ashes mixed with a snowy slush that lay in the grate so he could build a fresh fire to see his camp mates and him through another cold day laying siege to the city of Delma.

Methanlan and his comrade, Shaul, were both men of the Order, born to the line of Queteria, that had been assigned by Queen Kasnata to find out what was going on amongst the ranks of her husband's soldiers.

It was a task similar to those that Methanlan had performed many times for the Queen of the Order and one he was uniquely suited for. As a boy, Methanlan had found that lying came as easily to him as telling the truth. His father and mother had both been worried by this and had taken him to General, then Captain, Avner.

The captain had been a young man, but was able to recognise talent, despite his age. So Methanlan had been accepted into the ranks of the Order of the Hound and it did not take long for

Methanlan to not only develop his skills as a warrior but also to hone his silver tone.

So practised did he become at lying that often times his lies were more convincing than when he was telling the truth. It took several years before he was assigned tasks to infiltrate enemy camps under the guise of different identities that all had a root in his own past, just so that the lies had a narrow frame to work within, limits to stop the boy with a vivid imagination getting too carried away.

"You're awake early, Sidney," a tired voice greeted Methanlan as he stacked the wood that lay next to the fire pit, wrapped in shark skin to keep it dry enough to light in the snowy conditions.

"Morning, Jack. I won't call it good as it can't be when it's this cold," Methanlan replied grimly. His feet hadn't been warm for days and he was painfully aware of the snow melting through his sodden foot wraps that were more suited to desert climates than the tundraic conditions around the city of Delma. "How was night duty?"

"Cold. Dull. Those Delmarians are keeping their heads down. Think the sight of the barbarian horde is making them wish they'd never been born," Jack said sourly.

"Barbarians that are all snug in their little huts," Methanlan sneered in reply. When they had first arrived, the queen had ordered the camps set out in identical fashion, the sloping wooden roofs propped up on four posts over each tent, the snow packed into walls and breaks against the weather. For the first few days, all those under the banner of both nations had slept in warm and dry conditions.

This had not lasted though as the commanders of the army of Nosfa petitioned to move their camp closer to the walls of the city of Delma. Kasnata and General Rathe had agreed, but the same provisions had not been made for their new camp site as those in the rest of the camp. The merchant train had made a home between the two army camps, but had the sense to copy the design that the Order had created.

The shelters, which had been designed by Benaiah, were simple enough to construct and were lashed to the ground in the same fashion as the tents. Yet they were strong enough to bear the weight of the snow falls and leaves were spread across the ground in each of the tents beneath these shelters to keep them warm underfoot.

Since then there had been a lot of complaints from the men of Nosfa at sleeping in their flimsy tents in the cold weather when the Order were sleeping in shelters that were not only warm, but weren't prone to collapsing under the weight of freshly fallen snow.

After the first week of setting their second camp, there had been so many instances of men waking up to find their comrades in the next tent had been buried alive and died from the cold, or suffocated in their sleep, that men went to bed praying to their Gods and Goddesses that they wouldn't share a similar fate.

The commanders of Nosfa had argued that the Spregan heat would soon melt the snow and there was little point wasting the energy and time of the men when there was a siege to prepare for.

But as the days ticked by, the weather was no warmer, in fact, if anything, it was getting colder and the men of Nosfa began to grow discontented, their anger directed towards the barbarians of the Order as much as their own commanders.

"Sodding bastards," Jack spat as he huddled towards the small fire that Methanlan had managed to spark into life.

The heavy snowfall over the last few weeks had meant that their original camp had become buried so they couldn't withdraw to their previous camp without needing to put as much effort into clearing their old camp as it would to craft a new one.

"You seen them lately?" Methanlan asked as he retrieved some leaves and a small pot from his tent. He picked up a handful of snow and threw it into the pot and began to melt it over the fire.

"The wolf pack? Yeh, they were out there last night. Flaming crazy buggers, the lot of them. Even in this cold they still don't wear shirts or armour," Jack said shaking his head.

The wolf pack were the men of the Order of the Wolf, warriors under the command of General Yoav.

"What do you think they're doing?" They've been out there for several days now," Methanlan asked as the water started to boil and he threw in a handful of leaves.

"I dunno, but whatever it is, it's something important. Not even the commanders know what they are up to," Jack smiled to himself.

"Oh?" Methanlan replied, noting the look on Jack's face.

"Yeh, Harry overheard them the other night. They don't know what's going on and it's making them nervous. They say that the Queen seduced General Bird and now he's doing her bidding instead of the king's," Jack lowered his voice and leaned towards Methanlan in a conspiratorial manner.

"Never met a man that didn't do the bidding of a woman that seduced him," Methanlan said with a grin.

"But this is different," Jack insisted. "One of the other hands spotted a man who looked like the general dressed as one of the wolf pack. She's corrupted him, made him into her pet," he finished sending scandalised.

"The Bird's become a wolf?" Methanlan asked with scepticism, "Next you'll be saying the queen's an immortal with the powers of a witch during the full moon," he snorted.

"Don't talk about them!" Jack begged as he glanced around to make sure none had appeared. Witches had not been seen since before Queen Tsmara and King Jadow had chaired the council of nations. It was rumoured that they were extinct, hunted down by the wolf pack, the dog pack and the bear pack, but others were certain they were still out there, plotting with the dark powers until they could resurrect themselves to full power. "You might not think it's right, but no one has seen the queen since we arrived."

"I haven't seen Lieutenant Giles since we got here, but I'm not overly worried," Methanlan joked as another soldier crawled from his tent.

"You two don't half make a bleeding racket," the man complained as he clapped his arms around his body in the cold morning air.

"Harry, I'm just telling Sid about what you said about the queen and the general," Jack explained as Harry settled down next to the fire as Methanlan rummaged around for the small metal cups they had for the boiled water and leaves.

"You got to the part where the queen's pregnant yet?" Harry asked with a devilish grin and Methanlan dropped the cups and burst into laughter.

"That's more ridiculous than the queen being a witch," the Queterian looked at both men with disbelief as he gathered up the cups.

"No, it's true; Nifty was saying he saw her the other day, her belly swollen up like she'd been eating all the camp rations," Harry said earnestly.

"I heard that Commander Grice sent word to the king about it," Jack said solemnly.

"Well then, we should be happy we aren't the Bird then!"

Methanlan said with a grin as he poured out three cups of boiled water and leaves and sat drinking them with Jack and Harry until Harry reported for duty and Jack tried to get some sleep.

Methanlan cleared up the cups and pot, storing them in his tent. As he crawled back into the thin canvas Shaul was sat looking worried.

"You heard all that?" Methanlan whispered.

"Yeh, What do you think?" Shaul asked his old friend.

"We should walk the camp; see what others are saying about it," Methanlan said seriously.

"What is Wolfblood up to?" Shaul asked as the two men stepped out into the camp and began to walk between the different camp fires.

"I don't know, he isn't with the Order out in the woods right now though. Abendigo was leading them when I saw them the other night," Shaul said as he narrowly missed tripping over an anchor rope.

"I wonder if they are scouting around the city, looking for supply lines and weaknesses that could be exploited," Methanlan mused as he and Shaul waved at a few families faces from patrols and night duty.

"Would make sense, well we can be sure they weren't scouting for witches at least," Shaul grinned.

"You think they're really all gone?" Methanlan asked looking at his friend with great interest.

"I don't think those wars between nations would have started if they were still out there," Shaul smiled, "Or if they had, there would be reports of the dead coming back to life and stealing children off into the night."

"I see your point," Methanlan shrugged but offered nothing of his own thoughts on the matter, finding the eight children in the desert had set his mind wondering about witches returning and so far, nothing he had seen had done anything to change his mind.

The two men walked in silence, listening to snatches of conversation and soldiers' gossip. Most of it was theories on what the wolf pack were doing; most outlandish and some downright disturbing, but there were also a lot of rumours that the king was coming, that the queen was pregnant and the General Bird was guilty of treason.

After an hour of walking through the camp, Methanlan returned to his tent to prepare for the patrol Commander Grice had ordered Methanlan to take the vanguard whilst Shaul slipped into the merchants' caravan that lay between the two camps and surreptitiously made his way to the quarters of the queen to report.

General Rathe Bird sneezed for the fourth time in fifteen minutes. Abendigo had taken the general out with the other members of the Order of the Wolf to scout around for any signs of Duke Kelmar DeLacey returning to the city.

It had been weeks since the Queen had received the news of Renta's death at the hands of the Duke and that her daughters were now safely out of his reach in the village of Tulna. However, there had been no sign of the Duke returning to Delma and this worried the queen more than she wanted to admit.

The Order of the Wolf had been ordered to search for any signs of the Duke. During the day the warrior scouted the area on the far side of the camp and at night they searched the land between the city and the siege camp, but so far they had found nothing.

General Bird had been taken under the wing of General Yoav and was learning the techniques that the Order of the Wolf used in battle, which involved wearing their armour and traipsing through the snow as animals instead of men.

When he had returned to the tent that he shared with the queen, he had found Kasnata waiting for him with warm and dry furs as well as hot mead laced with lemon. He had been so cold and exhausted that he hadn't been able to thank her before he fell asleep and when he woke the queen had already risen. The general could hear the raised voices of Amalia and Misna coming from the war tent.

"Morning Pup," Yoav growled as Rathe stepped out of his tent in search of food.

"Wolfblood," Rathe greeted the grizzled general, who beckoned for the young man to follow him.

"There's going to be some trouble in camp today," the general of the Order of the Wolf explained as he led Rathe to where breakfast was being served.

"Oh? What kind of trouble?" he asked, trying to sound nonchalant, trying to hide that his stomach had dropped at the thought of danger.

"There's a small convoy under a flag of parlay coming in from the wilds, looks like the flag of Delma above the flag of parlay. Everyone is to stay on their toes," Yoav said in a low voice.

"What would a convoy be doing coming in from the wilds under a flag of parlay?" Rathe asked as he was handed hot water and a thick hot porridge that was full of chunks of meat.

"Who can say? Avner is going to meet with the convoy and see what they want as the queen is no condition to go charging about the landscape, and the less people who know about her current condition, the better," Wolfblood frowned at the general, who had the decency to blush.

The older general liked the heir to the seat of Afdanic; he found that he not only a man of honour but was incredibly gifted when it came to warfare and fighting now that so many of his bad habits had been broken. It would be a cold day on Celadmore when General Rathe Bird had to be rescued by the queen in the middle of battle.

But for all this, he did not approve of the relationship that the young noble man of Nosfa had developed with the queen. It threatened not only the safety of Rathe and Kasnata but also the people of the Order. Something that King Jadow and Queen Tsmara would never have allowed to happen.

"What are Misna and Amalia arguing about?" Rathe asked, changing the subject with as much tact as he could.

"That is a question you don't want the answer to, Pup," Wolfblood said grimly. Rathe took the hint and let the subject drop. He wasn't disliked by the people of the Order but it was clear to him that none of them trusted him and those that knew the queen was pregnant with his child, for the most part, treated him with tolerance that was a thin veil over their disdain and disapproval.

Rathe came from a world where politics was a national sport, but he had not expected to find so many amongst the Order that were concerned with it and the implications of something as trivial as a love affair.

CHAPTER 3

"It is not trivial!" Misna tried to keep her voice even as she spoke in the presence of her queen on such a delicate matter, but was finding it extremely difficult.

Kasnata was sat upon her throne, her hands clasped over her belly as she watched her two generals argue. The purple and silk robes that the queen wore rippled with every movement she made, the furs that lay over them causing the fabric to flow rather than float.

Her hair was pinned back, held in place by ravens' wings that sat behind the circlet of silver and onyx she wore, marking her as the ruler of the Order.

It has been three days since there had been any peace in her war tent and there seemed to be no end of problems to be argued over. The most popular point to disagree upon at present was General Rathe Bird and the children that Kasnata carried of his blood.

It was understandable that they were worried; under the law of the Order, there were no penalties to be paid, however, under the law of Nosfa, there were consequences that not even Kasnata would be able to avoid.

"Pretending that there are no issues to be dealt with or that this will simply go away if we ignore it is irresponsible," Misna continued.

"It IS trivial! There are other things we should be more concerned with at present," Amalia said, her voice quieter than Misna's, but her frustration was still apparent.

"You think that the weather being this bad this late in the year is more important than what could happen to her majesty?" Misna asked, sneering slightly.

"We are at war; the queen's life has been in danger since she left Anamoore, whether it is from the Valians or from the king, she is far better protected since she started sharing the general's bed," Amalia replied flatly. "How many assassination attempts have there been on her life since then? What the king may or may not do, what he is entitled to do, what the law of his people says he must do, these are all things that are trivial when we are faced with a siege of a city, a thaw that has not come and that we have still not uncovered who it was that sent Ariella to assassinate the queen."

"You are not a gatherer of information, Amalia. You are an archer," Misna spat.

"And you are a glorified assassin that should have the safety of the queen as her highest priority," Amalia glowered.

"You dare to question my loyalty?" Misna snarled and drew her sword.

"Enough," Kasnata said firmly. She didn't have to raise her voice in order to silence the two women. "Amalia, whoever the assassins are, then it is Misna's responsibility to discover their identities. If she would benefit from your help, I am certain she will ask. Misna, it is not for you or anyone else to question my relationship with General Rathe, he is my choice, the consequences of my actions are mine alone to bear. They will not affect my people," the queen said as she slowly rose from her makeshift throne and Misna sheathed her weapon.

"Your highness, the consequences of your actions will affect your people, I mean no disrespect, but -" Misna said in a much more even voice.

"But you think I have been foolish," Kasnata smiled. The queen of the Order was well aware of her folly in allowing herself to become so involved with the general from Nosfa. Lord Rathe Bird was an honourable man, but he was not a man of the Order and she was a married woman. Though considered barbarians by the majority of the people of Celadmore, the Order were more traditional than most realised and adultery, even when in the case of an unhappy, politically matched marriage that Mercia and Kasnata were locked in, was something that was still frowned upon.

Kasnata had spent her life living a lonely and miserable existence until she had met Rathe, and though she was aware of how dangerous and stupid her decision was, to her, the happiness she had enjoyed for the past weeks and days far outweighed whatever she would face.

She had spent her entire life thinking of her people, of putting others first, of place the needs of her people and those of other nations above her own. It was weakness and selfishness that led to her indulging her emotions, coupled with a naïve notion of romance.

Having been injured during an ambush and nursed by the general when the two had been cut off from the rest of her army. They were alone for days, living off what could be foraged whilst the queen healed. So removed from reality as they were, it had been a moment when the queen was free of the burden of her throne, the worry for the lives of her children and the shadow of her parents.

Kasnata's parents, Queen Tsmara and King Jadow, had been legends in their own lifetime, an idyllic couple that had not only been respected by their people, but by the other nations and their rulers across Celadmore. They had been taken when Kasnata had been little more than a child and many of the actions she had taken in her youth had been shaped and formed by straining to live up to the expectations of her people.

It had been in her attempts to reach the unobtainable mantle her parents had held that had led her to marry Mercia. He hadn't been a terrible man when she had first met him and there were qualities in his character that even to this day the queen found attractive, but when they had been wed, the darker side of his nature had been revealed.

His thirst for power and his desire to rule over all of Celadmore regardless of cost that verged on madness at times, madness that scared Kasnata more than she wanted to admit, had all developed over the years as they gained a more solid grip over his heart and mind.

Stories and rumours from the court all said that he had grown up as a spoiled child, murdered his father and his mother in order to seize the throne and silenced all those that would speak out against his rule. Many believed he had been born as wicked and cruel as he was, but Kasnata knew better.

She had watched her husband slowly disappearing into his obsession of ruling over Celadmore, watched the madness take over more and more gradually, yes, she had been a tool to acquire as far as he was concerned, a weapon to be wielded, but he had slowly been getting worse as the years passed and that concerned Kasnata more than the consequences of her affair with the general.

"I mean no disrespect, your highness," Misna apologised.

"But?" Kasnata asked with a raised eyebrow.

"But you cannot continue to conduct yourself in this manner; it is not fitting of a queen of our people," the general finished, pursing her lips as she spoke.

"Not fitting?" Kasnata toyed with the expression as she rose to her feet and walked to where the two women stood. Misna watched as she descended from the small dais that Benaiah had constructed for the throne to sit upon to elevate the queen above all those that would stand before her.

Though the general had misgivings about the wisdom of the queen's love affair, she respected and loved her monarch more than most realised.

"Your people expect you to be without fault," Amalia explained, though she disagreed with Misna on many things, she understood how the general felt.

"Then I have failed them every day since I was born," Kasnata said with a wry smile. "If I had not made so many mistakes we would not be at war, so many of our people would not have abandoned the Order for that of the Valians, my children would not be in danger, I would not be married to a man who was not of our people and I doubt I would have ever have met the general that you both find so disagreeable," the queen shrugged as she looked between her generals.

"But sadly, I am a mortal woman and it is the mortal condition that leads to so many mistakes and as I am set to continue as such, I am sure to make many more in the future. If the fealty of my generals and my people is so dependent on perfection then I am not fit to lead my people," she finished with a dangerous edge to her voice.

Both generals dropped down on one knee and bowed their heads as the flap to the war tent was opened and Shaul was announced.

"Your majesty," the Queterian bowed and looked at the two generals with a slight look of confusion but chose not to comment on their posture.

"What is it, Shaul? Has something happened in the other camp?" the queen asked as she focused her attention on the new arrival and signalled that both Misna and Amalia should rise.

"Your highness, I have no evidence to support what I have to say, but there are rumours circulating amongst the men of Nosfa that the king is on his way," Shaul explained in a worried voice.

"I see," Kasnata said as she turned and returned to her throne.

"Do the rumours say why he is coming?" Amalia asked as Misna moved to the entrance of the war tent and asked the guards to send a runner to summon the other generals.

"There are many different theories," Shaul shrugged.

"Then we must assume that he is coming because he knows of the queen's affair," Misna said shortly.

"Well there is some comfort to take in that," Kasnata said with a small measure of glibness.

"Begging your pardon, your highness, but what comfort?" Shaul asked.

"That whatever consequences that are to be faced, will be faced here and not in the city of Grashindorph where I have little influence. Misna, send for Samara. As the other generals are coming it is time I named Renta's successor," the queen sighed.

Misna nodded and did as she was bid as Yoav, Rathe, Shamgar,

Marissa, Hesla, Quisla and Kia all entered the war tent.

"Shamgar, I will rely on you informing Avner as to what we discuss here once he was finished dealing with the Delmarian envoys," the queen said as she looked at the generals assembled before her. She hadn't expected Rathe to attend on the summons of one of her generals but the queen was glad he had.

"There is news?" Kia asked as she looked at Shaul with suspicion.

"There is," Kasnata confirmed. "Rumour amongst the soldiers of Nosfa tells us that the king is coming."

Each of Kasnata's generals nodded grimly as they listened, each glancing at Rathe in turn. Rathe stared opened mouthed at the queen, the shock of the king coming to the front lines clearly etched upon his face.

"What will he do?" he croaked in a small voice.

"At worst he will sentence us both to death," Kasnata shrugged.

"What?" Rathe asked in disbelief. He had never taken time in his schooling to study the law of his people. He knew enough that he could avoid being arrested as a noble man, but with the number of mistresses he knew the king had taken over the years it seemed impossible to him that the queen and any lover she took could be subject to such penalties when there were no consequences for the king.

"Calm yourself, Pup," Yoav growled as he clamped his hand on the general's shoulder. "The king won't risk anything before the city of Delma is taken."

"You are sure about that, are you?" Hesla asked with a disdainful tone.

"I am," Yoav replied more gruffly than usual.

"Whilst there is war, he won't risk losing control of the Order," Quisla agreed.

"Unless he believes he can place a puppet on the throne that we will accept as our ruler, one that he can control," Marissa offered.

"Kasna and Kia are too wilful to be his puppets," Amalia shook her head, "They are the only ones with a claim to the throne."

"No, they aren't," Kasnata spoke quietly.

"Your highness?" Shamgar looked at the queen with a worried expression.

"There is another with a claim to my throne, one that many would accept if Mercia were to install them," the queen leant back on her throne and steepled her fingers.

"The last heir of Valia," Misna said grimly.

"You think that is his plan?" Shamgar asked, and Kasnata nodded.

"Then we have to do something," Amalia said firmly.

"No," Kasnata replied. "There are more important things that each of you should be concerned with. We are still at war, you have duties within the camp," the queen said firmly.

The flap to the war tent was pushed aside as a guard entered and announced Samara.

"You asked for me, your majesty?" Samara bowed and then saluted the queen, feeling slightly self-conscious amongst the gathered generals.

"I did, Samara," Kasnata confirmed. "Since the death of General Renta, there has been a vacant position of general that must be filled. I asked General Kia and General Marissa who would be the best replacement for General Renta. Someone who would not only be able to lead with authority and patience when it is called for, but also someone who would be able to step into the shoes of one so dearly loved, as the general was, and be respected, not questioned and compared. Both Kia and Marissa suggested you, Samara," the queen smiled at the young woman, who was looking utterly taken aback.

"Me?" Samara asked softly.

"Samara, will you serve your people and your queen and accept the position of Condor General in the army of the Order?" Kasnata asked as she rose to her feet and drew her Ralenetia Estral from its scabbard that was resting against her throne.

Samara was speechless. She blinked several times before meekly nodding and stepping forward, past the other generals, to kneel before her queen.

Hesla concealed a scowl behind a fixed smile. She had been certain the queen would ask for her help in selecting a replacement for Renta, but the Eagle General had been unaware that the queen had even met with Kia and Marissa on the matter. Since Ariella had failed in her assassination attempts, and General Rathe Bird had begun sharing the queen's bed, it had been much more difficult for Hesla to find opportunities to seize to remove the queen from power and replace her with the true heir, the last heir of Valia.

There were too many eyes watching, too many obstacles between her and the queen, so she had to be patient. The king coming to the forward camp would provide plenty of opportunity and even a feasible solution, but she needed to remain unseen and undetected until then.

Yoav and Shamgar exchanged an amused glance as Samara tentatively knelt before the queen. They had once knelt before Kasnata, as Samara did now, but the queen had been little more than a child, inexperienced and uncertain of herself, still grieving the loss of her parents and her ascent to the throne before she was ready.

Now she was very different. A life of struggling had forged a woman of impressive character and had crafted a reputation amongst those that had remained loyal as a wise and strong ruler. Amongst those outside of the Order, she had become known as an unbeatable force; unstoppable, relentless and unforgiving to those that would stand against her.

The concerns that many spoke of over her affair with the general of Nosfa were not born out of a lack of confidence in their queen, but out of fear of what would happen to her should the king of Nosfa choose to try and harm her or her children as a punishment for her indiscretion.

Misna caught Quisla's eye as Samara passed, a silent agreement that they would meet later to discuss what was happening in the camp and the dangers to their queen.

Shaul soundlessly slipped from the tent and returned to the men of Nosfa, his presence no longer required as the queen had been informed of the king's visit. There had been no point in mentioning the other rumours to the queen when she had so many other things to concern herself with.

Kia and Marissa smiled warmly as Samara place her hands on the hilt of Kasnata's sword and pledged her life and love to the queen and the people of the Order and as she rose, Amalia was the first to greet her as an equal, presenting Samara with new armour, robes and insignia that would mark her as the Condor General.

Kasnata dismissed her generals. Kia, Marissa and Amalia accompanied Samara to present her to her new command and to ask if they were willing to accept and follow her. The other generals all returned to their duties around the camp, save for Rathe, who lingered, waiting until he was alone with his lover before he spoke.

"What are we going to do?" he asked staring at the floor.

"What do you suggest we do?" Kasnata asked testily. "Tell him that I have been eating more than my fair share of the rations?"

"You cannot think that there won't be consequences, that he won't do something desperate and stupid," Rathe snapped.

"You don't think I know that there are consequences? That every time you make love to me, take me in your arms, even brush hair from my eyes that I don't think of what he might do to me and my children? What he will do to you?" Kasnata asked as she sheathed her sword and removed the temptation she was resisting to throw it across the war tent.

Rathe looked up at the woman he loved. Her eyes were seething with anger and her face was pale. He wanted to hold her every time he looked at her, to tell her just how much he loved her and what she meant to him, but at this moment the impulse was not one that he felt he should act upon.

"Then how can you be so calm?" he asked in a softer voice. "How can you not be afraid of him?"

Kasnata frowned. She had never been afraid of Mercia, he was a bully, but he didn't frighten her. She knew what he was capable of, possibly better than he knew himself, and she worried over the safety of her children, but she was not afraid of the man.

She had no reason to fear him, but had every reason to hate him and want him dead. She preserved her marriage for the sake of her children alone, so that they would be safe. She had never considered that he was a man she should be afraid of, but as she looked at Rathe, she could see that he was afraid of his king.

Kasnata's demeanour softened as she stepped down off the dais and took Rathe's hands in hers.

"You have spent your life living under the weight of fear of your ruler, of what he might do to your family," she said gently.

"You have spent half your life married to him, afraid that he will kill your children," Rathe replied as he squeezed his lover's hands.

"No, I have worried for their safety, but I have known he would not harm them, not out of his love for them, but because he needs my people to carry out his bidding. Leinad is safe as the heir to the throne of Nosfa, even if he did sire an army of bastards, Leinad would still be the rightful heir and there are those that would protect him, even in Grashindorph. My daughters, well, they are resourceful and finally free of him, safe in Tulna. I have never feared him, in fact, I am certain that he fears me more than I could ever fear him," Kasnata smiled, and placed Rathe's hands on her belly.

"You have never known what it is like living under a tyrant who sees your family as a threat to his rule because your father and his father had been as close as brothers," Rathe sighed and felt his child kick.

"He is strong, like you," Kasnata grinned as the baby kicked again.

"I fooled myself into thinking that I was finally free of him out here, that in his war I could finally stop fearing what he would do to my family and those that I love," Rathe admitted. "But I was wrong; I will never be free of him, will I?"

"Not whilst he lives," Kasnata sighed and leant her head upon Rathe's shoulder as he wrapped his arms around her.

"So what do we do?" Rathe asked again.

"We wait," Kasnata replied.

CHAPTER 4

Avner had ridden a short distance from the camp with a small detachment of men. The Dog of War was the father of the queen of Delma and understood the people of the country better than any of the Order or of Nosfa, but he didn't understand why they were fighting a war that they couldn't win.

He had met with his daughter when he and Queen Kasnata had returned the body of his grandson, Prince Jayden, to her after he had been killed in a skirmish, thrown from his horse. He had not expected the meeting to be a welcome one, but the ways in which his daughter had changed and the way she had spoken to him had made him begin to question whether there wasn't something else at work besides the greed of men sitting upon gilded thrones.

The envoys he had been sent to meet had travelled slowly, there was only one horse in the party and it was pulling a cart that was surrounded by a company of ten men.

"Hold," Avner called out. "What business do you have with the queen of the Order of Anagura and Queteria?"

"We come on behalf of the Regent of Delma, Duke Kelmar DeLacey," the man holding the flag of truce answered.

"Step forward," Avner replied as he signalled that his men should stay back unless the men of Delma attacked.

The envoy stepped forward leading the horse and cart

forward with him.

"The Duke sends his regrets and lamentations to Queen Kasnata," the envoy said solemnly as he pulled back the furs that were piled in the back of the cart to reveal the body of Renta.

Her skin was paler than a waning moon and flecked with her own blood. Her eyes had been closed though and her armour and weapons were intact. Avner nodded and pulled the furs back over the body of the fallen general.

"What does the Duke ask for in exchange for our fallen sister?" Avner growled.

"The Duke asks that we be allowed to return to the city of Delma unharmed," the envoy stammered. The Dog of War looked at the man who stood before him and noticed that the man was shaking so badly that he was barely able to remain standing.

The general of the Order of the Hound looked over to where the other nine men stood; they too looked as though they were shaking as much, if not more than the envoy that stood before him.

"I will send word to the queen and we shall stay here and await her response," he grunted. The general motioned for one of his men to approach and sent him with the message from the Regent of Delma to the queen. The man disappeared without a word or even a flicker of surprise showing on his face.

The envoy twitched as Avner pulled back the furs to examine the body of Renta.

"I'm sorry, Condor," he whispered to her and smiled sadly. There was a bond that existed between most of Kasnata's generals, one of respect that comes not only from serving together in war, but in leading together, of surviving battles that should have brought the end of their lives, of sharing the burden that command brought.

Renta had become the Condor General just before Avner's wife had died, and she had shown the Dog of War compassion that he had not expected. The two had been close since then, sharing their regrets over poor decisions they had made on the battlefield as well as confiding in each other in other matters; chiefly, Renta's relationship with Tola.

The thought of the Roencian caused a sharp pang in his heart as the general wondered how Tola was coping with the death of Renta. The two had been lovers for years, a relationship that could never be sustained for more than a few months at a time and only when they were in the same war camp. He had seen how the months apart, unable to write to one another in case the missives were intercepted, had tortured Renta, but he had also seen the joy that being reunited with the Hero of the war of the east had brought as well.

His thoughts were interrupted by the return of the man with the queen's response.

"What does she say?" Avner asked, pulling his thoughts back to the present situation.

"She says that the body of the general is to be delivered to the camp along with the envoys and the Order of the Bear will escort the men to the city," came the reply. Avner nodded.

"Have you eaten?" he asked the envoy, who still looked nervous.

"No, not since yesterday," the envoy replied weakly.

"Very well, we'll see you are fed before you go to the city," Avner grunted and began to lead the horse and cart back to the camp. The men of Delma still seemed nervous, but the Dog of War knew that if the queen had wanted to see the men dead, she would have simply sent a dagger instead of a reply.

The Abbott stood before his mother, pondering a suggestion that had been made by the guardians before they had left.

"Do you think it will help?" the monk asked as he tapped his chin in thought.

"It may be the only way to ensure they can be ready," Kania shrugged as she looked at her son.

"And Lavinia recommended this?" he said slowly, his lips purse.

"She did, though I am aware you do not hold the highest regard for her," Kania replied with a raised eyebrow. "It does not mean that she is wrong."

"True. It is more that I am dubious of the benefit to the princesses training in such a way, and if there would be any benefit to the realm," the Abbott shrugged.

"You doubt her motivation?" Kania asked, raising an eyebrow.

"Yes," the Abbott said flatly. "But in order for the girls to become better warriors, I don't see another way. Kasna is at least four years behind the other children of the Order, and Kia is two. The only downside is that they will age whilst they are training, they will become much older than they are supposed to be in a very short space of time."

"You are worried about the effect it will have on their longevity?" Kania smiled at her son, it had been some time since he had been concerned about the fate of individual mortals.

"Yes, we don't know what it will do to them," the Abbott shrugged, as though his concern should not be a surprise.

"Kasna will not be afraid of doing do, she has endured other horrors to protect her sister, and she is not even past the age of ten. Kia shows no fear and will follow Kasna into fire," Kania offered as she sat down in one of the wooden carved chairs that sat around the small wooden table.

"I will make the arrangements then. I will speak to them in the morning and if they agree, we will begin," the Abbott sighed.

Tola sat alone in his room. Mathias had tried speaking to his cousin many times since Renta had passed but the Hero of the war of the east had been merely responded with a mixture of grunts and dark looks.

He had lost people before in battle, war had a nasty way of taking people the people he cared about away from him, but in battle it was expected. He could prepare himself for it. Renta he had not been prepared for.

Tola had replayed the scene and events leading up to her death over and over again. He had not been there when Renta had stepped forward to hold off Kelmar and his men; he had been with the horses. Mathias had been and he had chosen to leave her to die at Kelmar's hands.

When she had not appeared with the three girls and two men, he had known what would happen, deep down he had known, but he had not admitted it to himself at the time. Instead he had clung onto false hope, hope that told him the Condor General was a warrior that could take on the small army that Kelmar commanded and live.

He wondered if she knew that she was giving up her life when she had stayed behind, whether she had felt scared at facing her own mortality. No fear had shown on her face when she was knelt before them, Kelmar's blade threatening her.

Tola began to weep as he watched her die again, his mind unable to let go of the image of her lying in the dust of the plain that was stained with her blood.

The pain at her being going clawed at him, raked at his inside, making him want to reach into himself and pull it all out. They had often talked about what the other wanted if they should fall in battle, how they would carry on after, but the reality of it, he didn't want to face.

His mind jumped from the image of Renta's disfigured body to that of Kelmar's face. The young duke standing over her dying form, his hand gripping the hilt of the blood stained blade, his face a caricature etched in Tola's memory. The hero of the east could see a self-satisfied expression gripping Kelmar's features, a look of malice and disgust.

Tola felt his anger welling up inside him, stronger than his grief. He had sworn he would avenge Renta, that he would cause the Regent of Delma of Delma to suffer; that he would revisit whatever pain Renta endured back upon him tenfold and there was no force on Celadmore that would prevent him from doing so.

He sat and brooded, plotted, withdrawing into himself, allowing his grief and his desire for revenge to consume him.

The small procession of Avner, his men and the men of Delma had grown as they had entered the camp and the people of the Order began to follow them.

Word had spread quickly that Renta's body had been returned and was being brought in by those that had delivered it to the camp.

The men of Delma were looking even more terrified than they had before; in their minds they were certain that the sight of the walls of their home city were as close as they would ever come to seeing it again.

Avner ignored all those who tried to push near enough to the cart to see if it really was Renta's body, his men turning aside those who weren't deterred by their presence with threats and even small altercations.

It quickly became clear that Avner had no intention of letting anyone touch Renta's body before he had presented it to the queen.

By the time they had reached the queen's war tent, most of the Order was stood around the cart. The onlookers had been murmuring to one another and casting dark looks at the men of Delma, but as the cart stopped, the crowd fell into a silence that was deafening to the terrified envoys.

The entrance to the war tent was pulled back by the guards and Kasnata emerged, her robes hiding her pregnancy well. She was flanked by General Bird and General Samara, both who hung back slightly as the queen stood beside the cart and nodded. The furs covering Renta's body were pulled back to reveal the full extent of what Kelmar had inflicted upon the general.

Her arms had been placed by the sockets that they had been cleaved from as a mark of respect and her sword was lying on her chest.

"Have her prepared," Kasnata said softly to Avner, who nodded and led the cart away from the prying eyes of the other members of the Order.

Kasnata turned her attention to the men of Delma who stood shaking before her, their eyes darting around all the disgust faces of those that surrounded them.

"One of you will not be returning to the city," she spoke clearly so all those gathered could hear her. "You will be returning to your master with a message. The rest of you will be escorted home by General Shamgar and the Order of the Bear. No one will harm you or try to stop you from returning to your home. Any that attempt to harm you will be punished under the penalties of violating the articles of war," Kasnata raised her voice to make sure that she was clearly understood by all those present.

She was glad that Tola was absent, though he would not be there for her funeral pyre, the queen had not wanted to endure her own grief and trying to control the hero of the war of the east.

General Shamgar stepped forward with the men he had chosen to act as the escort for the envoys back to the city. He carried a flag of truce to ensure that the Delmarian defences didn't fire upon their own men as they approached the city.

Many of the Order that were assembled seemed tempted to test the queen's resolve on allowing the men to live, but as the party set out, the remaining generals of the Order drew their swords and started to disperse the crowd, the queen stood with General Rathe beside her carefully watching her people.

"Send a message to Tola, he is needed back here," Kasnata whispered softly to her lover, who nodded in response.

"Will he want to return?" Rathe asked, his eyes watching the retreating backs of the Order of the Bear.

"No, he will not, but he is a soldier, he doesn't have a choice,"

"It is not something that either of you has to do. It is merely an idea, something that will help you to hone your skills," the Abbott explained.

"There are some risks involved," Kania said slowly. The two princesses were sat in a small room in the main building of the oasis. There was a square wooden table with chairs made of the same wood; the seats weaved from wicker surrounding it in the room. The walls were the same sandy colour as the rest of the village; a thin arch window was opposite the door with a tapestry on the wall to the right of the door.

The tapestry had caught the attention of both Kasna and Kia when they had been brought into the room as it was an extensive family tree of the royal line of the Order. The tapestry extended well past their names, but those that were to follow were blurred and appeared almost as smoke on the surface of the material.

Kania had told them to not study it too closely as the future was not set in stone and there were more pressing matters to attend to.

"What risks?" Kasna asked looking slightly worried.

"You won't be training in the world as you understand it," the Abbott was sat on the opposite side of the table to the two princesses and his gaze was fixed out of the window rather than on the two girls. "We would be in a time slip,"

"A time slip?" Kia frowned.

"It is a pocket of reality that we create where time is

manipulated to run at a different rate to the rest of the realm. It means that for every day that passes outside of the time slip, weeks or even months will pass in the time slip," Kania said as reassuringly as she could.

"So time will pass more quickly in the time slip?" Kania shrugged.

"It will," the Abbott agreed. "But it means that you will age more quickly in the time slip. At the end of every day in this reality we will emerge from the time slip and allow your bodies to rest for a day before we return to it, but in the space of two weeks in the time slip you may have aged as much as two years," the Guardian of the Spire warned.

Kia blinked several times and looked at her sister, expecting her to have already made up her mind. The thought of aging quickly frightened her, but if Kasna was sure that it was the right thing to do, then Kia would do what her sister thought was best.

Kasna sat in thought for a few moments before she spoke.

"It means that we would learn to fight in a shorter space of time?" She asked, looking slightly hopeful at the prospect.

"It would," the Abbott confirmed.

"Then it doesn't matter what the side effects are," Kasna said firmly. "When can we start?"

"I will make the preparations so we can begin in the morning. It would be a good idea to spend the day considering what it is that you both wish to specialise in. There are few warriors who are skilled to the level of master with every weapon. If you had been raised with your mother, then you would have chosen whether you wanted to fight with a sword, bow, or spear as your primary weapon."

"Will we only be trained to use whichever weapon we choose as our main one?" Kasna asked, sounding a little concerned.

"No, you will be trained to use all three weapons and in how to use different shields as well, but to be the equal of any of your people, you will need to specialise. If you have any questions about what the strengths and weaknesses of different weapons are, then Mathias will be able to explain them all to you," the Abbott said as he stood and nodded to his mother before he quietly left the room.

Kia looked at her sister and was glad that she had made the decision for them both. The idea of growing up and being able to fight was something that they had both always talked about and dreamed of doing, but not that it was to become a reality, and much sooner than either girl had realised, she was more than a little apprehensive about it.

CHAPTER 5

"They passed this way, not a few hours ago. We're close now. Neesa's horse is fairing badly under the weight of two riders without enough time to rest or feed properly," the Guardian of the Wilds said as she stood from where she had been kneeling over the tracks the assassin of Nosfa had left behind.

Weeks had passed since Lady Mia Bird had been taken from the Tulna Oasis. Joab and Cassandra had not been far behind the assassin, but she had fled on horseback with a clear destination in mind, whilst Joab and Cassandra had set out after her on smaller animals and were having to follow a trail in the dark. Neesa had brought supplies with her, Joab and Cassandra had none.

But it had not stopped them from keeping up their pursuit, and now they were finally closing the distance Neesa had managed to put between them.

Joab had lit a small fire to cook the rabbits that Cassandra had caught earlier in the day and was sat beside it. There had been little conversation between the two as they had followed the trail, save for warnings of danger, deciding who was to hunt and forage and relaying tracking information. Neither had a desire to engage in unnecessary conversation, nor felt the social pressure to chat out of politeness.

The Guardian of the Wilds looked over to where Joab was sat

and waited for some form of response. But Joab was not listening as Cassandra spoke.

He was lost in his own thoughts of what he would do to Neesa should any harm have befallen Mia. He knew Tola was hurting, his heart broken in the wake of Renta's murder. Joab too felt the keen sting in his chest and the lump of emotion rise in his throat when he thought about the sacrifice made by Kasnata's friend and loyal general.

She had willing died to protect the daughters of her queen, gladly given up her life for those she was sword to safeguard. She had not flinched in her duty or hesitated to do what was necessary to carry out the orders she had been given.

He had spent his whole life being trained by Cassandra, the Abbott, Kania, Nodarto and Layla for a single purpose – to protect the Lady Mia. The giftings of the immortals of Tulna extended far beyond what Joab knew of, but he knew that they had some capacity to see what was to come; at least Kania and Nodarto did.

The Abbott and Cassandra were more of a mystery, burdened with fewer reservations than their parents when it came to direct intervention. Cassandra seemed almost wild by comparison to Kania; the Abbott a rogue when put next to Nodarto, and yet there was nothing in their countenance that suggested they could not be trusted.

In his younger days, Joab could vaguely remember hearing

arguments between the four, arguments no other was supposed to hear; about what though he could never recall.

His training had given him all the skills he could ever need to serve the Gibborim, to obey the orders of Hermia, to protect Lady Mia. But the feelings that now stirred in him, the feelings that had surfaced when he discovered Neesa, these feelings were not the feelings of a man sworn as a shadow.

He didn't want to feel like other men did when they found themselves in the company of women that they were unable to express their affection for, but he wasn't entirely certain that he wanted to feel any emotions towards her either.

As a shadow he had to protect her with his life, to weigh dangerous situations that were difficult enough to predict without complicated emotions clouding his judgement.

"Why did you come?" he asked as he looked over to where Cassandra stood. She titled her head as she regarded him and began walking over to where he sat.

"I came because whilst in Tulna, the Lady Mia was under my protection as well as yours. I was so focused on the threat of Kelmar to the princesses that I did not protect Mia as I should have done. I am here to make amends for my lack of foresight," the Guardian of the Wilds shrugged as she sat down beside the fire. "Why do you ask?"

"I have not heard of any guardian or immortal taking

such trouble over a single mortal before. In my training, you and the Abbott always taught us that our duty should be our primary focus, that seeing those we protect as people can only weaken us," Joab explained as he checked on the meat.

"I see. What we told you wasn't entirely true," Cassandra yawned as she stretched out and gazed into the flames. "You came to us a child, like many others and children have a way of forming attachments to each other and to people. We needed to keep that from happening in order for you to be effective shadows. Seeing individuals as people can often be the reason we choose to keep protecting them as much as it can cloud our judgement."

Joab studied Cassandra's face as she spoke. The Guardian of the Wilds wore an almost impenetrable mask that effectively hid what she thought and felt from those around her. It made her an excellent teacher in combat, but infuriating when engaging her in conversation.

Joab lapsed back into silence and stared into the fire. The Guardian lay back and looked up at the stars that were being to spread across the sky above.

"Where is she trying to take her?" he asked as he took the rabbits from the fire.

"Neesa? She's heading to Fintry."

Marissa waited until the changing of the nightwatch, when there were conversations between warriors and movement throughout the camp to cover her whereabouts. She went unnoticed amongst all the other warriors moving between the tents, down the high walled passages that not only protected the camp from the fiercer Wentrus elements, but also from attacks from the city.

Quisla was sat in her tent, waiting for the general to arrive. The Vulture General did not smile as the Phoenix General entered her quarters, but she was glad she had come.

"What is it?" Marissa hissed in a low voice.

"I needed to talk to you about Samara," Quisla replied in hushed tones.

"Oh? You're worried about her being named as Renta's successor?" Marissa frowned as she sat down. "You doubt Kia's judgement and my own?"

"I'm curious as to why you chose her," Quisla shrugged.

"There is one thing that I know that neither you nor Misna have ever experienced and that is idle curiosity. When you are looking for information there is always a reason for it that runs to a much deeper course than something as pedestrian as your own piece of mind," Marissa said with a raise eyebrow.

"That is true enough," Quisla admitted as she poured out two goblets of wine. "It is not that I doubt your judgement, or Kia's. It is a possibility that I am being overly cautious, but with the assassination attempts on the queen's life still not resolved, I am merely trying to get a better grasp on those that are close to her majesty," she explained as she handed the goblet to Marissa.

"Then I am happy to tell you why we chose Samara," Marissa smiled as she accepted the wine. "I won't waste your time on discussing her exploits or her abilities, those I am sure that both you and Misna are well versed in. The reason I suggested Samara is that she does what she thinks is right, not what she is told is right. Renta used to tell me stories of Samara verging on disobeying orders because she challenged the thought behind them," Marissa smiled sadly at the memory. "She simply seemed the obvious choice for Renta's replacement."

"I see. So no one else knew that you were selecting a new general for the queen?" Quisla asked as she sat down and leant back in the crudely carved chair.

"No, I didn't even know that Kia was being asked for her opinion," Marissa sipped from her wine as she watched Quisla carefully.

"I see," the Vulture General looked thoughtful for a few moments as the two drank in silence. Quisla let her mind mull over the actions of the queen and where she was placing her trust. There was something that Kasnata could see, knew about or rather sense, that both Quisla and Misna had been oblivious to.

"What is it?" the Phoenix General asked as she noticed a shadow of confusion and frustration flicker across Quisla's face.

"There is a traitor in our midst," Quisla shrugged.

"There must be hundreds of traitors in our midst," Marissa laughed to herself, "Not least amongst out own people, but among the men of Nosfa as well."

"That's not what I mean. Of course there are traitors there, but I think there is a traitor closer to Kasnata than any of us realised, and I think she knows it as well," the older woman frowned and stared up at Marissa with cold eyes.

The young Phoenix General met her gaze and shook her head.

"Impossible, Misna would have noticed."

"Unless they became corrupted after they reached that position," Quisla countered, her gaze unwavering.

"You think that there is a more to this than that," Marissa said flatly.

"I think that we have been dealing with immediate threats to our leader without looking at the bigger picture for far too long," Quisla lowered her voice and leaned forward.

"The bigger picture?" Marissa frowned as she put down her

empty goblet.

"You don't trust Hesla, correct?" Quisla asked as she too put down her empty goblet and steepled her fingers.

"No," Marissa replied.

"Many people believe that my opinion of her was soured by what she did to my husband, but that was done out of spite on her part, a reaction to me refusing her," Quisla explained and sighed.

"I see. You think that our attention has been fixed on Hesla as a possible traitor when there are other forces at work?" the Phoenix General asked as she stood and began to pace around the tent.

"I do, I think there is someone supporting her from the shadows, making sure that things are done in a manner that benefits them, even when it does not benefit the general," Quisla mused.

"Trying to name herself steward being one example," Marissa agreed. "So the raised voices, the argument with Amalia-"

"A diversionary tactic. However, is behind Hesla must be drawn out and a clear divide showing between Kasnata's generals provides ample opportunity to strike," Quisla smiled.

"What is Misna doing in all this?"

"She is doing what she does best," a new voice entered the conversation. The Phoenix General paused in her pacing and glanced over to the entrance to Quisla's tent, where Misna stood with Amalia beside her.

"How long have the three of you been weighing all of this?" Marissa asked, raising an eyebrow.

"Too long. Amalia wanted to talk to you about this sooner, but I was wary of adding anyone else to our number," Misna shrugged. "But with the appointment of a new general, we needed to know if any pressure had been brought to bear against you in order to appoint Samara," the Raven General explained.

"There was no pressure, simply a clear choice. You find that suspicious?" Marissa questioned her comrades of many battles.

"Misna finds everything suspicious," Amalia jibbed.

"With good reason," Misna replied humourlessly, "As far as anyone else in the camp knows, Quisla is investigating Ariella's assassination attempts and whether there are others involved. We want it to stay that way."

"Who is investigating?" the Phoenix General asked, expecting that she already knew the answer.

"No one," Amalia replied. Marissa looked up sharply with a slight air of disbelief.

"No one?" she echoed.

"There is no need. Ariella is dead, and it is not the one who sent her to assassinate Kasnata that we want to find, but the one pulling their strings. That is being left to Misna and myself," Amalia explained.

"What do you need from me?" Marissa asked, knowing that

there was another reason behind her being informed of the investigation, other than trying to gain information about Samara's appointment.

"I need you to act as the queen's bodyguard in my stead. I cannot protect her and investigate this threat with Misna at the same time," Amalia said grimly. The weight of passing on her responsibility clearly told in the lines on her face.

"Very well," Marissa accepted the task with a deep intake of breath.

The four women looked at each other in the stillness of Quisla's quarters. The Raven, Phoenix, Vulture and Kestrel. There was no need for anything else to be said, Quisla refilled her goblet and Marissa's, the two silently toasting before passing them to Misna and Amalia to do the same.

Until the threat to their queen had been neutralised, the four women would not meet again.

"Pup!" Yoav roared in frustration and threw down his blade. "You are still dropping your guard. The next time you leave an opening like that I will skewer you like a boar!"

Rathe's training the Order of the Wolf had intensified since the news had been passed to them that King Mercia Nosfa VI was coming.

Whilst the king was in the camp, Rathe would be confined to his quarters with the men of Nosfa and not at liberty to spend as much time training with the Order of the Wolf or in the company of the queen.

Yoav had pushed the young general almost to his breaking point. He had assigned him to every night mission the wolf pack had been given in the last few weeks and then had refused to let the general retire to his bed, forcing him into the sword ring instead.

Thought Rathe didn't know it, his skills had improved greatly in a very short space of time and the more that Yoav pushed him, the harder Rathe seemed to apply himself.

Though he didn't show it, Yoav was impressed by Lord Bird. Most soldiers would have thrown down their weapons and given up, refused to rise to each new challenge that was presented. But with every passing day it became clearer to Wolfblood what it was that the queen saw in Rathe.

There was a determination and passion in his soul that was hidden beneath the courtly manners and a reserved nature that was the result of living under the rule of a tyrant.

He had been trained in combat, but not in battle. He was more than capable of taking on a single opponent, but the moment that he was faced with the reality of men dying in droves around him, the sound of battle cries, war horns and the rush of adrenaline that gave some warriors their strength, he froze, unable to fight or even move.

Yoav didn't know if it was because he had not served in war in the same way that those of the Order had to before being promoted to higher ranks, or whether it was just inexperience on the battlefield that paralysed the general, but Wolfblood was determined to train the young lord so that his fear would not be given a chance to take hold again.

Instead the general of the Order of the Wolf intended to ensure that his muscle memory would carry him through his panic until he recovered enough to find his courage.

Unfortunately for Rathe he still had his duties to attend to as commander of the Nosfa forces as well as his training with Yoav and the other warriors.

As a result, he found that he barely slept more than an hour and most of the time he was not sleeping beside Kasnata. The tiredness, training and his duties were all things that the young general could cope with, but he found that as the days went by and he saw less of the woman he loved that he became more and more irritable.

Rathe raised his guard and repeated the exercise that Yoav was drilling him in. He tried to keep his mind focused on the movements of the older man, but found that his mind started to wander to thoughts of his lover. The scent of her skin as she slept, how she felt in his arms and in the next moment he found himself lying on his back staring up at the sky with a sharp stabbing pain in his side.

"I warned you," Yoav barked. "Young idiot," He muttered as he knelt down beside Rathe and inspected the wound.

"I can't keep doing this," Rathe moaned as he tried to sit up and Yoav clouted him round the back of the head.

"Never say that again," the older man said sternly. "You're stronger than most of the whelps I am given to train and you can cope with a lot more than you give yourself credit for, as long as you flaming concentrate," He scolded the young lord.

"It's not the training," Rathe sighed.

"Get her out of your head, Pup," Yoav said hauling the general to his feet and helping him through the camp to where the healing tents were. "The king is coming, you won't be able to see her, talk to her, touch her or share her bed whilst he's here. You know that and she knows it. Take the advice of an old warrior, put her out of your mind and concentrate on what you can control. After all, your sister's safety is at risk if you don't do what the king wants," Yoav reminded him.

Rathe nodded weakly, he tried not to think about what his sister was enduring at the hands of the king, which had been made easier by the happiness he had found in the arms of the queen. But there were still nights when he would wake up in a cold sweat having nightmares about the punishment that Mia was being subjected to.

The nights when he didn't dream of Mia, he dreamt of his father being killed on the road to Afdanic, killed by bandits in the employ of the king. When he woke crying out, Kasnata had soothed him letting him drift off into a dreamless state, but without her there, the few hours of sleep he managed were turbulent, tortured and far from restful.

"I know," He sighed and winced as Yoav helped him to lie down on one of the beds.

"Do you want me to tell her majesty that you're injured?" Yoav asked as a healer can to inspect the wound.

"No. She has enough to worry about," Rathe said as he sucked air through clenched teeth, the healer oblivious to the pain that they were causing.

"It's shallow, no real force behind the blow. He'll heal in a few days; though it needs to be dressed and kept clean otherwise the infection could kill him," the healer said matter-of-factly.

"No night manoeuvres for a few days then, Pup. Take the opportunity to rest as when you are healed, I'll be making you suffer for the training time you've missed," Yoav growled and nodded to the healer.

Rathe winced again.

"Is there a reason you aren't gentler with our patients?" The young lord asked as the healer applied a salve with unnecessary force.

"My name is Payne for a reason," the healer said absently as he worked.

"Payne is the best in his craft but sacrifices in personality had to be made in one so – uniquely gifted," Yoav smiled.

"I see," Rathe replied as he almost cried out when Payne pour a liquid over the wound that caused his skin to boil around the edges.

"You warriors are all the same; tough until you're injured then you want pity and shadcrag gloves," Payne snorted as he dressed the wound.

"If you didn't seem to take so much pleasure in inflicting pain on those that were injured, you might find there are fewer complaints from your patients," Kasnata's voice sounded slightly amused as she appeared beside Yoav.

"If I was given more respect by those that I keep saving, then maybe I wouldn't enjoy inflicting pain," the healer said to his queen as he pulled Rathe's bandages slightly too tight.

"When you can wield a sword as well as you can wield your tongue then you shall have my respect," Yoav grunted, bowed to the queen and left the healing tent.

"I was born to the wrong people," Payne sighed and shook his head. "He'll be fine, your majesty. When I have made sure all my patients will survive the night I will come and see how you and your baby are, highness," the healer assured the queen who nodded her thanks.

"Dutiful as always,"

Rathe watched the healer blush slightly as he hurried away to deal with those that had more severe injuries.

"What happened?" She asked as Rathe stood from the bed he lay upon.

"I lost my concentration and Yoav's spear slipped through my guard," the young lord said sheepishly. The queen smiled kindly at her lover.

"I have missed you," She whispered.

"And I, you," Rathe replied, looking somewhat relieved.

"You need to rest tonight, allow your body to heal," she said, taking the general by the hand and leading him through the camp to her tent. She paused by the entrance. "Go relax, I still have things I must attend to, but I will be with you later,"

Kasnata made to leave, but the general gripped her hand, pulled her to his chest and held her for a few moments.

"I love you," he said as he buried his face in her hair.

"I know, I love you too," she sighed. "That is one thing you should be mindful of," Kasnata said as the two broke apart.

"Oh?"

"Not that I love you; that you should stop speaking in my tongue whilst Mercia is here. He will see it as an act of treachery," Kasnata warned. Rathe bit down on his lip and nodded.

"I should let you attend to your duties," he said formerly before ducking inside her quarters.

CHAPTER 6

It took two days before Avner had completed the building of the funeral pyre for Renta. He had chosen to work alone on its construction; he had wanted to ensure that it had been perfect for the fallen Condor General. Many had offered their assistance, but he had growled at each of them.

Avner wanted to build the pyre for Renta himself. She had been the one who had overseen the building of the pyres for those of the Order ever since her sister had died in battle, and the general wanted to make sure that Renta received the same care that she had awarded to others after their death.

Her funeral would not be like other celebrations of the Order, as she had not died in battle, she had been butchered for the sake of the princesses and she would be honoured for it.

When the pyre was completed, he sent word to the queen that it was ready and spent the rest of the day wrapping the body of the Condor General in linen so that she could be sent to Halsanda in one piece.

Haston awoke to the stillness of the Gibborim. Since the

discovery of Bracha as a traitor and the execution of Ilana, there had been a dark cloud of loss hanging over the people living underneath the city of Grashindorph.

The usual rhythm of their daily lives had been disrupted and there were concerns that Bracha was not the only spy amongst their ranks.

Haston had been treated with more suspicion in the last days than he had been when he had first arrived. Hermia had not been seen for days as she was questioning Bracha with the help of Layla.

Harman and Jephthah were left to the day to day running of Gibborim and dealing with the information that was filtering down from the surface. Jephthah didn't seem too concerned that his wife had been revealed as a traitor and his daughters, from what Haston had seen of them, had disowned their mother.

Neither of the girls wanted anything to do with the woman after she had not only betrayed the beliefs shared by the family as well as all those that lived and fought for the Gibborim.

Helez was in mourning for his sister. She had been a foolish and headstrong girl, but she had been an innocent life that Bracha had cruelly manipulated for her own gain.

Asahel had supported the man who was like a brother to him with patience and kindness that most often thought was lacking in their friendship.

Haston had found the reliance that Helez had on Asahel

rather comforting and refreshing. As a lord of the court of Nosfa, there had been no one that Haston could confide in since King Rosla had passed on. The aging lord saw a lot of himself in Helez and even more of Rosla in Asahel.

They were not inseparable, but when the other was in need, there were no questions asked before support was provided.

The lord of Afdanic had wondered if he would ever see that kind of camaraderie again in the borders of Mercia's kingdom and the sight of it gave him hope.

The time slip was almost undetectable to the naked eye. It was nothing more than slight shimmer, almost the same as heat rising but with the odd flicker of light that marked it as something different.

The two princesses were stood in front of the time slip waiting for the Abbott to appear.

"Are you sure this is a good idea, Nini?" Kia asked, trembling as she stood there.

"Yes, Kit," Kasna replied smiling and squeezing her sister's hand reassuringly. "I know you're nervous, but we will be fine, just older when we see mother."

"But it will still feel like years to us," Kia blinked, trying to hide the tears she was fighting against.

"I know, but just think, it will only be days for mother. She'll be surprised and we'll be able to help her," Kasna said warmly and hugged her sister. Kia pouted for a second, before she threw her arms around her sister's neck and hugged her tightly.

"Good morning," the Abbott greeted the two girls as he walked over to where the time slip shimmered. "Are you both ready?" he asked. Both of the princesses nodded.

The Abbott clapped his hands together and rubbed them together before holding his right hand out to the distortion of air. In seconds it moved, or rather it seemed to move to envelope the three figures. In reality Kia, Kasna and the Abbott were drawn into the time slip, which closed behind them.

The ground beneath their feet was as firm as it hand been in Tulna but instead it was covered with sand and dirt that was soft to fall on. There were wooden dummies set up with white and red circles painted on the torsos as well as sacks stuffed with straw that were suspended from wooden frames.

Beside the Abbott, there was a weapon rack that had swords, spears, daggers, lances, bows, crossbows, shields and other weapons that neither of the girls had ever seen before.

"Did you decide which disciplines you wanted to master?" The Abbott asked, smiling at the awe with which the two princesses had been struck.

"I want to be an archer," Kia spoke first, her fear having evaporated in the excitement of finding she was in a real training environment.

"Kasna?" the Abbott turned to the older girl and waited for her response.

"I want to be an assassin," she said shuffling her feet.

The Guardian of the Spire had expected that Kasna would have chosen to master the staff or the broadsword as she seemed to rely on brute force rather than skill and let her emotions guide her actions. To say that he was surprised she wanted to learn the skills of an assassin was an understatement.

"I see. There is more to being an assassin than simply mastering weapons," the Abbott warned the young Anaguran. "You will need to learn to read people, to use their emotions against them and use your own as a defence, to continually keep knocking them off their guard,"

"I understand, but I still want to be one," she said firmly.

"Very well. We should begin with the basics. Take a sword and we shall look at balance."

Mia shivered. It was much colder now than it had been when

she and Joab had left Grashindorph. When the assassin had taken her from Tulna, she had been wearing her night attire and the thin dress did not keep the cold night from biting at her skin. Neesa had not spoken a word to the girl, nor did she take any notice of her shivering. Her focus was ensuring her horse survived in the wilds and it seemed to Mia that her survival was a secondary focus.

Lady Bird had never seen the woman before she had appeared in Tulna, but there was something vaguely familiar about the way she moved that Mia couldn't place.

"Please, it's cold; can I have a blanket or maybe light a fire?" Mia asked, needing to break the silence for her own sanity. Neesa turned and regarded her taciturnly.

"If you had chosen to go to Fintry as the king ordered then you would not be cold," she replied without emotion.

Mia shivered and stared at the assassin, the icy feeling of dread creeping over her.

"You're taking me back to him?" she croaked her voice barely above a whisper.

"Had I not seen you fleeing with the two princesses, I wouldn't have believed you were stupid enough to defy him, but it seems that I was wrong. There is nowhere you could hide from him; nowhere you could run to where you would be safe," Neesa knelt down in front of Mia and stared into the eyes of the young girl. "When he decides that he wants something he will not be denied."

For a moment Mia thought she could see some regret flicker in the eyes of the assassin, but it was so brief that if it had been there, it was gone in an instant.

"Please, don't, I just want to see my brother," Mia begged, still holding Neesa's gaze.

"From what I understand, your brother will be returning to Grashindorph, whether he wants to or not," Neesa said standing.

"What do you mean?" Mia asked, but Neesa had finished talking to her. Lady Bird shivered again, no warmth was being granted to her and the brief conversation with Neesa had made her more afraid than she had been when she was being treated as an inanimate object.

The king departed Grashindorph amidst a festival of colour and music. Whilst he was visiting the army at Delma, the Baron of Fintry had been appointed as steward to the kingdom. Any decisions that needed to be made immediately were to be made by the Baron, but the majority of his duties revolved around Prince Leinad.

The son of Mercia and Kasnata was different from both of his parents. His hair was a startling dark colour that was a gift from his mother, whereas his clear blue eyes belong to his father, but that is where the similarities ended.

The boy was of a slim build that neither of his parents possessed. He was also far more gentle in spirit than the Baron expected the son of two warriors to be.

He spoke kindly to the servants, as though they were equals, not beneath him, and whenever he saw anyone upset, he would sit down and talk to them. Even if they were an enemy, the Baron supposed the princeling would still give them his time.

If he lived long enough, the Baron thought he would make an excellent diplomat, there would not be a nation that would be able to refuse a request from him, nor fail to tell him what he wanted to know. Without training, his gifts of diplomacy would be wasted though, they would not be applied for the good of Nosfa, but for the good of individuals instead.

The thought caused the Baron to shiver. There were plenty of enemies outside the walls of Grashindorph that would take advantage of such a leader, and Nosfa could not afford to have a weak ruler.

Rathe hadn't thought that he would see another funeral in the Order so soon after the last one. In war, it was inevitable that people would die, but he always thought that there would be battles to be fought before the funerals would be held.

His wound was healing nicely, though he was still being told by Payne that he needed to rest for a few more days before he could return to his duties.

Lord Bird had moved out of Kasnata's quarters, taking up residence in the camp of the men of Nosfa whilst he rested. He had barely seen the queen since he had been injured; it hurt him to be parted from her, but he also knew it was necessary.

Yoav had told him that his attendance at Renta's funeral was required in Tola's absence, so that the men of Nosfa were represented. It was added as an afterthought that both the queen and Tola would be offended if Rathe chose not to attend.

Like the funeral that had been held for those that had died in the skirmish with Prince Jayden's soldiers, the funeral was held at sunset.

The Order had all gathered, and some of the men of Nosfa that had served with the Anaguran General over the years, too. They stood arrayed around the funeral pyre that Avner had built. It was a smaller lean to than Rathe had seen before, but it was big enough for the three Queterian generals to stand in with Renta's body.

As the sunset a horn was blasted three times and Renta's body, carefully wrapped in linen, was carried on the shoulders of Avner, Shamgar and Yoav to the pyre.

There had been no celebration before the funeral pyre, there had been no dancing, no drinking or feasting, no celebration of life. If Tola had been there, Rathe would have asked why, but it did not seem like a prudent question to ask in the face of such reverence.

Renta's body was laid in the pyre and a few moments both Yoav and Shamgar emerged and stood either side of the entrance whilst Avner made his final farewell.

As the Dog of War stepped from the pyre he led the singing rather than the queen. The tune was the same that Rathe had heard Kasnata sing when the bodies of the fallen had been carried to the lean to, but this seemed to be an ode to the general rather than a tradition.

"She gave up her life, let her lie down and find final peace. She earned her place long ago, let her lie down. Let your hand guide her way, let her lie down. Her body was broken for the love of her own, let her lie down."

The voices of Shamgar and Yoav joined with Avner's as he continued to sing.

"We honour her memory, let her lie down. May we carry her courage, let her lie down. May we learn from her sacrifice, let her lie down."

Kasnata was stood some distance from General Bird, but he could see that she was crying, as were most of the Order as they listened to the voices of the three generals.

Rathe listened as Wolfblood, Cave Dweller and the Dog of War repeated the refrain three times, then let silence fall. Three torches were lit and carried forward to the generals, who accepted them. As the approached the pyre with the blazing torches, the rest of the Order began to sing.

"Let her be laid down, let her find her rest. She has warred for long enough, she has earned her place. Let your hand guide her way, let her feet carry her true. She is weary from battle, she has shed her blood. Let her be laid down, let her find her rest. Let the honour guard ride out to welcome her in, let the gates be flung open, let her come home. Let her be laid down, let her find her rest. She has warred for long enough, she has earned her place. Let your hand guide her way, let her feet carry her true. She is weary from battle, she has shed her blood. Let her be laid down, let her find her rest."

As the song ended the three generals set the torches to the corners of the funeral pyre and stepped back. Kasnata stepped forward and drew her sword.

"We live by the will of Arala, we die by the sword. Let those we give to her flames be welcomed into her arms and find peace."

"By the will of Arala, by the will of fire," the members of the tribes of Anagura and Queteria replied. Rathe expected the High Priestess to step forward and lead the prayers of the Order for Renta but instead, the generals of the Order stepped towards the pyre and formed a ring about the burning pyre.

Rathe watched as those that were officers in each of the generals' commands line up behind their leaders in another ring and yet more warriors behind them until there were seven rings of warriors surrounding the pyre.

Kasnata and the High Priestess stood on the outside of the rings.

Avner closed his eyes and blinked away the tears that were welling up behind his eyes. He drew in a deep breath before letting a long mournful howl escape his lips.

Rathe stared in amazement as the other generals joined the howl, then the circle behind them, and the next until the night was filled with a chorus of voices howling as the waning moon rose.

"No sacrifice shall be forgotten, no life is lost that we do not remember," Kasnata spoke as the howling died. "For the love of each other, those we fight to protect, those that we would die to defend," the last of her words were barely out of her mouth before war cries began to ring out in a deafening cacophony of sound that carried to the walls of Delma and echoed back to the camp.

Rathe was certain that the sound of so many warriors would terrify those who were tucked up in their beds in Delma as much as it would those who were stood guard on the walls.

Music began to play and the High Priestess led prayers as the seven circles around the pyre began to dance. There were practised steps that each circle were performing slightly out of sync so that there was a ripple effect of movement to anyone watching.

"They will dance until dawn," Kasnata explained as she appeared at Rathe's side. He watched as those who were not part of the dancing slipped away. There were many faces her recognised that were dancing in different circles that included Benaiah, Oswin, Serra and Cara.

"Tola would have appreciated the respect that she has been shown," Rathe replied.

"He would have demanded that we burn him along with her," Kasnata said with a serious note to her voice. Rathe hadn't considered how badly the Roencian would be taking the general's death, but then the queen had known him for a much longer time and fought beside him for many years.

"If they are to dance until dawn, I should depart and rest," Rathe changed the subject and took his leave of the queen.

"As you wish," she tried to sound aloof as she replied, hiding how much she wanted to tell the general to stay.

Rathe began to walk away from the queen when he heard her gasping for air. He turned to see she was collapsed on her knees. The High Priestess was rushing over and had begun issuing orders to those that were not dancing.

In a heartbeat, Rathe was kneeling beside her.

"What is going on?" he asked as the High Priestess tried to

examine the queen.

"I don't know, we need the healers," she replied looking pale in the firelight.

Rathe picked the queen up in his arms and carried her through the camp, as he left the light that the funeral pyre cast, Payne came rushing towards him flanked by two of the Order that the High Priestess has sent to find the healer.

"What happened?" he asked abruptly as he placed a hand on the queen's forehead.

"She collapsed and was struggling to breathe," the High Priestess answered. Payne muttered under his breath to himself.

"Your highness, are you in pain?" he asked as he held her wrist.

"No, it feels like a rope is trying to cut me in half," she gasped.

"Take her to the tent," Payne ordered the general.

"What is wrong with her?" Rathe demanded as the queen screamed in pain.

"It's the baby. I need her to lie down so I can do what I can. Take her to the tent, then you'll need to leave," Payne said in matter-of-fact manner that made Rathe want to punch the healer, but he did as he was told.

"Fetch water," Payne ordered as Rathe laid the queen down on one of the beds. A small crowd had begun to gather outside of the healing tent to find out what was happening. "And tell those outside, if they step in here whilst I am working, I will poison their next meal," Payne snapped.

Rathe went in search of water, panic rising in his chest. The crowd outside glanced at the general and a ripple of muttering ran through the assembled crowd. The general heard some of the derogatory remarks that were being made about him as he went in search of water. The High Priestess was keeping people back from the tent with calm persuasion, which would only be hindered by Rathe responding to those in the crowd.

He collected several skins of water from around one of the camp fires and hurried back to the healing tent. He could hear raised voices before he saw Amalia arguing with the High Priestess.

"Go back to the dance. The queen would be very upset if she discovered you were dishonouring the memory of Renta by abandoning her funeral when there is nothing you can do," the High Priestess was clearly losing her patience.

"I am her bodyguard, whatever is going on, I should be with her," Amalia said trying to push past her.

"You will only be in the way," the High Priestess insisted.

Rathe toyed with the idea of waiting until the argument had finished before trying to enter the healing tent with the water, but not knowing how long the general and High Priestess would argue for, he didn't want to keep Payne waiting.

As she watched him approach, the High Priestess allowed him

to pass, which antagonised Amalia further, but Rathe left dealing with the Kestrel general to the holy woman.

"Here," Rathe handed the water skins to Payne who merely grunted in reply.

Kasnata was still struggling to breathe as she lay there. Payne had rolled up several furs and placed them under her feet and was in the process of uncorking the water skins.

"You need to drink, your majesty," Payne urged as he held the skin to her lips and helped to support her head as she drank.

"Do you know what it is?" Rathe asked, trying to stay out of the healer's way.

"Is that better?" Payne asked the queen, ignoring Lord Bird's question.

"Yes," the queen replied.

"I see. Your highness, you need to rest more," Payne scolded his ruler as he offered her another skin of water that she drank from without complaint.

The healer stood and motioned that Rathe could sit with her if he liked, whilst the healer went to deal with the crowd outside.

"Are you all right?" Rathe asked as he knelt next to the dark angel. She smiled weakly at him and nodded.

"Payne thought I might give birth, but the baby wasn't ready. Just my body thought it was," Kasnata tried to sound reassuring as she spoke.

"I'm glad you are both all right," Rathe sighed with relief.

"Don't worry," she said as she moved so she was sitting and could lean her head on her lover's shoulder. "I have no intention of leaving you."

Rathe wrapped his arms around her and held her in silence, relief flooding through him.

CHAPTER 7

Kasnata was ordered to rest for a few days by the healer, but there was much that had to be done before her husband arrived at the camp.

Samara stood before the queen in her war tent. She had been training with the Condor warriors since she had been appointed as general, but she had yet to receive an assignment for the queen. She had felt a tingle of excitement when she had been summoned, but there was no hint of what the dark angel had in store for her.

"Samara, when was the last time that you were on Anamoore?" Kasnata asked as she sat upon her throne, Marissa stood a few feet away from her.

"It has been four years since I was last in the homeland," Samara replied. "My father is in Queteria and keeps sending me messages asking when I will be returning," the general smiled to herself at the thought.

Messages were dispatched with the movement of troops, which meant that they were often delayed in reaching their destination. This meant that few in the Order sent messages to one another unless they were important.

"He clearly misses you," Kasnata smiled and waved in the direction of the map that lay on the table at the side of the room. "I have been making plans for changes to Anamoore and our garrisons on the mainland," the queen explained. "The map has the locations I think are most suited for what I have in mind."

Samara waited for the queen to rise and followed her over to where the map was pinned to the table. There were eight locations that Kasnata had marked on the map. Two were on Anamoore, whilst the other six were on the mainland.

"The two locations on Anamoore, I think they would be ideal for two new villages to be established. I want you to go to Anamoore with a handful of warriors and oversee the start of the construction," the queen smiled as Marissa brought over a pile of papers.

"Only the start of construction?" Samara asked as Kasnata looked through the papers.

"Yes. Here, these are the plans for the two settlements. Once you are satisfied that they are under way, I want to you to establish six garrisons on the mainland. Five of them are to act as trading posts for the most part, places our warriors can find supplies and rest in briefly as they travel across Celadmore. But this one, here, close to Roenca, I want that to be a fully-fledged fortress," Kasnata pointed at the map to an area of woodland that was to the west of where Roenca lay.

"A fortress so close to Grashindorph, your majesty?" Samara asked innocently as her eyes looked over the plans that she had been given.

"I think that an outpost that we control within the borders of

Nosfa may be useful," Kasnata replied with a slight smile.

"As you wish, your highness," Samara saluted the queen. "I will leave in the morning."

The banners of Nosfa's party could be seen when they were still a few hours from the camp. The imminent arrival of the king cast different shadows across the men of Nosfa and the people of the Order.

There was a sense of foreboding that had settled over people in both camps, not all the men of Nosfa were anxious to see the king that ruled over them with so little regard for those that lived and worked in the kingdom.

The commanders were looking forward to the king visiting, expecting their loyalty to be rewarded and the general to be punished for his treasonous acts with the barbarian queen.

Kasnata had ordered a welcoming party for the king that would be comprised of members from both armies. Yoav volunteered to stand with Rathe as representatives of the officers of each army. Methanlan and Shaul had brought some soldiers from the camp to act the soldier component, though all the warriors of the Order had been ordered to ignore Methanlan and Shaul whilst they were still acting as though they were soldiers of Nosfa.

Mercia had brought a small entourage with him, though the muscular man that rode to his right caused Kasnata to frown.

"Welcome, my husband. What an unexpected pleasure this is," Kasnata smiled at the king, though the warmth of it was not reflected in her eyes.

"My dearest wife, how wonderful to see you again," Mercia replied in the same manner.

"You must be tired after your journey; quarters have been prepared for you with your men," Kasnata said making it clear that the king was not welcome in her quarters.

"You are too kind, my darling," the king bowed to the queen in an overly dramatic manner. "General Bird, if you would be so kind as to escort me to my quarters," the king ordered without taking his eyes off the queen. He searched her face for the tiniest reaction to taking her lover away from her side and felt a smug satisfaction as he watched her eyes narrow and the corners of her mouth twitch with annoyance.

"As you wish, your highness," the general bowed.

"Oh and may I introduce General Seaton to you, my dear wife, he has proven to be a valuable asset to my forces in other climes, I felt that his experience could only help you in your campaign against the Delmarians," the king waved in the direction of the muscled man.

"Your highness, your reputation as a warrior is without

parallel, but the stories of your beauty have not done your highness justice," General Seaton bowed to the queen, who barely managed to conceal her disgust. The king watched as Rathe's jaw tightened into a firm line and his eyes filled with jealous anger.

"You are too kind," Kasnata spoke with disdain. "When you have rested, my king, we shall hold a feast to welcome you," the queen said dismissing the welcoming party.

The king turned to General Bird, who led Mercia and his entourage through the camp to the quarters that had been prepared.

The dawn was breaking, the weak Wentrus sun struggling to brighten the sky, when Joab and Cassandra caught their first glimpse of Neesa and Mia since the chase had begun.

Mia was slung over the withers of Neesa's horse, her hands and feet had been bound. The assassin was a few paces away, dusting away any sign that the two women had stopped there.

Cassandra had dismounted and crept through the scrub that shielded the camp site from the worst of the wind from the north. Joab was waiting, just out of sight of the camp, for the signal from the Guardian of the Wilds.

She had made the young assassin swear he would be patient

and wait, not charge in like a common soldier. The immortal watched Neesa and tried to judge how long it would take her to reach her horse.

Timing was essential when dealing with enemies that were as dangerous and skilled as Neesa was. If Cassandra moved too soon then she would risk Neesa taking flight or even harming the Lady Mia, then it would be up to Joab.

The Guardian didn't like the idea of the shadow chasing after Neesa on his own, she had far more experience than Joab and Cassandra knew that it would take a moment of distraction on the shadows part to bring an end to his life.

Neesa could feel the eyes of someone watching her. The hairs on the back of her neck all stood on end as she went about clearing the site. There were no ashes or remains of a fire to dispose of, it was more of an excuse to find out how close her pursuers were.

The assassin of Nosfa couldn't be certain who had been following her other than Joab, she was certain that the shadow of Lady Mia would follow her to the ends of the earth. She smiled to herself and Cassandra sprang from the scrub.

The assassin rolled as the Guardian of the Wilds came at her, the two women tumbling across the dust and fine powdered snow. They scuffled, neither gaining the upper hand.

Mia could hear the fight behind her and as the two women fought, the horse began to snort nervously, becoming more agitated.

Joab heard the sound of fighting and didn't wait for Cassandra to signal, he kicked his mount hard so that it sprang forward, protesting momentarily at having Joab's heels dug into its sides.

Neesa grabbed a handful of dust and aimed for Cassandra's eyes, the Guardian of the Spire darted backwards, away from the assassin, so that she was between Neesa and her horse.

Neesa felt she was being toyed with, the Guardian didn't seem to be trying to kill her, merely delay her. Joab's horse sprang through the scrub and the Roencian hauled Mia off the assassin's horse and held her tightly.

Cassandra nodded to Joab, who reined his mount around and cantered away to where Cassandra's horse was waiting. Neesa tried to get passed the Guardian one more time, but Cassandra simply smiled and nimbly kept her back.

Joab trusted that Cassandra would be more than a match for Neesa, so slowed his horse to a walk so that he could remove Mia's bonds.

"You came for me," she gasped as she massaged her wrists, glad to have her limbs free again.

"Of course, I told you I was here to protect you, to keep you safe. Leaving you in Neesa's hands to be given back to that beast would have been going back on my word," Joab spoke evenly, though he was smiling broadly, happy that Mia was safe, at least for the moment.

Joab and Mia waited for a few minutes by Cassandra's horse until the Guardian of the Wilds appeared.

"What happened to Neesa?" Joab asked, Mia still sat in his arms.

"She ran," Cassandra shrugged. "She'll go back to Grashindorph or she'll regroup, ready to try again. But I wouldn't worry about her right now. We should be getting back to Tulna."

Nosfa looked at his general with a sneer. The man who was second in the line of succession to the throne of Nosfa was more of a threat in the bed of his wife than he had been in the court of Nosfa.

Lord Bird allying with his wife had not been what the king had imagined when he had sent the general to fight on the front lines. He had planned for the general to die in battle after compromising his wife, but the irritating man had failed to do either.

"What have you to report?" Mercia demanded in an icy tone.

"Prince Jayden fell in the first assault he made against our forces, the Regent of Delma is not within the city and the supply lines have been cut, they will not be able to last more than a few months before surrendering, your highness," Rathe reeled off the report in a flat tone. He knew that the king would already be aware of most of what Rathe had to say, but talking about the war was much more preferable to talking about what he had been doing with the queen.

"Is that all?" Mercia demanded.

"Sire?" Rathe asked, not wanting to say more than he had to.

"Your subordinates had other things to report in their dispatches," the king said pointedly.

"What things, sire?" Rathe asked calmly.

"They report that you have been spending a lot of time with the queen," Mercia said lightly, "that you have been training with General Yoav, that you have been seen dressing as animals and running about the land with the barbarians, that you have violated my wife and finally, if violating my wife was not enough, that you have impregnated her," the king finished, sounding as though he was reading an interesting story. "What have you to say in response to these accusations?"

Rathe stared at the king, unsure of what to say or do.

"Do you have nothing to say?" the king asked, his patience turning quickly as Rathe seemed unable to respond.

"I acted to serve the best interests of the nation of Nosfa, your highness," Rathe stammered.

"You have acted in your own interests for long enough, general," the king spat back. "Seaton is here to act as the head of my army. You will act as his aide, at least until he feels that you are no longer needed. You are dismissed, general."

Rathe felt his heart pounding in his ears as he stepped out into the cold night air. He was being replaced, as soon as General Seaton knew all that was required to lead the men of Nosfa alongside the queen of the Order, Rathe would be summoned back to Grashindorph, and whatever fate the king had in store for him.

CHAPTER 8

When Hermia was finished with her interrogation of Bracha, the date of her trial was set. She was being held as a prisoner of war, and would face the justice of the Gibborim for her treachery.

Haston had been asked to preside over the trial as both Haman and Hermia would be involved in presenting the events to the people.

The system was modelled on the law courts of Nosfa; the defendant was brought before a lord who would read out a list of the crimes they were accused of. Those that had brought the charges would then call witnesses to substantiate their claims and the lord would decide based on the stories the witnesses and the defendant told whether they were innocent or guilty.

If they were found guilty, then the lord would then decide on the most suitable punishment for the individual. In some extreme cases, the lord asked the people who had been wronged what they required the law to do in order to punish the guilty party.

Bracha was brought before the Gibborim to a chorus of jeers and Hermia stood up to speak.

"Bracha, wife of Jephthah, a woman we all once trusted betrayed our people. She passed information about us to our enemy and tried to corrupt my shield, tried to turn him against me and against all of you," Hermia spoke clearly and her words received cheers as a reply.

"Not only is Bracha guilty of treason, she also sent Ilana, an innocent, a young woman, to the surface to be arrested and hanged. She did this knowing what would happen to the young girl and as an act of revenge against those closest to Jephthah," Haman continued for Hermia.

"You have witnesses who will speak to the truth of this?" Haston asked. He already knew that Bracha was guilty, he had been there for at least some of what had happened, but he was determined to follow the correct procedure.

"I present, to the people, Asahel, comrade of Helez, the brother of Ilana," Hermia said, summoning Asahel to speak.

After Asahel was called, Helez was summoned, and then Jephthah and Layla before Bracha was given an opportunity to speak.

"This is not justice, you are all criminals, you have no right to pass judgement on me. You will all be caught and all be punished under the law of King Mercia Nosfa VI," she said defiantly. "You have all fled here to escape justice; you are nothing more than thieves and murderers," she spat.

The Gibborim erupted into noise as curses and insults were hurled at Bracha.

"You offer no explanation for your crimes? No remorse for ending the life of an innocent?" Haston asked from his seat of judgement.

"I did what was best for my country," Bracha said firmly, her convictions unwavering.

Helez had managed to keep a thin mask of calm in place as he spoke of his sister's death and Bracha's part in it as well as the betrayal, but as he listened to her indignance, he felt his anger rising.

"Let Haston do what is right," Asahel warned him in a whisper, standing next his shoulder. If Helez did try and break through the crowd to get to Bracha, Asahel would be able to stop him before her got too close.

"Bracha, wife of Jephthah, you have offered no explanation, no apology and displayed no remorse for the actions you have taken," Haston had to shout to be heard over the cries from the Gibborim. "However, your death would serve no purpose. I sentence you to a life of imprisonment, where you will have to think about what you chose to do every day for the rest of your life. You will be confined in silence; no living being will ever speak your name again.

"For betraying the Gibborim to our enemy, your tongue will be cut out and your fingers broken and bound," Haston was resolute in his judgement; but Helez felt cheated.

He had been certain that Haston would give her a death sentence as was befitting treason and causing the death of his sister, but Haston had shied away from it. Asahel watched his friend and saw the look of frustration as the sentence was passed.

"Don't do anything stupid," Asahel warned Helez quietly.

"She deserves to die," Helez replied through gritted teeth.

"I know," Asahel replied with a sigh. "But that is not what has been decided, we have to live with the judgement Haston passed,"

"No, we don't."

Kasna opened her eyes to find a blade lying across her throat and her eyes looking into those of Duke Kelmar DeLacey. She could hear Kia struggling against some of the Regent of Delma's soldiers in the darkness.

"Let her go," Kasna spoke evenly without fear as she met the gaze of Kelmar.

"You are in no position to make demands," the Duke smiled at her without warmth and pressed the blade against her throat so that Kasna could feel it bite into her soft skin, causing a warm trickle of blood to flow down her neck and onto her pillow.

"Let her go, unharmed, leave her here and I will go with you without any resistance," Kasna seemed even calmer as she spoke a second time. Underneath her bed sheets, her fingers grasped the hilt of the sword she slept with.

"And why should that be any different to the situation that we have now?" Kelmar asked, frowning, not understanding why the princess was so calm and confident under pressure. It was true that the princesses both looked much older than they had since he had seen them at the fortress of Abergorlech and when he had pursued them across the plains of Celadmore.

He had assumed it was down to the influence of the village, there was something about it that troubled him, made him nervous, more than the woman who had so easily bested his men when he had first arrived here. But as he looked down on the eldest daughter of the barbarian queen he felt there was more at work here than he had dreamed possible.

"If you don't let her go, I will scream and the man who wants to gut you for killing General Renta will tear your men apart to get to you. You may kill me, but Tola will certainly kill all of you," Kasna replied with a satisfied smile and a note of triumph.

"Know this, princess, if you break your word, I will kill you, and your sister will not be left unharmed. She will know unending torture for the rest of her life that will be inflicted upon her by those that are well practised in keeping people alive whilst inflicting the most gruesome punishments imaginable," the Regent of Delma spat with menace and Kasna nodded her assent.

"Very well. Kia, go back to bed. Don't raise the alarm until morning," Kasna said firmly.

"You would do well to listen to your sister," the Duke warned. Kasna released her grip on her sword as Kelmar withdrew his blade.

She gracefully rose and was instantly tied and gagged by the soldiers of Delma. Kia was thrown to the floor as the Regent hoisted the bound form of her sister onto his shoulder and disappeared through the window that he had entered through.

Kasna kept her eyes on Kia's until the wall of their quarters in Tulna obscured her from view. In the dark of the room, Kia began to whimper as she took her sister's sword from where it was hidden amongst the sheets and held it to her chest, wishing it was Kasna instead of the blade.

"Be still, little one," a voice from the shadows soothed.

"Abbott?" Kia asked as she sniffed to hold back her tears.

"Yes, do not be afraid," the monk moved to lay a comforting hand on the princess' shoulder.

"They took her; you have to help her, why didn't you stop them?" Kia let her questions tumble from her mouth as she collapsed on her bed, still clutching her sister's sword.

"Though it may seem I have been callous in letting her be taken, be assured, she is in no danger from those men. She is more powerful than you or your mother know, and she has her own path to walk before this is ended. She saved you from pain and suffering without a second thought," the Abbott comforted Kia as he tucked her in.

"But what if she – what if I never get to see her again?" Kia yawned.

"You will, little one, you will, and until then, you must take care of her sword. She will need it when you meet again. In the meantime, get some sleep. I will awaken the others and tell them of what has happened here."

Kia closed her eyes as the Abbott bid and soon drifted off into a dreamless sleep. The Abbott stood over her for a moment and sighed, knowing that Kasna had saved her sister, but in doing so had visited more pain upon herself than she could yet realise.

"How could you let them take her?" Tola roared. "That cretin escaped, not only did he escape, but he took Kasna! Why didn't you stop him?" the Roencian was so angry that he paced the room, uncertain of what to do with himself, his braided hair flicking out behind him every time he changed direction.

"Peace, Tola," Kania warned gently. "There are things at play here that you do not understand."

"What I understand is that Renta's murdered was here, in front of you and you let him go with one of Kasnata's daughters that we were sent here to protect!" Tola fumed and made to charge at the Abbott, his sword drawn, but Mathias stepped in front of his cousin.

"Listen to what he has to say," Mathias tried to calm the larger man as he caught Tola's sword arm mid-swing.

"The princess chose to go with the Regent. She made a choice to shy away from violence in order to save her sister's life. She chose to protect Kia and bargain her own capture to ensure her sister remained free. If Kasna had chosen to fight against Kelmar and the men he brought, then I would have helped her. We cannot intervene, you know why better than most, Tola," the Abbott said, motioning to Mathias to stand aside. Tola's cousin let go of the arm he was holding, letting Tola sheath his blade.

"It is frustrating, we understand, we know that there are some things that have to happen, that must be, even if they lead to painful situations," Nodarto soothed as he patted Tola on the shoulder.

"I will kill him; I will find him and rescue Kasna from him," Tola said through gritted teeth as he shrugged off Nodarto's hand.

"You will not," the five occupants of Tola's room turned to look at the small figure of Kia.

"Princess –" Tola began, but the slight girl held up her hand for silence. The Abbott smiled to himself as he saw her mother reflected in the young princess.

"Kasna knew what she was doing. The Regent will take her to Delma; he won't harm her if she is to be used as a bargaining chip against our mother in the war being waged. If you go to rescue her then you will needlessly risk your life and go against the expressed orders of my mother. She asked you to bring us to her," Kia said firmly.

"And your sister is in the hands of the enemy," Tola retorted, his eyes alive with a thirst for revenge.

"And I am not. My mother needs to know where Kasna is and that I am safe. See me safely to her and then ask for her permission to hunt for Kelmar and Kasna," Kia's voice carried the weight of her ancestry as she spoke. Tola opened his mouth to reply, but after a few moments of standing before the assembled company he closed his mouth and simply nodded in agreement.

"Do you wish to remain here for further training before you are reunited with your mother?" Kania asked as Tola moved to sit on the edge of his bed, shaking his head with resignation.

"For as long as you think there is still something I can learn," Kia replied.

"There will always be something you can learn, but for now there are reasons that you should remain here for a few months more," Nodarto said slowly, glancing at the Abbott who closed his eyes for slightly too long, indicating his agreement.

"So whilst one daughter is in the hands of a murderer, the other remains here and Renta is still dead," Tola spat bitterly.

"And whilst that is so, you shall come with me, Tola," the Abbott smiled. "We leave in the morning and there is much to be done."

The camp of the Order was as quiet at night as Nosfa had expected. He walked between the tents and covering structures without meeting a single challenge from someone on watch.

He slipped quietly through the camp until he reached the tent that the note he had received had mentioned. He ducked inside without calling out to whoever was inside, he had no need.

Hesla was waiting for the king and bowed to him as he entered.

"Your highness," she said in a low voice. The king gave her a wry smile as she returned to standing and motioned that the king should sit in one of the two chairs that stood either side of a small table. The king shook his head and instead grabbed the general by the throat.

"You summoned me for some reason?" he asked pulling the general's head to within inches of his own.

"Yes, highness," she gasped, her fingers clawing at his hand.

"Remember who it is that you are dealing with," he said in a threatening tone as he released the general and watched as she collapsed on her knees gasping for breath.

"Of course, Sire," Hesla replied. "I must beg your forgiveness, the general lives as does your wife."

"So I noticed," the king replied with a sneer. Hesla had caught her breath but she remained on her knees at the feet of the king. Experience had taught the Valian that she was safer submitting to the wishes of Mercia.

"I placed my trust in the wrong people and I am prepared to suffer whatever punishment you deem necessary," Hesla grovelled.

"Punishment I deem necessary? It isn't I that you should fear retribution from," the king said with a cruel smile. "It is the last heir that is more displeased," he said turning away from the general to pull back the flap of the tent.

Hesla looked up at the last heir of Valia.

"I'm sorry," she whispered. The last heir of Valia simply stared at her with cold eyes. The king stood beside the heir and looked down on the general.

"Do you have anything to offer that might redeem you?" Mercia asked.

"I, no, sire," she closed her eyes as the last heir of Valia struck her across the face.

"Failure is not something that we can tolerate," the king said firmly as he sat down in the chair he had been offered and watched as Hesla learned what happened to those that disappointed the pretender to the throne of the Order.

Chapter 9

2431IGL 79th Sagma/Sumar

Kasnata awoke to pain in her belly that told her the baby was coming. Marissa was close at hand and fetched Payne as soon as she heard the queen call out to her.

The healer confirmed that the baby was coming. Marissa woke Yoav and Shamgar, who in turn woke Rathe and the High Priestess.

By the time Rathe had dressed and made it to Kasnata's sleep quarters, her contractions were close together and her brow was matted with sweat.

Marissa was knelt beside the queen, but stepped aside as Rathe came to take Kasnata by the hand.

"Has anyone else been told?" Kasnata gasped between muffled cries.

"No, your highness," Marissa replied.

"Make sure there is no one lurking. I will be safe enough with General Bird," She breathed deeply as another wave of contractions began.

"I'll wait outside; turn away anyone that gets too close," Shamgar spoke to Marissa and Yoav as the three generals moved into the cold night.

"No thaw is coming," Marissa shivered as saluted Cave Dweller and Wolfblood, and began her patrol of the camp.

"I'll wake Avner. He'll want to know," Yoav whispered to the shorter man.

"Let him rest, it'll be dawn soon enough and we can tell him then. No point all of us losing sleep tonight," Shamgar clapped his old friend on the shoulder.

"True, he'd only antagonise the High Priestess," Yoav grinned before turning and patrolling in the opposite direction to Marissa.

Shamgar rolled his shoulders and drew his broadsword and planted the tip in the earth in front of him. His sword was almost the same size as him, making him a more imposing figure than a man twice his height.

He tried to block out the sounds of the queen in pain as he glanced around the camp. He didn't think that there would be any spies or assassins lurking now, but with King Mercia Nosfa VI in the camp and the threats that were being dealt with by Misna and Amalia, the general didn't think that taking any precaution when it came to his queen's safety was being too careful.

"The baby is coming, your highness," Payne tried to soothe the queen as the pain intensified. She had given birth to three children and found that each delivery was worse than the one before.

Kasna had been the easiest by far, but she had been born early and was much smaller than other babies. Kasnata had feared that her oldest daughter would not survive but thanks to the efforts of

Cassandra, Payne and the Abbott, the princess had survived.

The queen wished she was back on Anamoore, in her home, her own rooms where there were walls, not canvas. She found that she missed her homeland more as the days of the siege of Delma dragged on.

The blockade had cut off the city and scouting parties had ensured that any supply lines were no longer usable, but that did not mean that they would surrender soon. The queen silently cursed her husband's vain ambition, though it had brought her some happiness in the form of Rathe.

She could hear the general whispering to her, encouraging her, reassuring her. His hand was grasped firmly in hers, no matter how tightly she squeezed it, he didn't flinch. Kasnata wasn't sure whether it helped or not, but she was glad that he was there.

The sound of a baby crying, and the lessening of pain, brought a wave of relief washing over the queen. She was exhausted, but her baby was crying.

"A boy, your highness," Payne smiled, and for a moment, the normally grumpy healer seemed genuinely happy.

The High Priestess stepped forward and took the baby from Payne. Rathe watched as his son was wrapped in blankets that had been prepared for him and he was presented to the Queen and her lover.

"Your highness, by the will of Arala, I present your son," the

High Priestess smiled as Kasnata took the baby into her arms, it still crying and screaming.

Rathe was surprised the child could make so much noise, being less than a few minutes old. He felt pride he couldn't explain as he looked down at the woman he loved and his son.

Kasnata felt exhausted and an unexpected wave of pain. She handed her son to Rathe and looked at Payne in alarm.

"Something's wrong," she gasped as more contractions began.

"Your highness, I am afraid you are not done," Payne frowned and motioned that the High Priestess should take Rathe and the child elsewhere.

"What's going on?" Rathe asked, trying to turn back to Kasnata's side.

"There is another child," the High Priestess said grimly.

"Then I should be with her," Rathe frowned.

"No," the High Priestess was firm with the general. She forced him from the tent, to the surprise of General Shamgar.

"A new prince of our nation?" Cave Dweller asked as he looked down at the blotchy bundle that was held in Lord Bird's arms.

"Yes," Rathe replied; his attention focused on what was happening inside the queen's quarters. He heard her screaming in pain and sighed in frustration.

"Don't do it," Shamgar warned, as he reached down and stroked the face of the new prince with his large stubby finger.

"What?"

"Don't go back in there. If the healer and High Priestess removed you, they have their reasons. You're better off out here," Shamgar said as he made funny faces at the baby, who had finally stopped crying.

"I want to know what is happening, they said there is another baby," Rathe tried to explain, working himself into a frenzy.

Rathe felt a hand impact with the back of his skull. For a moment, he was dazed and had to shake his head several times before his vision returned to normal.

"The queen doesn't need you to hold her hand, Pup. She has more important concerns than keeping you calm. Let her do what she has to, let the healer and the priestess take care of her now. You've got a son to look after," Yoav growled from behind him.

Rathe looked up at the grizzled man with a look of complete helplessness as the general lifted the baby out of his arms.

"Ah, now a little whelp, soon a great warrior," he smiled at the baby. "Needs a name, a good strong name,"

"Like Yoav, perhaps?" Shamgar needled his friend.

"It's a good strong name, but this whelp isn't a wolf, he's the son of the dark angel, he needs a grander name," Wolfblood grinned and handed the baby to Shamgar as the short general sheathed his sword.

"A name of our people?" Shamgar asked as he rocked the baby gently.

"I need to ask Kasnata what she thinks," Rathe said, trying to go back in the tent. Yoav hit him again.

"Nonsense, man. Children are born with their names, they aren't chosen for them. We just need to discover what this young princeling is called," Yoav said marching Rathe away from the queen's tent and sitting him by the fire. He left Rathe for only a moment before returning with the baby in his arms.

Yoav was a gruff man, but he knew when a man needed to be distracted and never believed that mollycoddling was an appropriate thing. Indulging in self-pity was a dangerous thing for any warrior, even more dangerous for a man who supposed to be leading others.

Shamgar watched Yoav playing with the baby and distracting Rathe in the dancing firelight. For the moment, the baby could not be in safer hands. The general of the Order of the Bear often wondered at how a man that was so gruff with people and so fierce on the battlefield could be so gentle with babies and young children.

Shamgar could understand Rathe wanting to return to Kasnata's side. As he stood guard on the tent and listened to Payne and the High Priestess trying to coax and calm the queen as she screamed in pain, it took all of his self-control not to abandon his post to try and help.

"How is she?" Marissa asked as she appeared out of the darkness.

"Struggling. She has a son and another baby that is yet to come,"

Shamgar replied.

"I'll wake Avner; he may be needed after all," Marissa sighed and vanished again. Shamgar looked up at the sky and wondered if anyone within the camp of the Order was sleeping with all the noise that the queen was making.

Kasnata prayed that the pain would be over. Payne had a worried look fixed on his face as the second child of the queen and her general was finally born.

He glanced at the High Priestess who looked white as she looked down on the child. Kasnata collapsed on the bed, so tired that it took her a few minutes to realise that she had given birth but her second child was not crying.

"What's wrong?" the queen demanded as the silence caused panic to bubble in her stomach.

"Your highness, I'm sorry, your daughter -" Payne said gently as he handed the baby girl to Kasnata. She was barely breathing or moving. Her body was cold to touch.

"Blankets," Kasnata ordered. The High Priestess stood still staring down at the child. Payne shook his head and tried to reason with the queen.

"Your highness, there is nothing we can do," he said calmly.

"Blankets. Now," Kasnata said raising her voice.

Avner stepped into the tent and picked up a pile of blankets that the High Priestess had prepared for the baby. He scowled at the

High Priestess and Payne as he pushed them aside and knelt beside the queen. Marissa and Shamgar stood either side of the entrance watching the queen and the Dog of War.

"She is alive," Avner confirmed as he placed his large hand on the baby's head. Kasnata wrapped the baby in the blankets and held her close to her chest.

"She can't breathe," Kasnata chewed her lips as she looked at Avner, the general held the queen's gaze. She was not panicked or hysterical; the dark angel was as calm as when she led in battle.

"Then we should help her lungs as we would any that had taken water instead of air," Avner took the child from the queen's arms and laid her on the floor beside the bed. He tilted the head of the child back ever so slightly and gentle blew air into its lungs.

He was careful not to let too much air flow into the baby's lungs and damage them. He could feel the beating of the baby's heart as he helped the baby to breathe.

Liquid was bubbling in the infant's throat, so the general picked up the child and tilted her so that she was on her side and the liquid could drain out of her throat and lungs. As the last of the liquid was gone, the crying began.

"Thank you," Kasnata breathed a sigh of relief as she lay back and closed her eyes.

"She has a strong will, just like her mother," Avner beamed at the queen as he handed her the baby.

"Do you know what she is called?" the dark angel asked as she gazed down at her youngest daughter. Rathe burst into the tent to see his lover holding his second child. Yoav was behind him, carrying the prince.

"Deshanna," Avner looked up at Rathe and motioned that he should sit with the queen.

"Your highness, by the will of Arala and the grace of her love, I present Deshanna, princess of the Order," the High Priestess said as she remembered herself. Avner cast a dark look at the woman that told the priestess she should leave quickly.

Yoav handed the prince to Rathe and nudged him towards his daughter and the queen.

"Deshanna?" Rathe asked as he looked down at the child in Kasnata's arms.

"Yes," the queen smiled and looked at her son.

"Gildow," Rathe said as he handed the baby to her. Kasnata looked pleasantly surprised as she cradled both children. "Yoav helped me find his name," the general whispered as he put one arm around the queen.

Payne let the scene unfold for a few moments before he began ushering all but Marissa out of the queen's quarters.

"She needs her rest."

The twins slept soundly in the crib that Yoav, Shamgar, and Avner crafted for the new prince and princess. It had taken them less than a day working together to create the crib the children shared. It was made from a single log that they shaped and carved bears, wolves and dogs on the inside the crib for the babies to grab hold of when they lay in it.

The crib sat next to Kasnata's bed, where she lay, her body still recovering from giving birth to her two children. Each of her generals had visited and brought gifts for each of the children, but they had not stayed very long. Marissa stood on the inside of the tent, protecting the queen whilst she was resting. Outside the tent, two guards had been placed.

Kasnata had gotten used to people trying to argue with the guards about visiting the queen, but as she was woken by raised voices, she nodded to Marissa to let the visitor in.

King Mercia Nosfa VI entered the queen's quarters in a flustered state.

"You people should have more respect," he snorted as Marissa slipped in behind the king to resume her position guarding the queen. "Is her presence really necessary?" Mercia demanded, as he glared at Marissa.

"He won't hurt me here, Marissa," the queen smiled at her temporary bodyguard, who nodded and went to wait outside. "You wanted something?" the queen asked brightly.

"Your camp is a mess," Mercia sneered.

"What is it you want?" Kasnata asked in frustration. "You want my army to march on your enemies, my army marches; you hold my son hostage and I do as you ask. You have a parade of mistresses in order to sire bastards to give you an heir that is free of my blood, and I say nothing. So, what is it that you want, Mercia?" the queen hated having him in her war camp; she wanted him as far away from her as possible.

"You have embarrassed me," Mercia growled.

"Have I? I have exposed to your enemies that our marriage is not one of bliss and contentment? Or is that I have taken one of your generals into my bed, one you wanted to see dead, one you didn't send to seduce and control me?" Kasnata shot back.

"Women in my nation do not betray their husbands. They do not take lovers. Queens that engage in adultery are tried and executed for treason," Mercia said as he advanced on the crib where Kasnata's children lay.

"Then have me executed," Kasnata climbed out of her bed and stood in Mercia's path. "Do what you will to me, but you will not harm my children," she spoke each word deliberately, and the king paused.

"It is not only the queens that are punished. It is their children and their lovers," Mercia stood a few inches away from the queen. Somewhere deep down, he had once loved the woman that was stood before him.

Their marriage had been something he had engineered in order to cement his power, but when he had courted the queen, he had loved her. He found it easy to hate her from a distance, easy to convince himself that she was his enemy, a tool he could use, but when he was stood in her presence, when he could see the fire burning in her eyes, he was reminded that once he had cared about this woman.

"So what is it you want?" Kasnata asked again.

"You will take the city of Delma and capture the king. You will drag him back to Grashindorph where he we fall at my feet and beg for the lives of his queen and his people. You will forsake your lover and deny that these are his spawn. You will return to my bed and show all that would oppose me that you stand ready to defend my throne. You will give General Seaton whatever he desires and willingly submit to my rule," Mercia could feel his desire rising as he knew that he had his wife completely trapped.

"And what if I don't?" the queen asked, her eyes still fixed on Mercia's.

"Then all your children will be publicly executed, your lover will be executed and you will be broken, beaten until you can no longer raise your voice, let alone a blade against me. You will never see your homeland again and will end your days locked in my dungeons where the jailers will be able to abuse you for their own pleasure and amusement," the king whispered in the queen's ear. Kasnata closed her eyes and tried to suppress the repulsion she felt as her husband kissed her and forced her down onto her bed.

Kasnata's body ached, there was no pleasure in her husband's thrusting for her. Mercia grunted and looked down at the queen of Nosfa and the Order.

"At least pretend you are enjoying yourself, my dear," he groaned in her ear as she dug her nails into his skin. She intended to cause him pain, but Mercia demanded more.

When he was finished her collapsed on top of her, pinning her down on the furs, panting heavily.

"You should know; your daughters will not find their way to you," Mercia whispered. "My garrisons watch the roads and Kelmar stalks the wilds, they will die before you ever see them again,"

Kasna could hear the men of Delma making loud comments about her around the campfire that they were huddled about to keep out the cold of the night.

She was still bound and gagged but had no idea where she was now. She had been thrown across the knees of Kelmar on his horse and the princess had soon drifted off to sleep, rocked away by the motion of the horse.

She had awoken when the party had halted and she had been roughly thrown to the ground.

"You two, go back down the trail and keep a lookout for anyone following us from that village," Kelmar ordered as he dismounted. "The rest of you make camp. We rest for five hours and then move on."

The men had been quick about their business, food had been hunted for, water found and a fire built in a much smaller time frame than Kasna would have expected from men that were not of the Order. Though there were some who were skilled warriors outside of her mother's people she knew about, Kelmar being one of them, from what she had been told none could match the ability of the Anaguras and Queterians when it came to living off the land and discipline.

The Duke stood over Kasna and oversaw the actions of his men whilst not taking one eye off the princess. In the two hours it had taken for the night to draw closer to dawn, Kelmar had not moved and had not spoken a word to her.

Kasna found herself feeling drowsy and so drifted off to sleep again.

"You think that the Duke will let us have a little fun with her before we have to turn her over to the king and queen?"

"Do you think we should ask or just wait for him to disappear into the forest and have some fun."

"You really want to get your hands on a barbarian spawn?"

"Why not? No other women out here to play with."

"She's barely a woman at all."

The voices of the men seemed to be coming from inside her head, much louder than they should have been, given the distance she was from the men and the fire. She opened her eyes, half-expecting the men to be stood over her, but they were still a good distance away from them and the fireside.

"Not used to sleeping outside, princess?" Kelmar asked with a measure of disgust in his voice. Kasna tried to reply, but the gag in her mouth muffled her words. The Duke looked down at her with a bored expression for a moment or two before he knelt beside the eldest daughter of Kasnata and roughly pulled off the gag.

"Not used to sleeping outside in the cold desert night in nothing more than a slip," Kasna replied dryly.

The fact that the princess was barely dressed had not escaped Kelmar's notice, but he had been working hard to ignore how light and revealing the girl's night attire was.

"Your time in Tulna has made you soft," the duke sneered.

"And you have spent weeks living through Wentrus and Spregan leaving your men half-starved and nurturing their baser desires with no outlet," Kasna made no effort to try and sit up from the position she had been thrown into on the floor by the rough hands of the men.

"Scared they may take liberties?" Kelmar half-laughed, the icy tone of his voice as cold as the desert night.

"I have lived my life as a prisoner in my father's palace surrounded by guards, treated as though as I am expendable. My father allowed his men to take liberties with me; I can only pity those who feel the need to satisfy their desire that way," the princess replied hotly.

"You're lying," Kelmar said with amusement. Kasna opened her mouth to protest, but the Regent of Delma had dropped to his knees and pulled her up onto hers. "No matter what you may have gone through at the hands of your father and his men; you would still be afraid of it happening again as you know what it feels like and can only imagine how much worse it can get."

Kasna stared at Kelmar, her eyes unblinking and filled with contempt. Kelmar felt a jolt run through his body as he looked into the princess' eyes for the first time. They were eyes that held wisdom beyond her years and the wisdom they held gave them a beautiful quality that the Regent of Delma had never seen before.

He kept his eyes locked with hers to avoid them scanning every inch of her body through the slip that she was wearing. He was painfully aware that it was not only his men that had been denied pleasurable company and having a young woman so ample in form as his prisoner, he knew he would have to work harder than normal to keep his desires in check.

The urge to kiss him was almost overwhelming as the moments she held his gaze lengthened, but Kasna was not going to break eye contact first, it was a matter of stubbornness and pride. Though she did not have to resist the urge for long, as Kelmar looked down. His fingers fumbled with the clasp of his cloak.

In a fluid motion, he removed his only source of warmth and wrapped it around Kasnata's body.

"Get some sleep," he ordered as he roughly gagged her a second time and pushed her back to the ground.

CHAPTER 10

"There are rumours circulating," Amalia sighed as she met with Misna. The two generals had assigned themselves to the nightwatch so that they could meet without attracting too much attention.

"I know," Misna pursed her lips and gazed out at the city of Delma. People had started to try and flee the city. Those that had been captured by the combined forces of Nosfa and the Order had revealed that the city was well stocked but there was a madness descending on the people that was more terrifying than running into the arms of the vast army that surrounded their walls.

"Have your people gotten any information yet?" Amalia asked.

"Some, but it makes little sense," Misna replied, shaking her head. "There is lots of hysteria rather than solid information, talk of spirits and witches,"

"Do you think they have been sent out to damage our morale? To cause the army to break and run?" Amalia looked at the Raven General with worry creasing her brow.

"It's a possibility," Misna admitted, "but I don't think so. On the other matter, there has been something."

"You've questioned Hesla?" Amalia couldn't hide her surprise.

"She was found beaten and bloody in her own quarters," Misna looked seriously at Amalia. "She was attacked, but not by any from among our number," she dropped her voice, so it was barely above a whisper.

"Who was it then?" the Kestrel General hissed.

"She won't say. Payne is dealing with her injuries, so I can't question her properly. But I have a theory," Misna said with a sly smile.

"Oh?"

"I think she was punished for her failure to assassinate the queen. I think the last heir of Valia is getting ready to make their move."

The oasis of Tulna was buzzing with life as Mia, Cassandra, and Joab arrived. Kania was waiting and took Mia into a hug as Joab lowered her down from his horse.

"I'm glad you're safe," a girl with dark hair and dark eyes smiled at Mia. She looked to be about sixteen and there was something familiar about her that Mia couldn't place.

"Thank you," Mia blushed, unwilling to admit she didn't know the girl.

"Where are Kasna and Kia?" Joab asked as he dismounted.

"That is Kia," Mathias smiled in amusement as he pointed at the dark-haired girl. "Kasna, well, she's not here any more."

"I see my brother has been hard at work," Cassandra said, jumping down from her horse. Kia beamed at the Guardian of the Wilds, who smiled back. She had lost the edges of youth and the soft naivety that marked her as a warrior. She wore a blade at her waist, a bow on her back, and a knife was strapped to her leg.

She looked every inch a warrior of the Order, save for the armour she wore. She was dressed in reinforced leather, the armour that the defenders of Tulna often wore.

Tola was standing some distance away from the welcome party that had assembled. To Joab's eyes, he looked much older than he had before Renta's death. There were deep, dark circles around his eyes that spoke of a lack of sleep and new lines across his face that were born out of grief.

His long hair was streaked with more grey than it had been before, his shoulders were slumped forward and the people of Tulna seemed to be moving around him, giving him a wide berth.

"He has," Mathias agreed.

"Where is he?" Cassandra asked as the horses were led away by the stable boys.

"Gone," Nodarto shrugged.

"As we are soon to be," Mathias' skin had darkened in the sun of the desert.

"Oh?" the Guardian of the Wilds asked absently as she licked her teeth. The weather in the oasis was warm, the sun bright.

Wentrus was long since ended in the village, even though it still seemed to persist beyond its borders.

"Tola has received word that he is to return to Kasnata. This being so, we thought that it would be an opportune time to reunite Kia with her mother," Mathias explained.

"The Abbott departed after my training was done. He said there was still much for me to learn, but that I could learn from my people rather than him," Kia said as she rested her hand on the hilt of her sword.

"Then it would seem we arrived back at the right time," Joab observed.

"If you will excuse me," Cassandra took her leave of the group of travellers as they began to discuss their plans for the journey to Kasnata's camp.

The Guardian of the Wilds moved into one of the small buildings that lay behind the largest building in oasis.

"What is it?" Kania asked her daughter. The leader of Tulna had followed her to the small building, where Cassandra had begun rifling through stacks of paper.

"I don't know yet," Cassandra sounded frustrated as she found what she was looking for.

"You think the answers lie in the records that Allamonto left to us?" Kania asked as she sat down.

"When Valia sacrificed Ina, something happened to the

realm," the Guardian of the Wilds was struggling to remember the exact sequence of events.

"Yes, it was not only to ensure her place on the throne, it was part of a ritual to grant her enough power to defeat those that she believed were arrayed against her," Kania frowned at her daughter. "Does this have something to do with Kelmar?"

"No, I don't think so. Delich may be after her blood, but it is not that I am concerned about – at least not at this moment," Cassandra spoke slowly as she read through the piece of paper in her hand.

"There is something more?"

"The blood moon rose and the land became dark. Wentrus came, as if unending and abominations stalked the earth," the Guardian of the Wilds read aloud.

"There has not been a blood moon for centuries. Not since the texts of the coven were destroyed," Kania tried to reassure her daughter.

"The texts of the coven were weaker spells than those practised in Oran. I found a book in the library of Grashindorph that was filled with the rituals and spells of that land. If there is one here, why not more?"

"Sagma/Sumar is waning and Antompne is approaching, Wentrus is not holding sway," Kania argued.

"Not within Tulna, but beyond our borders, the snow has not

thawed, the dawn barely breaks," Cassandra snapped as she thumped the wall.

"The abominations were destroyed with the coven," Kania sounded confused as she took the paper from Cassandra.

"The coven was formed of Valians, those that stepped away from the desire to place an heir of Valia on the throne and instead sought to increase their own power. As long as Valians exist, the coven could always rise again."

"We have forgotten much," Kania said softly as she let the paper fall from her hands.

"No, we forgot what it is we were here for," Cassandra countered.

"What will you do?" Kania asked her daughter.

"My brother left, he knows he has walked his path better than I, he will be where he is supposed to be. I need to discover what I have missed and go where I should have been for some time," Cassandra replied.

It was not difficult for Helez and Asahel to slip into the prison that Bracha was being held in. Asahel had argued with his friend for days about whether they were doing the right thing, but had given up when it was clear that Helez would not be dissuaded.

There was no reason for the prison guards to deny the two men entrance to the prison cells. They held positions of power within the Gibborim as part of Hermia's entourage and with no orders from Hermia about denying them entry, the guards let them pass.

Bracha was hung from the ceiling by chains wrapped around her wrists. Her hands had been broken, crushed between stones and left to heal without splints, if they ever would.

Asahel made sure that the door behind them was not locked. The guards had seen them enter, knew who they were, whatever they did, Asahel knew that they would be held accountable.

Helez felt anger rising in him as he laid eyes on the wife of Jephthah. She parted her lips and a gurgling sound came from her throat that sounded something close to laughter. Helez's lips curled as he stepped forward and struck her across the face.

No matter how many years that Bracha lived in this condition, Helez knew that she would never regret the actions she took. She would always congratulate herself from bringing about the death of Ilana, for inflicting such pain upon Helez and Asahel.

No matter what the young man did, every time he closed his eyes he saw his sister, terrified, standing with a noose around her neck. He watched her die again and again. In part he blamed himself for not paying more attention to her, for not protecting her, but he knew that, ultimately, it was down to Bracha.

He had imagined over and over again what he would do if he ever came face to face with the woman, what he would say, how he would act. He knew that he would never be given a second opportunity to do what he felt needed to be done.

"Are you sure you want to do this?" Asahel asked one final time as he looked between his friend and the traitor.

"Yes," Helez said firmly as he drew a dagger from down the back of his collar.

"Helez, stay your blade," Jephthah warned as he appeared in the doorway. Asahel looked over his shoulder to see his mentor had been accompanied by Layla and Hermia.

"The guard sent for you?" Asahel asked and Haman nodded.

"Put down the blade, Helez. Justice was done," Layla said slipping past Asahel and her hands resting on her own daggers that were slung at her waist.

"No, it wasn't," Asahel said from behind Layla. "None of you were there when Ilana was hanged. You didn't have to see, you aren't still tortured by it,"

"Justice has been served," Hermia said firmly. "Doing this now will not take away what you saw, you will not punish her, you will release her,"

"She doesn't have any sense of remorse," Helez argued.

"Do this and there will be no way back," Jephthah warned. "You will be considered traitors to the Gibborim. You will no longer be welcome amongst our number,"

"You would exile us for this?" Asahel asked.

"No, just Helez, you have done nothing but support a friend," Hermia assured the older of the two men.

"If you exile Helez, you exile me," Asahel said grimly.

"Headstrong fools. Helez, put away your knife. Asahel, stop being so pig-headed," Jephthah barked at the two men.

Layla was within arm's reach of Helez, and creeping closer, when Helez darted forwards and stabbed Bracha in the chest. Layla moved faster than Asahel thought possible and within the blink of an eye, Helez was lying on the floor, Layla straddling him with her daggers at his throat.

"You leave me no choice," Hermia said sadly as she walked over to look down at Helez. Jephthah stepped forward and pulled the dagger out of his wife, her lungs already filling with blood.

Helez wasn't paying any attention to Layla or Hermia. His eyes were fixed on Bracha. He waited for satisfaction to fill his chest, for the pain of losing his sister to subside. The light faded from Bracha's eyes, but Helez's pain remained unchanged.

"Jephthah, take them to the surface," Hermia ordered. The man mountain hauled Helez to his feet as Layla sprang back and half-dragged him from the cell.

"Farewell, my lady," Asahel bowed to Hermia and followed.

"It was always going to happen," Layla said quietly to Hermia.

"Because he has always been a victim of his own folly?" Hermia asked.

"No, because revenge promises to bring closure and end to pain that it seldom delivers. He knows that now, a little too late for the sake of the Gibborim. But the death of Bracha -"

"Murder of Bracha," Hermia corrected the shadow.

"- murder of Bracha, it will celebrated, not lamented," Layla looked at her leader, her lips set in a thin line.

"I know, it's the only reason that they are being exiled instead of executed," Hermia sighed. "Send in the guards to clean up this mess. Her body can be floated into the sewers, the king's men will find it eventually."

Jack and Shaul walked through the camp. The two men had been excused from night duty and we reporting to Commander Grice for further orders, both hoping that it would mean they could turn in for the night.

Shaul found that living amongst the men of Nosfa was not as disagreeable as he had originally imagined it would be. There was camaraderie that was not dissimilar to that of the Order and the songs that were sung around the campfire were lewd and often far more enjoyable than those that the Queterian had been raised on.

The snow falls had been getting worse over the last few days, and General Seaton was proving to be a tyrant when it came to warfare.

He had ordered that the camp be moved back to its original location, which meant that men who were not on watch were sent to dig out the wooden structures and construct new walls and pathways.

Men had been found dead, buried by sudden collapses of snow, or had died from exposure to the cold. It had been bloody work but it had been finished a few days earlier. Morale had sunk to new lows and more than one voice was lamenting General Rathe being reduced to an advisory capacity.

"It's typical," Jack cursed as he shivered in the wind. "We spend years marching in battles in scorching heat, but the moment we lay siege to a city, Wentrus decides it's taking over. Then we get a power man general to replace a general who has fallen under the spell of a witch queen and now we can't find the commander,"

Shaul smiled at the man. He always found something to complain out, no matter what was going on or how well things were going, Jack would always be able to find something to moan about.

"We'll find him; then there are a campfire and a bedroll that are calling my name," Shaul smiled.

"Tam, there are more adventurous things you could be doing

with your time between watches that do not involve sleeping," Jack said, clapping the Queterian on the shoulder.

"And this coming from a married man," Shaul replied with a raised eyebrow.

"What can I say? I miss the comforts of home," Jack shrugged innocently.

The two men laughed as they trudged through the snow to where the duty sergeant had told them that Commander Grice was eating his supper.

A few feet from the tent, Shaul stopped abruptly. He could feel the hairs standing up on the back of his neck, and there was a metallic taste in the air.

"What's wrong, Tam?" Jack asked frowning at him

"Can you taste that?" Shaul asked as he glanced around at the brilliant white snow fall that lay on top of the black and grey slush they had dug out of their camp.

"Taste what?" Jack asked impatiently.

"Blood," Shaul pursed his lips and slowly moved towards the tent that the Commander dined alone in. He slowly pulled back the flap to reveal the tent was covered in the Commander's blood. His neck had been cut along with the arteries in his arms and legs. "Fetch the lieutenant," Shaul instructed as Jack peered in and recoiled from the sight of all the blood.

"What the hell?!" Jack gagged as he spoke.

"Jack, we need the lieutenant," Shaul repeated himself to get his friend to focus on a simple task. Jack looked at Shaul with wide eyes and nodded slowly before running off through the camp.

Shaul shook his head as he looked over the commander's remains.

"Typical."

King Mercia Nosfa VI bid farewell to his wife and General Seaton with a smug expression on his face. He left knowing he had extended his control over the queen of the Order and ensured that not only had he placed a general in her camp that he could trust, but that he had destroyed an alliance between the Order and the house of Afdanic before it could become a threat.

The last heir of Valia was in the camp, and Mercia was certain that even if the assassination of Kasnata led to civil war amongst the Order, they would no longer be a threat to him.

Kasnata watched her husband's party departing and caught the eye of Rathe, who was stood a little way from her. She had not seen the general since Mercia had made her position clear. General Seaton was keeping Rathe busy and Methanlan had passed information to the queen that one of the commanders had been found murdered.

She wanted to keep General Bird close in case the leadership of the men of Nosfa was being targeted, but the queen trusted that Misna and her command were more than capable of discovering who was behind the murder and if any more would occur.

"Your highness, we should meet to discuss the siege of the city," General Seaton said, his gruff voice muffled by the giant beard on his face.

"General Seaton, my commanders and I are already meeting to look over the state of the siege, if you wish to be part of our gathering; I would talk to General Marissa," the queen said in an even tone, she could see Rathe making his way over to her out of the corner of her eye.

She moved swiftly away from General Seaton and whispered something to Yoav. Wolfblood nodded and moved to intercept Rathe before he could speak to the queen.

General Seaton smiled to himself and marvelled at how easy it was for the king to manipulate the queen.

Chapter 11

General Hesla was unable to attend the meeting of Kasnata's generals, but her presence was not seen as suspicious by any of those assembled. She was still in poor condition after being attacked and unable to walk without searing pain.

General Seaton and Bird had been invited to join the discussions and each of the generals had brought two or three of their commanders with them. Horsemistress Cara, Swordmistress Anna, Bowmistress Serra, Horsemaster Horace, Swordmaster Oswin and Bowmaster Wist had all been invited to attend.

There were close to thirty people assembled around Kasnata's war table as plans for attacking the city were laid.

"We need to dig trenches close to the city to launch attacks from," General Seaton argued. They had been assembled for several hours and the discussions had become circular.

General Seaton and General Kia had been arguing about how best to launch an assault on the city, whilst General Shamgar had been abdicating starving out the people in the city.

"If the people leaving the city are telling the truth, then the madness that is descending over the city could be dangerous to anyone going over those walls. We need time to discover what is going on," Misna said flatly.

Kasnata could feel her temples throbbing as a headache

developed. She had listened to all the different opinions that her generals had to offer and could see that there was no way in which they would be able to reach a consensus on how best to proceed with their assault on the city, not without arguing for hours.

"Enough," the queen said, leaning on the table they were stood around.

"General Misna is right. We don't know what is going on in the city and we need more information before we launch any form of assault. However, we cannot sit and do nothing forever. General Seaton, have your men dig trenches around the city, make preparations for an assault. I will not order it to begin until General Misna can tell me what is happening on those streets. It has been a long day; you should all get some rest," Kasnata sighed and dismissed her generals.

No one argued with the queen, but they muttered under their breath as they left the tent.

"You have been avoiding me," Rathe said from the corner of the war tent. The other generals had left, so the two were alone for the first time since the birth of their children.

"You shouldn't be here," Kasnata warned and made to leave the tent.

"You told me I wouldn't lose you," Rathe said, catching her arm as she passed him.

"That was before -" Kasnata shook her head as she spoke.

"Before what? Before the king threatened your life? Threatened mine? Told you he would execute your children, our children, before your eyes?" Rathe looked at the queen with compassion in his eyes.

"I will not give him an excuse to hurt any that I love," Kasnata had her eyes closed and her voice was rich with emotion.

"He does not need an excuse," Rathe said as he gently pulled the queen into his arms. "I will die before I let him harm you or the children as well as any that are loyal to you," he whispered into her ear.

"What about General Seaton?" Kasnata buried her head in Rathe's shoulder.

"He will be overseeing the siege works for several weeks," Rathe smiled, tilted the queen's chin upwards and kissed her.

As forge master, Benaiah was charged with forging the blades for those who earned them. Each blade was crafted from the bearer, the metals chosen, the design, the balance and weight all brought together to give the wielder the advantage.

He had not crafted a blade in many months, but the queen had come to him with a special order. She wanted a blade forged for

General Bird that was befitting of the new skills he had acquired under Yoav's instruction.

Benaiah had never forged a blade for anyone who was not of the Order, but he bowed to the request of his queen. The forge master had not seen the general fight, so he went and watched the general train. He spent weeks watching how Rathe moved, which had he used to fight, if he switched sword arm during a fight, when he chose to lunge, when he chose to defend. Benaiah studied every aspect of Rathe's fighting style for many weeks.

After weeks of watching, he drew out plans for the blade he was to forge. There were few raw materials in the camp, so he requested leave from the queen to gather them. It did not take a few days or even weeks for Benaiah to forge a blade. He was not a smith that cobbled together armour and blades to be wielded and worn by any that passed by.

The forge master was an artist; it took him years to craft a blade. He made weapons that were only to be wielded by those they were crafted for. They were given names, they passed into legend, and when their owners passed on to Halsanda, the blades were hung on the walls of their kin and in the great halls of the Order and in the Castle Anamoore.

When Benaiah forged a blade, it was not just for who the wielder was now, but also for who they were to become. Kasnata's blade, the Ralenetia Estral, had taken five years to forge and it was feared by all those that had met the Order in battle and lived to tell of it after.

Kasna and Kia's blades had been forged for them without Benaiah having ever seen the daughters of Kasnata fight; they were forged as variants on their mother's blade, one of the daughter who would be queen and the other for the daughter that had a different path.

The Talmer and the Tallana; the Star of Earth and the Star of Heaven.

Now that Princess Kia was in the camp, Benaiah could see how well the Talmer suited the princess. The Tallana had been returned to him to look after until Kasna was found and freed from her captor. The Tallana was mounted over the door to Benaiah's forge, waiting to be claimed.

Cas Carlan was the name that Benaiah gave to the blade of Rathe, before he had finished sketching the blade; he knew what it would be called, Heart of the Hunt; a mighty blade for a man of great destiny.

"How well guarded is he with the king absent?" Haman asked. He was sat with Hermia and Haston. With the king away from the city, there was an opportunity for the Gibborim to strike a blow to the king and remove his son from the palace and away from danger.

"The Baron of Fintry is the steward, the king's guard is all but absent from the city. There are a few servants that will still be in the castle, from whatever Bracha has told the Baron, it will be assumed that we intend to assassinate the king, not kidnap the prince," Haston said leaning back in his chair.

Hermia stood whilst the men sat. She hadn't said a word since their meeting had begun, simply listened to the two men. She had spent her life listening whilst men made plans, many of them doomed to fail. Rosla had spent many nights sat with Haston making plans from the early days of their marriage.

The thought of her husband brought a pang of heartbreak, having Haston join the Gibborim was a constant reminder of the days that had once been. Of the days when they had talked of the future and prosperity for the kingdom of Nosfa, not domination, when their enemies had been brigands, pirates and bandits, not her son and the people she had once ruled.

"We should move the Gibborim out of the city," the queen mother said as she stared at the walls of the old water passages.

"My lady?" Haman looked over at the leader of the Gibborim. She had never suggested leaving the city before.

"If we are to take the prince, they will search the throughout the city until they have found us and then those who are innocent amongst are number will end up dead. Haman, lead they out of the city, take them south, through the forest. We have friends in Afdanic that have been preparing, in case we were discovered," Hermia turned to face the two men.

"I will remain here with Jephthah, Layla and Haston. Even if they search this place, with only five of us to conceal they will not find us,"

"What about the rebellion?" Haston demanded.

"Once they have searched the tunnels, then we can call everyone back to the city," Hermia looked between the two men, who nodded their agreement. "Give the order."

Kelmar hadn't slept; instead he had stood guard over the prisoner whilst she slept. She was a barbarian and the daughter of Delma's greatest enemy, but she was right about his men. They had been away from their wives and civilisation for more than 200 days and though they were well trained, a young woman amongst them dressed in nothing more than a slip was something that even he was struggling with, even with all his breeding, he found it hard to focus on his mission.

His mission.

The thought of his mission caused him to shake his head. The Duke had been raised in the royal court of Delma and charged with one of the most sacred tasks of guardianship and no matter what his personal feelings might be, he would die before he failed in his task, but, for the moment he had more pressing concerns.

When he had first met Kasna in the fortress of Abergorlech, she had been little more than a child trying to stand up to a man, but mere months later she had aged at least eight years by his reckoning, if not more.

He knew the people of the Order and that they were not immortals or magical beings. They were human and aged in the same way that the people of Delma and Nosfa did. There was something else at work in this, something that scared Kelmar and made him feel glad he had not taken on the warriors of Tulna.

He could feel the cold of the night biting at his flesh, but the cold only served to help keep him awake. Kasna stirred in her sleep beside him. She was still gagged and bound, but the princess seemed to sleep easily despite this.

"Sir, we've had some moorin sightings," a sergeant announced gruffly as he approached, disturbing the Duke's thoughts. At the mention of moorin, Kasna's eyes snapped open and she rolled herself onto her knees.

"Build the camp fires higher, make sure the sentries and sleepers are all well within the circle of light. The moorin won't come too close to the flames," Kelmar ordered. The sergeant saluted and scurried away as the Duke pulled the gag out of Kasna's mouth.

"What is it?" he demanded impatiently.

"Fires won't keep the moorin away," the princess replied as she tried to free her hands from the ropes around them.

"I've spent more time living in the wilds than you've spent on Celadmore. I know how moorin behave," Kelmar said dismissively.

"If it were a small pack, then I wouldn't disagree, but with all the war and death, there has been more food for the scavengers and their numbers have swelled. If this is a moorin pack it will be far larger and bolder than those you are used to," Kasna said earnestly, but Kelmar simply smiled and thrust the gag back into her mouth.

"Don't leave the light, and you'll be fine," he said, pushing her back to the ground. War horns sounded in the night before the attack began and giant war hounds the size and colour of moorin ripped out the throats of sleeping men. Kelmar did not miss a beat as horses burst into the light of the campfires bringing with them riders from the north.

Men screamed as they died, dogs howled and horses whined. Kelmar was raised for war, just as Kasna was, and his training was making short work of the raiding party, but the raiders had surprise, and numbers, on their side, and even Kelmar was beginning to become overwhelmed.

His men, that fought in pairs and threes, were slowly winning, but the duke was isolated. He heard the singing of metal before he felt the warm trickle of blood as a sword grazed his ear.

"You should be more careful," Kasna said in a low voice as she forced back the attacker that had been aiming for Kelmar. She had slipped between the duke and barbarian to parry the strike, deflecting the blade from Kelmar's skull to his ear.

"Moorin would have stayed outside the firelight," Kelmar grunted. The princess had worked her way free and picked up the blade of a fallen fighter so that the duke was no longer fighting on his own. With Kasna loose, the raiders turned and fled, their losses too high for them to sustain their attack and the element of surprise had long since been lost.

"Count the dead, see to the wounded," Kelmar barked with exhaustion, when he was sure that the raiders were gone, then turned to where Kasna was kneeling in a breathless state. "You never killed before."

It wasn't a question as the Duke knelt down beside the princess and took e blade away from her. Kasna shook her head as she tried to stop herself from shaking as adrenaline coursed through her veins.

"Where did you get the sword?"

"Off one of the corpses," Kasna said shakily.

"Are you hurt?" Kelmar asked, putting his arm around her shoulders and helping her to her feet. Kasna shook her head and leaned into the duke. "Thank you," He said quietly.

"For what?" Kasna asked, looking at him for the first time.

"Saving my life."

Kasna smiled in spite of the nausea she could feel welling up inside of her.

"You're welcome."

The Gibborim was evacuated days before Hermia instructed Layla and Jephthah to attempt to remove Leinad from the palace. The shadow and shield of Hermia had spent the days in which the other members of the Gibborim left the undercity to explore further afield.

They were looking for a way into the tunnels that ran beneath the palace that was still passable, a way of entering the palace that the servants wouldn't know of and would be unguarded.

But no such route could be found.

"You will find that the garden entrance by the wall will not be guarded. The door is locked, but it can easily be lifted off its hinges. When we were young men, it is how King Rosla and I used to sneak in and out of the palace. None of the servants knew about it, and I am certain Mercia wouldn't know," Haston had offered them the information when they had questioned him about what he knew of the palace.

There was an entrance to the undercity that was not far from the garden wall. The shadow and shield stole over the garden wall without being seen and found the door was as Haston had described.

No guards were set on either side of the door. There was a long passage that sloped slowly upwards to the foot of a staircase that led up to a trapdoor in the west tower. With a small amount of convincing from Jephthah's shoulder, it opened.

Having lived in the palace for many years before the attempted murder of the queen, Layla knew the corridors of the palace better than most, but she was certain that there were many secrets she was unaware of.

She led Jephthah silently through the corridors until they reached the rooms that Hermia had told her Leinad would be using.

They were at the heart of the palace. The windows opened onto an enclosed courtyard that was guarded at all hours. When the full retinue of the king's guard was in the palace, the shadow may have been able to reach the rooms without being found, but she would not have been able to remove the prince without being seen.

"Be careful," she warned Jephthah as they approached the door.

"You think this has been too easy?" the shield grunted quietly.

"I think that the prince's room would be guarded, even with

most of the men absent from the palace," she hissed in reply.

"That would be a safe assumption to make," a voice called out from the darkness. Layla looked up with a malicious smile and drew her daggers.

"Neesa, what an unpleasant surprise," the shadow narrowed her eyes at the assassin of the king.

"Stealing from the king now, Layla? How the mighty have fallen," Neesa replied.

"Can you deal with her?" Jephthah asked Layla. She nodded in response. "Be quick about it,"

Layla leapt at Neesa, and found she stabbed at nothing, the assassin struck out, trying to hit Layla from behind, but the shadow ducked and rolled out of her reach.

"It has been a long time since you last crossed me path, do not think that age has made me weak," Layla warned Neesa, who chuckled to herself.

"You were never a match for me. I only let you believe you were," the assassin sneered.

As the two women fought, Jephthah forced the door to the prince's quarters open. The room was exactly as the queen mother had described, save for the prince was not in the room. Instead there was a jet black crystal set on a stone pedestal.

The pedestal was flecked with blood and being in its presence made Jephthah feel like his soul was being slowly drained from his body.

"You won't escape from here," Neesa crowed as she kicked Layla's legs from under her.

"Jephthah, what are you doing?" Layla shouted as she rolled out of the way of Neesa's blade.

"He can't hear you. In a few minutes, he won't be the man you remember. He'll belong to me," Neesa smiled as she crouched in the darkness between the shadow and the door to the prince's room.

"What have you done?" Layla scowled.

"What I have done for centuries," Neesa replied.

Jephthah was vaguely aware of someone calling his name, but the crystal seemed to be the only thing that mattered. He couldn't help but stare at its smooth surface, the light in the prince's room reflecting dancing patterns across the wall.

"Jephthah, you blundering oaf!" Layla yelled. "Your wife was right; you are too stupid to see what is right in front of you."

Neesa leapt at Layla again, the shadow narrowly escaping a backward strike by blocking it with her own dagger, but leaving her side open. Neesa took the opportunity to strike and caught Layla across the ribs.

The knife merely grazed the surface, but in sacrificing her skin, Layla could sink her own dagger into Neesa's arm. The assassin slunk back into the shadows trying to stop the flow of blood as Layla darted into the room.

She paid no attention to the crystal; instead she struck Jephthah across the back of the knees, dropping him to the floor. The shield blinked several times and frowned up at the shadow.

"Woman, what do you think you are doing?" he growled as scrambled back to his feet.

"As dumb as an ox," Layla muttered as she darted back to the door.

"Where's the prince?" Jephthah asked as he followed Layla.

"I don't know," Layla replied. "We need to leave. Neesa expected us, who knows what other traps she has in store."

"I didn't think you were afraid of anything," Jephthah observed as the two darted back to the west tower and dropped down through the trap door.

"This isn't fear. We have no information, no way of knowing if the prince is even in the city and an enemy who knew we were coming," Layla replied shortly.

CHAPTER 12

2431GL 19ᵀᴴ ANTOMPNE

The black staff the Abbott had presented to Kasnata had sat gathering dust with Kasnata's bow and other weapons. Whilst she had been carrying her babies she had refrained from practice and training with her people, but now her body had recovered, she knew she had a new weapon to master.

The staff looked no different from the wooden training staves that the Order of the Bear used, save for the runes that were carved into its surface and the colour of it.

When the queen touched it, she felt as though the weapon was a part of her, an extension of her body. Shamgar had been only too happy to train the queen in how to use the weapon, the queen not exempt from his brutal teaching style.

But as she become more adept in using the weapon, the more that she felt she was missing something. The staff sang to her as she used it, a melody that seemed to coarse through her veins and needed a release.

As she trained, she felt as though the words were almost forming on her tongue that would unlock something more, but every time she tried to grasp what was happened, the sensation slipped away, the power fading.

So she trained harder trying to focus her mind on other things as she fought.

"Goss."

The word slipped off her tongue without her realising what has happening. In an instant a wave of fire erupted from the staff, lashing out at Shamgar.

The short general ducked as the wave of fire licked at the air and he stared in amazement at the queen.

"Your highness, are you all right?" He asked with wide eyes.

"Yes, I'm sorry, Cave Dweller, I don't know what that was," the queen looked as astounded as the general did.

"Goss. That's what you said and then there was fire," Shamgar stepped slowly towards the queen, looking at the staff with suspicion. "If you summoned fire, then maybe you can control it too," he posited.

"Summon fire? Impossible," the queen snorted.

"I know what I saw, your majesty," Shamgar said firmly. "It is a gift you shouldn't squander, though talking to the Guardian of the Wilds about what it is and how it works might be wise before experimenting with it too much," he advised.

"Misna, you're needed in the camp of Nosfa," Methanlan

shouted as he found the Raven General.

"What is it?" Misna asked as the Queterian paused to catch his breath.

"There has been another murder, the same as the others. There is blood everywhere and the men are starting to panic. They are superstitious as it is, but there is talk of demons and monsters being spread and there are some that are starting to panic," the spy explained. Misna sighed and shook her head.

"Foolish, but with six of the nine commanders dead, it is not surprising," she picked her sword up from where it lay on the table outside her quarters and strapped it around her waist. "You should go on ahead, and keep your eyes open. With so many being murdered, I am being to question how safe you and Shaul are in that camp."

"Neither of us holds any rank," Methanlan shrugged with indifference. "It is the commanders who have been targeted."

"For the moment, but when the commanders are all dead, what is to stop whoever is responsible from coming after you?" Misna asked, looking at the man who had served with her for longer than any other.

"We'll keep our eyes open," Methanlan assured his general.

"Go, I'll be along shortly."

The city of Grashindorph was very different to how Asahel remembered it in his childhood. The smells of the lower streets were the same, but the faces in them seemed more menacing than in his memory. There was desperation on the streets, people kept to themselves and avoided anything that looked like it could attract the attention of the city watch.

It had been almost two weeks since the men had been exiled from the Gibborim, and they were both still adjusting to life on the surface. People did not stop to help each other here; they barely looked up as they passed each other on the street. Beggars were ignored or attacked. More than once, a small group of people had turned on a beggar that ventured too close to them.

Fear. It had seeped into the fabric of the lower streets, broken the spirits of the people and removed any form of trust that might have once existed between neighbours.

The lower streets were safer for the two men because of this. People didn't recognise faces, as they barely looked up long enough to register who those around them were.

The market streets were packed with people, a press of individuals that made life easy for pickpockets and sneak thieves, as well as a place that information could easily be collected by those who listened carefully enough.

The middle streets had been where Ilana had found herself, dangerous streets for those that had not lived these for many years, and a place where the city watch soon arrested those that didn't belong.

"If we can't go back to the Gibborim, then what do we do?" Helez had asked Asahel once they had taken quarters in the lower streets.

"We try to help these people. Unless you have abandoned what you once believed about this city and its people," Asahel had replied.

Every soul that passed by the two men every day seemed completely devoid of hope, empty vessels that trudged through everyday life.

Neither Asahel nor Helez knew where they should begin, or even how to bring hope to the lives of those around them, as they had no interaction with them. There was no interaction between people save for between market sellers and the people, though this too, was limited.

"Don't worry, we'll find some way," Asahel said firmly as the two watched the city watch march through the crowds to grab hold of one of the men. They listened to his screams of protest as he was dragged from the street, not a single person looked up as he was taken, no one cried out to stop it, in fact, the only evidence that any of those that swarmed the streets knew the man was a shadow of a grimace that passed over several faces.

"What was the crystal?" Hermia asked as she sat in the hiding place she had chosen to wait out any inspection of the tunnels in.

"I don't know," Layla and Jephthah had reported their failure to Hermia without embellishing any aspect of the story. "But what Neesa said about centuries, that I am not sure I believe."

"From what you have said about the crystal, it is very dangerous. How long has Neesa been in the service of the king?" Hermia asked hugging her knees to her chest.

"Shortly after the queen gave birth to Leinad. Mercia had designs on expanding the borders of the kingdom and was looking for an advisor. She appeared at court not long after that," Haston recalled. He had never thought very much about the assassin before now. Her name had been mentioned a handful of times, but he had never really seen her. "She kept herself to the shadows, but I seem to remember overhearing some of the generals talking about her."

"Long enough, then," Jephthah grunted.

"Long enough for what?" Haston frowned at the shield.

"Long enough to have learned how to influence the king's

mind and the kingdom," Layla said through pursed lips.

"You think that the reason the king is so bent on destruction and war is down to Neesa?" Hermia looked between her two bodyguards. "He always desired power; after all he tried to have me killed."

"Wanting to be king and securing his place on his throne are almost to be expected," Layla replied with a shrug. "There is not a throne on Celadmore that people are not coveting and plotting to take from others."

"It was his throne, being held in trust," Haston replied sharply. "He thinks he had his mother killed and has victimised my family for years because of his own paranoia."

"Paranoia that comes with the position," Layla shot back. "When the time came for Mercia to take his throne, could you have given the power back willingly? Would you have been so quick to give away ruling a country for the memory of a man that you adored to a son that was never going to be the ruler that the people of Nosfa deserved?"

Haston held Layla's gaze but didn't reply, he knew that the shadow had a point, that had Mercia not seized his throne back from him, he may not have given it back to the prince at all.

"When he met with Kasnata, what was he like then?" Jephthah asked sensing that Layla was ready to continue the argument even if Haston backed down.

"He was always ambitious; he wanted to be united with a powerful queen rather than a weaker nation that was afraid of invasion," Hermia said as she tapped her fingers against her bottom lip. "Before I left, she was all he could talk about."

"We were winning the war against Hespan, the war of the east, their army had been completely decimated, but Mercia didn't sack the capital, he called for peace talks instead. I always wondered why he didn't destroy them entirely," Haston frowned and glanced at Hermia. "I assumed at the time it was part of his plan to get Kasnata to marry him, she was keen on re-establishing the council and bringing back peace between the nine kingdoms."

Hermia rested her head on her knees and thought quietly for a moment.

"Maybe he really did want peace after seeing the reality of war," she sighed as she looked up.

"Then the war against Delma, the war against Vasknar, the plans to invade Zenix, they all came after Neesa arrived?" Layla surmised, looking at Haston for confirmation. The Lord of Afdanic nodded and the four sat in silence, each pondering what possible reasons Neesa could have for plunging Celadmore into war.

"You think that the murders have something to do with the assassination attempts on the queen?" Quisla asked. Misna had called for Amalia, Quisla and Marissa to meet with her as she returned from the camp of Nosfa.

"No, I think this is something else," Misna said firmly as she sat down next to Amalia.

The four women had built a new fire some distance away from the tents but within the nightwatch picket lines. They didn't want to be disturbed and they could see people approaching long before they would be within earshot.

"Oh?" Quisla tilted her head slightly with curiosity.

"The murders of the commanders of Nosfa are too ritualistic to be the work of an assassin. They are killed in the same way and their bodies are left to drain of blood," Misna had a sombre tone as she spoke.

"All bodies are left to drain of blood once they have been run through," Marissa shrugged. "I don't see why that makes these deaths suspicious,"

"They are disfigured so that blood would drain from the body, so that it was nothing but a shell of flesh by the end," Misna explained.

"It wasn't the work of wild animals scavenging for food?" Amalia asked as she warmed her hands by the fire.

"No, there were no teeth marks on any of the bodies," the raven general shook her head. "There is something else as well. The amount of blood around the bodies was wrong."

"What do you mean?" Quisla asked as she stood and stretched out her back.

"At first I thought the blood had seeped into the ground, it was a few hours at least after the first commander was murdered that the body was discovered. But the other bodies were found minutes after they had been killed and the ground is too solid to absorb that amount of blood so quickly," Misna leant forward and stared into the flames.

"Do you think something is drinking it? Killing the bodies to drink the blood?" Amalia shuddered at the thought.

"No, you said the killings looked like they were part of a ritual," Marissa said slowly.

"Someone is taking the blood from the bodies?" Quisla sounded disgusted as she sat down again.

"I believe so. The only beings that I know that take the blood of creatures are witches, but not in this quantity," Misna whispered.

"The witches are gone, they were hunted to extinction," Quisla dismissed the notion out of hand.

"Witches were born of the blood of Valia, as long as our people exist, they shall always be a threat," Marissa sighed and poked at the fire with a stick.

"Even if it is a witch, what would they want with so much blood?" Amalia looked at Misna for answers.

"I don't know, though there is no doubt that it is Hesla who is behind the assassination attempts on the queen," Misna sighed. "My spies report that not only is she suspected of being a Valian, but she is also having an affair with King Mercia."

"What do you suggest we do? Have you told the queen yet?" the vulture general asked.

"No, I asked Misna not to, I will deal with Hesla," Amalia said firmly.

"There are several of her operatives within the camp, but the one we should be most concerned with is General Seaton," Misna warned. "She has been observed visiting the general several times in the last few days. I suspect that she has taken him as a lover on the orders of Mercia to ensure that he doesn't take to the queen's bed as General Bird did."

"It doesn't matter what she is doing with him and on whose orders. She is a traitor and she will be dealt with. As for General Seaton, I suggest that we ask Kasnata to have General Bird assign Methanlan or Shaul as an aide," Amalia said sharply.

"Are you sure you want to deal with Hesla by yourself?" Marissa looked at the kestrel general with a worried expression on her face.

"I am," Amalia said firmly.

"Will the assassination attempts cease once she is dealt with?" Quisla frowned, doubting it would be so easy to end the attempts on the queen's life.

"Without Hesla, it will be easy to find the assassins hiding within the camp," **Misna assured her.** "I am more concerned with the murders. Whoever is killing the men of Nosfa is targeting the commanders of the army rather than our own people and could be any amongst our number."

CHAPTER 13

Kelmar had not tied the princess up. She had escaped from her bonds and saved his life instead of fleeing, so the duke did not feel that he needed to restrain her any further, though he wished he had her gagged still.

Instead of being thrown across the withers of his horse, Kasna sat in front of Kelmar as they rode, she seemed oblivious to the effect that she had upon the man and was perfectly content to simply lean into Kelmar's body for warmth.

The Regent of Delma was trying to focus his mind on other things as the movement of his horse rocked the princess against his body. He needed to remain focused on his duty, not allowing his lust to get the better of him. At the very least, the princess was no longer dressed in a simple slip. There had been enough clothing to spare after the bandits had attacked, as there had been deaths on both sides.

Kansa was dressed in tight hessian trousers that reached down to her, the top of her calves and soft leather boots that came up to meet them. She had fashioned her slip into an under shirt that made the chain mail vest she had found more comfortable to wear. Around her wrists she had leather armguards that matched her boots and trousers.

Her long, dark hair was now plaited tightly from the crown of her head and fell so it lay across her shoulder. To help keep out the cold, she wore furs around her shoulders that had belonged to one of the bandits but had clearly once belonged to someone of a much higher station.

If anyone were to see the party travelling across the plains of Celadmore, it would look as though the Regent was accompanying a lady of Delma rather than taking a prisoner back to the city.

As they rode, Kasna asked Kelmar questions that the duke managed to give short and curt responses to, but despite the abrupt manner with which he treated her, she persisted in trying to establish conversation.

After two days in the saddle, Kelmar was glad to finally dismount and able to put some distance between himself and the princess.

Instead of resting every night, Kelmar had ordered that they spend two days in the saddle for every night they rested. He was anxious to return to Delma with his prize and prove himself to his king.

The camp was set as efficiently as any party used to travelling as a unit could manage. Foragers were sent out to gather what food and water could be found, though it was becoming harder the further north they rode. Though it was Sagma/Sumar, there were signs of thick snow in the north and no thaw that would allow farmers to plant and sew their crops for harvesting in Antompne.

The duke worried that as they drew closer to the city that they would face problems with the snow drifts as well as unseasonable snow fall, but he knew there was little point in wasting too much time worrying about it when there were still bandits in the area.

Since the attack on the camp, Kelmar had not seen a single sign of any bandits following them or even lurking ahead, but this hadn't stopped him from sending a scouting party to check the area before they made camp.

As the weather was turning, it was necessary to set a proper camp instead of sleeping under the stars, as they had done in the desert.

The watch was set and the duke did not envy the men that were to stand guard. After two days of riding he felt exhausted and wanted nothing more than to climb into his bed, he imagined that his men felt the same.

The regent entered his tent and was about to lie down when he remember that the princess of the Order was not tied up and lying somewhere nearby. He sighed to himself and made to search for where she had gone to, when she walked into his tent carrying a skin of water and an arm full of cooked meat.

"What is this?" Kelmar asked crossly. He was fed up of dealing with the woman who still seemed to be so childlike in her behaviour.

"Food," Kasna said holding out the meat, "and water," she smiled as Kelmar took the offered skin and drained half the contents without stopping.

Riding across the desert had left sand and grit lodging in his throat that had refused to move. He knew that his skin was covered with dirt, but that would wait until he found one of the streams that flowed down from the mountains. He would not waste their precious drinking water.

He accepted the meat and sat down to eat. After a few mouthfuls he looked up to see that Kasna had gone again, returning a few moments later with oatcakes that were still hot from the fire.

Kelmar felt his mouth water at the scent of the oatcakes. The smell reminded him of the markets in the lower streets of Delma where there were a wide range of bakers and spicers, who created culinary delights that even the king and queen could not resist.

"Where did you get these?" he asked as he greedily snatched them from Kasna's hands.

"I made them," she said simply. "One of the things we had to do when we were cooped up in that fortress was learn how to cook. There wasn't a lot to work with, but one of the men found some sugar and oats in the remains of a trader's caravan that had been attacked and another found butter and milk at a small farm to the north."

Kelmar coughed as he swallowed in surprise. He hadn't expected either princess to have any skills that would prove useful. In his experience, women that were raised as nobility were brought up to look pretty, produce children and do very little else.

From what he had seen so far, Kasna could not only fight well, but was able to cook more edible food from inedible ingredients than Kelmar had thought possible.

"Did you roast the meat as well?" he asked as he finally managed to stop coughing.

"Yes. Everyone else seemed busy setting the camp, so I thought I would make myself useful," Kasna shrugged as she sat down and drank from the water skin.

"You didn't think of running away?" the regent asked sounding surprised.

"I thought about it many times," Kasna said with a broad grin, "but I have no idea where I am, not a clue about where I should be headed and I haven't got any weapons. You'd find me within hours of me disappearing, if not sooner and running away would just waste energy."

Kelmar laughed inspite of himself.

"So being my prisoner makes your life easier," he asked without only the slightest touch of condescension to his voice.

"For the moment, yes. Besides, I am much better here if bandits are lurking out there," Kasna said sensibly as she stood up and disappeared from the tent again.

That at least was true. The men of Delma were under strict orders that no harm was to come to the princess whilst she was being delivered to the city. Bandits would not show the same restraint when it came to keeping the princess alive or unspoilt.

The regent felt himself flush at the thought of Kasna as unspoilt. It had not occurred to him before now that she would still be a virgin and her childlike behaviour was due in no small part to her naivety about the world and the effect that she would have being close to a man, even when fully dressed.

Kelmar closed his eyes out of shame at the lustful feelings he had been suppressing whilst riding with the princess and was glad that he had come to this realisation whilst she was absent.

Kasna was not gone too long though. By the time Kelmar had finished eating she had returned with four jugs of water and a handful of rags that seemed to have been formed from shredding the shirts of the bandits that some of the men had been carrying to change into.

"And what is this?" Kelmar asked with frustration. Having eaten, all he wanted to do was fall asleep.

"You're filthy and starting to smell," Kasna said in a singsong voice as she placed the rags and water at the duke's feet and started to dip the rags into the water.

"What are you doing?" the regent cried out in alarm as the princess advanced on him with the wet rags.

"Washing your face," she replied in a matter-of-fact way.

"Why?" Kelmar asked grabbing her by the wrists to stop her

getting too close.

"Because I can see where the dirt on your face is and you can't. Now, let go and let me help," she said flatly. Kelmar wanted to protest, but the look that the princess wore on her face told him that he was better off simply agreeing.

He held his breath as the princess moved her body closer to his and gently began to rub the dirt off his face. She used one hand to move the rags in soft circles across his skin, whilst the other gently tilted his head to different angles so that she could see what she was doing in the dim light of the tent.

Kelmar found himself becoming increasingly relaxed as the princess washed his face and didn't even notice when she moved on to washing his hair. Her touch was incredibly light and the duke felt tension melting away from his body as she worked. With the slightest pressure from her fingers on his chest, he found himself lying down as Kasna removed his shirt and began to wash his torso in the same way she had cleaned his face.

Though the water was icy cold, it felt refreshing on his skin and more than once the Duke shivered slightly. The princess worked in silence and Kelmar felt the weight of the last two seasons of searching for the princesses lessening with each movement of her hand.

"Sit up, please," she asked softly and Kelmar obeyed, the princess moving around to wash his back. When she was done she moved onto his feet.

A wave of panic suddenly overwhelmed Kelmar as he realised that once the princess was done with his feet that she would move onto his legs and from there - he blushed and pulled his feet back from the princess.

"That's enough," he stammered as he stood and paced nervously for a few moments.

"What's wrong?" Kasna asked. She was still kneeling on the floor with the rag in her hand, not having moved.

"I can manage washing the rest myself," Kelmar said with a weak smile.

"Oh," Kasna said sounding slightly hurt. "I'm sorry,"

Kelmar blinked several times and looked at the princess with a look that displayed complete confusion.

"What? What are you sorry for?" Kelmar asked shaking his head slightly.

"I thought you were enjoying the attention. I wouldn't have carried on if you had said," Kasna said, setting down the rag and standing up.

"What are you talking about?" Kelmar was completely bewildered.

"I'm your prisoner," Kasna frowned. "I'm supposed to do things to make you happy."

In that moment, Kelmar wanted to be sick. He felt nausea rise in his throat, but suppressed the reaction as he stared at the princess. She had been a prisoner of her father from such a young age that it had not even occurred to Kelmar that men would think it was acceptable to force either of the young girls to pleasure them.

"Kasna, on the horse -" Kelmar began to ask, but he couldn't bring himself to finish.

"Oh, you didn't like that either? I thought men enjoyed that," she said, looking disappointed. "I'm sorry. Tell me what I should do, and I will do better, I promise," she begged.

Kelmar closed his eyes and rubbed his hands over them. It seemed so surreal to find himself in a situation like this. He had no idea that the princesses had been so badly treated, but then again, it was possible that it was only Kasna who had been treated that way. She had protected Kia by bargaining with the duke to give him what he wanted whilst sparing her. It hadn't occurred to him at the time, but it seemed to be something she was well practised in.

"Kasna, you are a princess. You shouldn't be doing anything to make me happy, least of all as my prisoner," Kelmar said gently.

"That's not true. I am supposed to make sure you are happy and then I won't get tied up again or punished," Kasna half-shouted. Kelmar suppressed the urge to move across the tent and put his hand over her mouth to keep her quiet.

"No, Kasna, I'm not going to tie you up or punish you, what other men have done to you was wrong, they aren't supposed to do things like that or tell you that you have to make them happy," Kelmar assured her.

"It wasn't just men who said it," Kasna said quietly. Kelmar closed his eyes and prayed that when he opened them, this would all be some horrible nightmare. It was clear that the princess had never had anyone to tell what was being done to her, no one to confide in save for her sister. It seemed unlikely to the duke that she would divulge the details of such abuse to someone she was trying to protect.

"I think maybe you need to rest," Kelmar said slowly. "Sleep for a while and you'll feel better."

Kasna looked at him and nodded, doing as he told her. Kelmar sighed heavily and waited until he could hear her breathing heavily before he went to lie down on the opposite side of the tent.

He slept soundly, his body feeling more relaxed than it had for weeks, until Kasna's voice woke him.

"Open your eyes," she said coldly. Kelmar opened his eyes to find the princess straddling his chest hold his dagger to his throat. She was looking down on him with disgust and hatred that she had skilfully hidden underneath a childish mask.

The duke realised that he had been deceived, that the princess was much more calculating than he had given her credit for. Though he was certain she had been abused in the way she had described, she had turned it into a weapon to disarm him with, so that he would let down his guard, promise not to tie her up again and treat her with trust that he had never afforded to any prisoner before.

"Not the naïve and helpless little princess after all then," Kelmar sighed and felt annoyed with himself.

"You think that I would have survived if I had remained naïve and helpless?" Kasna asked turning up the corner of her mouth into a half-smile that looked far from endearing.

"How far were you prepared to go in order to disarm me?" Kelmar asked out of interest. He was not in a position where he could do anything; the slightest movement he made was met by Kasna digging the dagger into his neck.

"To get to here I was prepared to do whatever it took. You surprised me though. I didn't take you for a man of honour," she replied with a small measure of disgust.

"So this is how you plan to escape? Kill me, take my weapons, my clothing, my horse and disappear?" the duke asked sounding disappointed.

"No. I never intended to escape; I already told you I had thought about it," Kasna shifted her weight ever so slightly so that her legs could pin down Kelmar's arms as she leaned forward.

"Then why all this?" Kelmar felt slightly exasperated, not only had she fooled him, but even when she was showing her true self to him, he couldn't read her.

"For Renta," Kasna spat at him. "You murdered her without

hesitation, you savoured it, enjoyed it, you tortured her for your own amusement and for that I will make sure that you pay." Anger flared in her eyes and Kelmar felt the blade bit into his neck so that a warm trickle of blood began to flow.

"I see," Kelmar spoke quietly. "I'm sorry for what I did to Renta. I once thought of her as a friend, before all of this started."

"But you killed her anyway,"

"I didn't just kill her, it was like a madness was being unleashed, a madness I never knew I had. It happened in Abergorlech as well, it was like something else was taking over my body and spilling blood for the sake of it," Kelmar tried to explain. He sounded so genuine that Kasna dropped her guard. The instant that Kelmar felt the blade drop away from his neck slightly, he flipped the princess from his chest on her back, pinning her wrist to the floor, keeping the knife well away from them both.

Kasna struggled in vain against the duke. She had gotten stronger from the training and the aging of her body, but Kelmar was still far stronger than she could ever hope to be. After a few moments she stopped struggling and cursed the duke under her breath.

His body had her trapped against the floor and he had an arm free that he used to take the dagger from her. She expected to find it at her throat but instead, the duke threw it away.

"You lying swine," she scowled at the Regent of Delma, who shook his head in response.

"No, I wasn't lying," he sighed.

"Then let me go," she demanded and tried to struggle free again. Kelmar laughed and stroked the side of her face with his free hand.

"If I did that you would try and kill me again," he said with a smile. Kasna shut her eyes so she wouldn't meet his gaze or see him smile. The way he looked at her and smiled seemed to be designed in order to endear him to her, to make her trust him, forgive him for what he did.

The princess didn't care about the people he had slaughtered in Abergorlech, they had tortured her daily, punished her, and abused her. Though it felt like a lifetime ago now, she didn't regret their fate at the duke's hands. But Renta, Renta was another matter and no amount of smiling or letting him gaze deeply into her eyes would change that.

"I am sorry," Kelmar whispered in her ear and Kasna felt chills run through her body, her chest tightened and her breath quickened. She could feel his breath on her neck and was suddenly very aware that he was wearing only his trousers.

She felt his grasp loosen around her wrist and his fingers gently traced lines down her arm. Kasna clenched her teeth, determined not to enjoy what was happening.

"Open your eyes, princess," he whispered, his lips brushing against her ear. Kasna opened her eyes without wanting to and found herself staring straight into the duke's eyes. His lips were inches from hers and before she could stop herself, she kissed him.

Kelmar was shocked by how aggressively Kasna embraced him; her lips were desperately crushed against his, her arms wrapped around his body, her nails biting into his neck and her fingers pulling at his hair.

Her body was lithe and smooth beneath him, the soft contours of her body almost demanded that he caress them. He moved his hands slowly, gently down her body and firmly grasped her hips. He felt her hands move down his chest and he gasped as she removed what remained of his clothes, the soft touch of her hands more arousing than he had imagined they would be.

Kasna felt the duke release her hips as his hands moved to tear at her clothing. With practised ease, Kasna rolled the duke off her so that she could undress, each time Kelmar sat up to try and help, she pushed him down again.

The Regent of Delma watched the princess of the Order undress, her every movement made him want her more. As she removed the last of the clothing he had secured for her, Kasna crawled forward until she was straddling the duke.

She leaned in and kissed him tenderly; his fingers brushed against her thighs as he slowly moved his hands up to her hips and pushed her body into position.

The Abbott had set out from Tulna without saying a word to anyone, not even to Cassandra. There were things he knew that were coming, events that needed to unfold without the interference of himself or the Guardian of the Wilds.

There were also things that the Abbott had to attend to at the Spire. It was easy for mortals and even those in Tulna to forget that there were other things that the Abbott had a multitude of duties to attend to that went far beyond dealing with the immediate future and the lives of individual mortals.

He was sat in his room in the oasis one moment, then after closing his eyes, he opened them, having been transported to the three pillars.

He smiled and shook his head as he approached them. No matter what else happened in the realm, he was always drawn back to this spot.

He reached up and touched the emblems on each of the pillars, the worn surfaces of the stone feeling familiar, almost comforting beneath his fingers.

After a few moments the air around him began to ripple and the doors to the Spire appeared before him, the cold dark stone looking almost forbidding in the fading light. He waited for a few moments for the doors to change from the navy colour that looked almost black to the iridescent pale doors with a smooth surface that he was used to seeing, but they remained unchanged.

As he waited the rest of the Spire began to materialise. The great monument looming out of the darkness, overshadowing the land that surrounded, a stark contrast to the snow flecked landscape.

"I see," he murmured to himself and placed a hand on the stone door. It swung open under the pressure and revealed a single room that was as dark and forbidding as the exterior of the Spire.

In the centre of the room was a pedestal, a long slim knife lying across it and at the base of it a large round basin that was shallow but etched with runes that the Abbott had only ever seen in books before.

Behind the pedestal was a vast altar that had a variety of different artefacts from the nine nations of Celadmore displayed upon it.

The Abbott entered the Spire without a word and carefully examined the room, trying to fathom why the Spire had presented him with such a terrifying and intimidating room.

Chapter 14

2431GL 78th Wentrus

Warning horns sounded in the camp of the Order, causing a flurry of movement. The nights had been quiet for the last few days as the cold of Wentrus had worsened.

Those who were not part of the nightwatch had spent their time huddled around large fires and grumbled about how long it was since they had been able to keep warm without the use of fire or needing to wear their heavy furs.

But as a party was sighted approaching the camp, all feelings of cold had been forgotten and warriors prepared themselves. Kasnata had not been asleep when the warning horns sounded, she had been nursing her children; the twins growing much faster than she would have liked.

She had thought about returning to Anamoore with the babies and placing them in the protection of her people, but she was certain her absence from the camp would be reported to her husband, and the queen did not trust General Seaton to be left in the camp without her there to keep him in check.

The general had made many demands and even tried to give orders to those of her people. Methanlan had been installed as his aide and had reported on some concerning attitudes that the general seemed to have towards war.

Shamgar had taken a small detachment of his men to meet the party as they carried no flag of parlay and the Nightwatch could see no sign of a larger force following behind the party.

It did not take long for Shamgar to return, accompanying the small party into the camp.

"Send for General Rathe," Kasnata instructed Marissa as she recognised Tola riding beside Shamgar and Cassandra on the other side of Cave Dweller.

"Greetings, your majesty," Cassandra called out as the party stopped in the centre of the camp. "I have found many strays on my travels and felt that they should be returned to you," the Guardian of the Wilds smiled as she dismounted.

"Tola, it is good to see you are well," Kasnata greeted the hero of the war of the east, who saluted as he dismounted.

"I am sorry about Renta," Tola knelt before the queen. "She died because I was unable to do anything to save her. I -"

"Peace, Tola. Rest, we will talk of these things later. Your body and heart are both weary and need rest," Kasnata said gently.

"Your majesty, may I present to you, the Lady Mia Bird of Afdanic," Cassandra indicated that Mia should come forward and meet the queen.

Mia felt nervous as she stepped forward and curtseyed.

"Mia?" Rathe shouted as he pushed his way through the warriors that had assembled to welcome the small party to the camp.

"Brother?" Upon hearing Rathe's voice, Mia felt her heart leap in her chest. The moment she saw him standing in front of her, Mia began to cry. Relief flooded through her at finally having been reunited with her brother. Rathe rushed over and hugged his sister tightly.

"It's all right, I'm here. You're safe now," he whispered to her as she sobbed into his shoulder. Kasnata allowed herself a slight smile at their reunion. Tola was still kneeling in front of Kasnata, his eyes fixed on the ground.

"There is more I have to say, your majesty," he said as he looked up at the queen. "Your daughters, I failed them."

"Where are they?" the dark angel asked, her attention snapping back to the hero of the war of the east.

"I'm here, mother," Kia said as she dismounted and stepped forward. Kasnata frowned as she looked at the young woman that stood before her. The frown faded through shock to joy as she recognised her youngest daughter stood before her, a child no longer.

"Kia?" Kasnata blinked in disbelief as the princess knelt beside Tola. "Where is your sister?" Kasnata asked as she realised that only one of her daughters had made it to her camp.

"The Regent of Delma has her, your highness," Tola said glumly. "Renta sacrificed herself to allow them to escape, so that I could take them to safety, but I failed them, I failed Renta and I failed you. I will await whatever punishment you deem necessary," Tola said solemnly.

"It is not Tola's fault," Kia shook her head as she looked up at her mother. "Kasna allowed herself to be taken by Kelmar to protect me. She was the better fighter; she had mastered many of the skills that the Abbott was teaching her. I was slower to learn. If I had been a better warrior then Kelmar would not have taken her. It is my fault," Kia defended Tola.

The hero of the east hadn't thought of how Kia must have felt when her sister was taken or that she would have laid such blame on her own shoulders. He looked at the young warrior with ambivalence as his own guilt mixed with relief.

"This not the place for such discussions," Kasnata said firmly, her face masking the worry and pain that was stirring in her heart. "Mathias, it was been a long time since you last graced our people with your presence," the queen turned to the Roencian with a smile.

"May I introduce Joab, the shadow of Mia, awarded to her by the Gibborim of Nosfa and the only reason that she is now free of the king and able to rejoin her brother," Mathias smiled.

"You are most welcome here, Joab," Kasnata greeted the young shadow. Kasnata nodded to Marissa and Shamgar, who began to dismiss those that had assembled. The queen beckoned for those newly arrived in her camp to follow her to her quarters where they would be able to talk.

Amalia and Quisla were waiting in Kasnata's tent as the party entered, the two generals watching over the newborns whilst the queen had greeted her guests. They offered a warrior's salute to Cassandra, who smiled and returned the gesture, but said nothing.

Mia was clinging to her brother as she was steered into the tent.

"Marissa, Amalia, Quisla, Shamgar, if you would keep watch, I do not wish to be overheard," Kasnata gave her command as a request and the four generals moved instantly to patrol the area around the queen's tent.

"It seems there is much to be done still," Cassandra sighed. "I had thought that there would have been a respite to the cold weather here, but it would seem that whatever is causing this weather is stronger than I thought," the guardian shook her head as she sat down beside the babies. "But neither of these two seem to mind the cold," She smiled as she gently picked up the children and cradled one in each arm.

Kia frowned and looked between the two babies and her mother.

"Who are they?" the princess asked, unable to hide how cross she felt at seeing two babies in her mother's room.

"Deshanna and Gildow, your brother and sister," Kasnata explained. Kia's eyes widened in rage at the idea that her mother had allowed her father to sire more children. "Or rather I should say that they are your half-brother and sister," Kasnata soothed, reading her daughter's mind.

"Half-brother and sister? Then who is the father?" Kia demanded. Cassandra grinned as Rathe removed himself from his sister so that he could take his daughter from the guardian.

"I am," Rathe said firmly. "Mia, come meet your niece and nephew," he smiled. The lady of Afdanic squealed in delight as she was handed the baby and gazed down at the small face of her niece.

Kia looked at the general who claimed to be the father of her siblings. Rathe could feel Kia's eyes judging him as she watched him, but he ignored the princess as he took his son from Cassandra.

"Tola, come and meet the warrior that one day will put us both to shame," Rathe could tell that Tola was taking the death of Renta much harder than he should be. He had seen what grief had done to his father and it had taken years of loneliness and regret building for him to be as depressed as Tola appeared to be.

Kasnata moved to Rathe's side and slipped her hand into his. She looked at Tola holding her son and placed her free hand on the warrior's shoulder.

"You are not to blame," she whispered. "For whatever wrongs you think you have committed against me, I forgive you. For all those wrongs that you think you committed against Renta, the dead do not hold grudges, you are forgiven."

Tola's eyes brimmed with tears as the queen spoke so he could not speak. Instead he fixed his eyes on Gildow who was grabbing for the long hair of the hero of the east and nodded his thanks to the queen.

"Tell me how my youngest daughter has grown to such an age whilst the rest of us have barely felt time pass," Kasnata stepped away from Tola, Rathe moving with her, his hand still grasped in hers.

"The Abbott played with time," Mathias shrugged. "I do not understand what he did enough to explain it, but he created a space for the princesses to train, to allow them to become as proficient as they should be with weapons for the age of their bodies. It seems to have worked," the Roencian spoke in an offhand manner that Kasnata had missed.

"I see, we shall put your new skills to the test tomorrow, I am sure that Oswin and Anna will want to see the extent of your training, to help you develop further," the queen smiled at Kia.

Kia wasn't sure what she had expected from the reunion with her mother, but she had not expected to be have two siblings, her mother's lover and a host of warriors all present. Part of the princess understood that there was a war being fought and here were more pressing concerns than a mother and daughter falling into each other's arms and embracing, but she was disappointed none-the-less.

She nodded to her mother, but any comment she was going to make was prevented by Mathias speaking.

"Your highness, Kelmar's pursuit of your daughters was

relentless, I fear there is more to it than simply having a bargaining piece to end hostilities against Delma."

"I would agree. There is much that is happening that seems to be connected by a tie I cannot yet name," Cassandra sighed as she stood. "There are a handful of places where knowledge exists that may help in discovering what is going on before it is too late."

"When will you leave?" Kasnata asked.

"I think that I should leave as soon as possible, though I would request the aid of Tola, if he can be spared," the Guardian of the Wilds glanced sideways at Tola as she spoke.

"With General Seaton in the camp, I think that removing Tola as quickly as possible would be wise," Rathe volunteered. "He has asked a lot of questions about where Tola is and why he is not in the camp. I have avoided answering as best I can, but the general seems determined that Tola is a traitor and should be executed as such when he returns."

"Then leave as soon as you are ready, I will have Avner keep the two of you out of sight of the general. I have no doubt that he will know you have re-entered the camp," Kasnata agreed.

Tola looked between the general and the queen and nodded, without saying a word he handed the baby back to Rathe.

"It may also be wise to keep the presence of Kia a secret, the general will not be expecting the princess to be as old as she is now, Mercia should not be told that she has managed to enter your camp,"

Cassandra advised.

"What about Mia?" Rathe asked. "She was a prisoner of Mercia and has escaped, she is not safe her when General Seaton is reporting back to Mercia."

"Kia and Mia will sleep in here tonight. I will have Misna take them in as members of the Raven squadron, they will both be safe and hidden amongst her warriors and none of them would betray their general or me," Kasnata said firmly.

"I should return to the Nosfa camp," Rathe said squeezing Kasnata's hand. "Sleep well," he said as he laid his son down in the crib and Mia laid Deshanna down beside him. Kasnata released his hand so that Rathe could say goodbye to his sister.

"Send in Shamgar and Marissa as you go," Kasnata ordered as Mia and Rathe embraced.

"Your highness, if Mia is to remain in your quarters this evening, I request that I stay by her side," Joab bowed as he spoke, his cheeks burning slightly at the thought of addressing the queen of Nosfa and the Order.

"Very well, Joab," Kasnata nodded. "Mathias, have you any preference as to where you wish to sleep?"

"I will find a billet amongst Shamgar's men. There are a few I need to speak to amongst their number," Mathias yawned and stretched.

"I will arrange for Methanlan and Shaul to speak with you too.

They are currently in the Nosfa camp, I am sure you will have questions for them too," Kasnata added. Mathias nodded his thanks, bowed and left the tent in search of a bed as Rathe left with him.

There were only a few moments before Shamgar and Marissa entered.

"Highness?" Marissa asked as she looked around at those gathered.

"Marissa, I need more bedding to be brought, Kia, Mia and Joab will sleep in here tonight," Kasnata explained. Marissa saluted and vanished. "Shamgar, please wake Avner, take Cassandra and Tola to him, I need them to be kept out of sight until they are ready to leave. Quisla and Amalia can retire unless they have anything to report,"

"Very well, majesty. Tola, your worship, follow me," Shamgar said gruffly. Cassandra suppressed a grin at being addressed so formerly. The Guardian of the Wilds gave Kasnata a warm smile before she followed Tola and Shamgar into the night.

Marissa returned moments later with a few warriors carrying extra beds and bedding, Payne following behind them.

"Is there a problem, Payne?" the queen frowned, as she had not sent for the healer.

"No, your highness," Payne sighed. "However, I was told that the two young ladies that arrived looked pale and so I was dragged from my bed. If there is plague being brought into the camp, I would sooner know now, before half the camp is struck down or your highness becomes too sick to lead and we are saddled with the direction of the idiot general."

CHAPTER 15

Samara had never known of any ruler that had asked for an expansion of the empire of the Order on quite the scale that Kasnata had suggested.

They had almost no presence on the mainland save for the war camps that the army inhabited. When they came to the other nations of Celadmore, they would stay with allies in Tulna, Roenca, and when Kasnata had first been married, in Grashindorph.

Something had changed in the queen since she had met General Bird, her passion and fight had been stirred, something Samara had never seen before, but had heard Avner, Shamgar and Yoav speak of it many times when they spoke of the queen in her youth.

She seemed to be stronger than she had been, more concerned with the people of Celadmore now that the weight of keeping her children safe from Mercia was lifted from her shoulders.

Samara had been given several locations that would be suitable to see the construction of a few small settlements and some larger fortresses. It seemed wise to her to send out a small party of scouts to each of the locations whilst she rode for Roenca.

Though the queen had not specified having a fortress within her husband's domain, it was a strategic location that the Order could not afford to be without if Mercia were to ever remove

Kasnata from her throne.

The fort she had planned for Nosfa was nothing elaborate; it was functional, with deep moats and pits dug around the exterior and big palisade walls that hid a complex system of ramparts. Inside the fort, there were to be no buildings close to the wall.

Samara had ensured that the plans had all buildings a distance that was at least twice what any man could jump away from the way. She had also laid out a design for sharpened stakes to be placed from halfway between the wall and the buildings up to the buildings.

She also ensured that there was no ledge or edge of any width around the roofs of the buildings so that no invaders could place a ladder between the wall and the buildings. Samara knew the value of high ground and just how important it was that the defenders keep it.

It would be built out of wood rather than stone, though a fire risk, there was plenty of wood to be found in the forest around Roenca and quarrying stone from further afield would only attract the unwanted attention of Mercia's patrols.

Haras, though gruff in her attitude, was a gifted engineer and had spent hours helping Samara plan the forts and settlements that Kasnata had asked for.

Nasus had helped by writing to her friends and allies across Celadmore, the dark haired Benadroccan had written asking for help and support for Kasnata. The war of the nine kingdoms had worn down the spirits of many and though they were weary of the turn the politics of Celadmore had taken, the slightest glimmer of hope was enough to inspire them to action.

Nasus was certain that Kasnata sending Samara out on such a quest was a sign that something was changing.

Akiva organised the Roencians into groups, some to cut down the trees, others to plane the logs into planks, stakes and palisade, a third group to transport the materials to the site of the fort and a fourth group to help in the construction.

As the last of the scouts returned to Roenca with news of the other locations for settlements and forts, the work had almost been completed on the first fortress. Samara was impressed with how hard the Roencians worked and how skilled they were in military construction.

"Is there anywhere on the flood plain that is suitable?" Samara asked of the last scout.

"Here, towards the coast is preferable," He replied, pointing at the map that the general had marked the areas for the other settlements and forts on.

"That is the only suitable site?" Samara frowned.

"I'm afraid so, it would have to be a settlement that would rely on guerrilla defence rather than a fort. Any fort would need a garrison that outnumbered the enemy to hold it as it is a site vulnerable to attack on every side and in the dip of a basin so an enemy with enough ranged weapons could pour fire into the fort and the defenders would be slaughtered," the scout shrugged.

"A settlement it is then, I will talk to Haras and see if she can't think of some ways of reducing the weakness of having it in a basin," Samara sighed.

"You seem to be making good progress," Akiva said warmly as he approached the general.

"Thanks to you and your people," Samara agreed. "What can I do for you, Akiva?"

"Epoch has sent something for Kasnata, as have the leaders of the Free Cities. As you have orders to build these forts and settlements, I have come to ask your permission to send Nasus to Kasnata with the gifts," Akiva said as he looked over the map and nodded his approval at each of the chosen sites.

"Will she be safe travelling to the war camp on her own?" Samara asked the scout saluted and left the two to talk as he went in search of food.

"Nasus and Haras are more than capable of reaching the war camp of Kasnata," Akiva assured the general.

"I have no objections, though I would set the condition that I send dispatches to her highness with Nasus, then I can be certain they haven't been intercepted," Samara looked expectantly at Akiva, who nodded his agreement.

The flap to Kasnata's tent opened and closed. The queen was stood with her back to the entrance and felt the cool night air against her legs.

"They have come to take me back," Rathe's voice betrayed nothing of the fear he felt swirling around inside him.

Kasnata nodded without saying a word. She had known that Mercia would recall Rathe as soon as he was certain that General Seaton was in command of the army and had learnt all that he could from General Bird.

She felt Rathe's arms encircling her body and leant back into his arms. The two stood in silence, neither knowing what to say, neither wanting to speak the fears that they harboured inside.

The sound of Deshanna and Gildow crying broke the lingering silence. Kasnata made to move towards her children, but Rathe held her back.

"Let me," he whispered and kissed his lover's cheek. Kasnata tilted her head and wrapped her arms about her chest, rubbing her upper arms, her eyes fixed on Rathe as he cooed over his children.

The general gazed down at the twins and smiled as they scrambled and crawled over to where he stood by the edge of their cot. He picked the two up with ease, their tiny fingers reaching for his face as he held them.

Rathe kissed their foreheads in turn and closed his eyes, trying to fix the scent of his children, the sound of their gurgling, trying to form words and what it felt like to hold the prince and princess he had fathered.

He regretted he would not be there to hear their first words, to see them learn to walk, to lift a sword and challenge their mother in many futile battles, attempting to prove their abilities as warriors.

He laughed at the thought and tears began to escape from beneath his eye lids. He felt Kasnata's hand on his cheek as the queen gently brushed away the tears. Rathe opened his eyes and tilted his head so he could kiss the queen's hand.

He looked at her and wondered, not for the first time, what it would have been like if she had never married Mercia, if he had met her first, what it would have been like to be married to her.

"This is no time for regrets," Kasnata said softly, reading the general's thoughts.

"I love you," Rathe told the queen as Deshanna tried to leap from his arms into Kasnata's.

"I know, and your children will know how much you love them too. I will make sure of it," the queen replied as she took Deshanna from her father. Rathe looked down at Gildow, who was clawing at the claps on the general's cloak.

"Thank you," Rathe nodded and leaned in to kiss the queen.

"I love you," Kasnata breathed. Rathe slipped his free hand into the queen's hair and crushed her lips to his. As they broke apart, Rathe leant his forehead against Kasnata's.

"This is not the last time we will see each other," he said firmly. Kasnata nodded as Rathe kissed her forehead and handed Gildow to his lover.

"Rathe, I am more your wife than I have ever been his," the queen blurted out as the general made to leave.

"Keep Mia safe."

Was all that the general could say in reply before he turned away from his family and strode out to where the envoys from Nosfa waited for him.

Kasnata watched Rathe leave the tent with tears in her eyes. She held her children close to her chest, praying silently that her lover would live to hold her and them again. She placed the two babies, fast becoming toddlers, back in their crib. She closed her eyes tightly and cringed as she heard Mia scream from the other side of the camp.

He was a stronger and greater man than her husband would ever be, no matter what the king would do to the general, Kasnata would always love Rathe. The babes before her yawn and punched the air with their tiny fists.

The queen smiled in spite of herself. No force on Celadmore or in the heavens would have been able to stop her from dethroning her husband and bringing stability back to the land if it had not been for her children held captive.

"Ssssh," she soothed as the twins began to cry again. "Sleep soundly, my little ones, you need not fear. No danger can reach you whilst you rest your heads here. No beast, fright or monster, creature or man may pass by my blade. I will defend you in the darkest of night. Let your dreams carry you, like the swiftest of steeds. Let joy dance around you like the hounds of the hunt. Your sword arm be strong and your shieldmate be true. Rough warriors stand proud as they watch over you," the queen sang the lullaby her mother had sung to her as a child.

"Nightmares will flee from the new light of day. No horror can harm you whilst our vigil is held. Honour with courage, brave, strong and proud, born of the blood, sleep now my little ones, be still like the dove. Let your dreams carry you, like the swiftest of steeds. Let joy dance around you like the hounds of the hunt. Your sword arm be strong and your shieldmate be true. Rough warriors stand proud as they watch over you.

"Gentle, gentle, sleep creeps your way. Whispers through the darkness cannot be heard as you are wrapped in the Goddess' arms. No creature of night, no vision of man, can break through my steel and bring you to harm. Let your dreams carry you, like the swiftest of steeds. Let joy dance around you like the hounds of the hunt. Your sword arm be strong and your shieldmate be true. Rough warriors stand proud as they watch over you.

"Gentle, gentle, dawn creeps this way. Darkness will flee when you open your eyes. Let your dreams carry you, like the swiftest of steeds. Let joy dance around you like the hounds of the hunt. Your sword arm be strong and your shieldmate be true. Rough warriors stand proud as they watch over you,"

Marissa stood outside the queen's tent and listened to her sing to her children. She knew many within the Order, and in the nine kingdoms, who would sacrifice their children without a second thought, that would rush to battle without giving any credence to consequences for those being held hostage.

Though she knew many thought her children a weakness she should rid herself of, Marissa admired her queen for her compassion and her patience. She also knew that General Bird was not a man that would stumble blindly into any traps King Mercia had laid for him.

Marissa was more concerned with General Seaton. From what Methanlan and Shaul were reporting to Misna, he was displaying an unhealthy interest in the queen's children, as was Hesla. Yoav had taken an oath that no matter what happened to the rest of the Order, he would protect Kasnata's children as Amalia and Marissa protected the queen, and as the Phoenix General stood listening to the lullaby, she vowed to Arala that whatever she could do to protect the five children of Kasnata, she would do, without hesitation.

Mercia could feel the familiar clawing at the back of his eyes. It was a feeling that seemed to ebb and flow like the tides. There were times when it was nothing more than a slight nagging thought at the back of his mind, something he could almost ignore, but these times had become a rarity.

Most of the time the compulsion completely dominated his mind, talons that were sunk so deeply into his grey matter that his head felt like it was being slowly crushed between two rocks.

The king of Nosfa couldn't remember a time when he hadn't felt the sensation lurking in his consciousness. His father had noticed something odd in the young prince, Mercia had never spoken to Rosla about his darker compulsions, but somehow the late king had known.

He had done all that he could to protect his son, to try and help him without drawing attention to the oddities in Mercia's behaviour, but it had been for nought.

When his father had told him that Lord Haston Bird was to act as regent until he was old enough and wise enough to inherit the throne, Mercia had felt certain that his father was trying to keep him from his birth right; that the king was ashamed of what he had fathered and confided in Lord Bird what Mercia was.

It had been this and this alone that had fuelled Mercia's hatred of Lord Bird and his descendants. His mother had been no better either, from the way that she spoke to him and looked at him; it was clear to the prince that his mother knew too and would do what she could to keep him from ever becoming king.

He spent months living in a paranoid fear that he would be abducted from the palace, or slaughtered in his bed or worse, so he decided to strike first.

When he had become king, things had changed; his mind had cleared to a certain extent, especially when his mother had been dispatched. Then he had met Kasnata.

The queen of the Order had been a pawn that he could use before he met her. All his advisors had extolled the virtues of having an alliance with such a strong military in a time of war and the need for peace that was enforced when necessary.

The first time he had met her, he had been overawed by her and those that travelled in her entourage. They were the stuff of legend, warriors that were renown throughout Celadmore for their skill in battle and heroic deeds.

Kasnata was bred from a line of warriors that any man of royal blood would have boasted, but she was gentle, for all the skills she had been taught, for her ability to deal death swiftly, there was a softness to her. Her decidedly calmer nature was something that

Mercia's advisors saw as something to exploit, and to begin with, so had Mercia. There had been a plan to bring about securing for his people through peace and a force that could conquer any enemy that decided to move against him.

He had originally thought that he would have to trick and manipulate the queen to get her to marry him, to agree with him. But through their conversations together, it soon became apparent to Nosfa that the barbarian queen shared his desire for peace and the security of her own people.

He also found that the more time he spent with the queen, the more distant the clawing became. His paranoia seemed to melt away and he began to understand what it meant to have a clear mind and peace from the urges that drove him to cruel actions and protected him from guilt with a shield of a callous attitude and a lie of necessity.

It was a different way of living that opened a more prosperous time for Nosfa and Grashindorph, but the king's change in attitude concerned his advisors.

Mercia had not intended to fall in love but as he spent more time with Kasnata, he realized that he wanted to marry her for more than political gain.

Shortly before they were to be married, Neesa had arrived. She had been sent for by the former Baron of Fintry. The aging noble had been out of favour in King Rosla's court for warmongering and an attitude that showed Rosla the Baron was only concerned with increasing the size of his own purse, regardless of the cost to the lives of those that lived on his lands.

The baron had recognized the paranoia developing in the young prince and saw an opportunity not only to regain favour in the court, but to also turn the focus of the kingdom of Nosfa to his own advantage.

The marriage to Kasnata had been his idea, but the effect the barbarian queen had on the king was not what the Baron had anticipated. It was a mistake he needed to correct and Neesa was the solution.

The baron had known her since she was a small child, he watched as she was trained as an assassin, and in forbidden arts. She was loyal to her own people and code that the Baron found more than acceptable.

As soon as Neesa had appeared, Mercia had felt the clawing intensify. He would wake in the night with a pounding pain in his head that would drive him to fits of rage.

But the Kasnata had been there to calm him, to hold him and soothe his frustrations. Neesa spent hours gradually and subtly increasing her influence over Mercia until Leinad was born.

The joy the king felt at having a son banished the darker side of his nature, if only briefly. Neesa saw the effect that the queen had on the king, how the assassin's work was being undone by the slightest smile or lightest touch from the queen, and so Neesa began to drive the two apart.

By the time Kia was born, Kasnata could no longer calm the king's rages and rather than finding his way to the queen's bed each night, he went to Neesa's, and eventually exiled the queen whilst keeping their children where they would be of greatest advantage to him.

When Neesa was around, the king had no comprehension of what it was like when his mind was still. Instead it was a constant swirling mass of pressure, noise and aggression.

Hatred bubbled under his skin that could be directed at anyone, including the assassin, though she was most adept in deflecting his ire onto a different target.

When Mercia had arrived at the forward camp of Kasnata's army, he had begun to feel slight twinges of emotion for the queen, though her gentle regard for him was all but gone, he had felt jealous beyond reason that General Bird had bedded his wife and that two children had resulted.

The king had tried many times to sire children from other women, but had never been able to. He wondered if he was cursed and question if his children by Kasnata were really his own.

On the journey back to Nosfa, the king had begun to feel his control slipping. Only Leinad remained in his hands, his only heir that he could not harm unless he had another to replace him. Kasnata now had two heirs to her own throne that were not of his blood, that her own people would gladly recognise, and Kia and Kasna were both still unaccounted for.

The Lady Mia had been Nosfa's chance at siring a new heir, but her escape and disappearance had left the king with only the threat of destroying Kasnata's lover and new-borns to keep her from breaking their alliance and making new alliances with Nosfa's enemies.

But he also wanted to punish his wife, to make an example of her for all his people to see and know that betrayal would not be tolerated. Not even from barbarian royalty.

Neesa was waiting for him as the king arrived in the city of Grashindorph. There has been no great procession through the streets, no smiling faces lining the streets to welcome the king home.

Instead the people were in their homes, the doors bolted, keeping the streets clear whilst the king passed. Even the beggars had withdrawn from sight, slipping into whatever dark, dank holes they could find.

Mercia dismounted in the courtyard of the city palace and nodded to those in his entourage, dismissing them until he was ready to travel to his own palace.

Neesa had requested they meet in the old palace as there were no spies lurking amongst the decaying walls of stone, unlike amongst the servants that stalked the halls of Mercia's palace. Neesa glanced about constantly as she waited; certain she was being watched, but not knowing from where.

"You failed," the king said sharply as he and Neesa walked slowly through the palace corridors.

"Sire, there were many obstacles I didn't anticipate. The Guardian of the Wilds -" Neesa began to explain.

"I don't want to hear pathetic excuses. My daughters have escaped and are now free, the Lady Mia is gone. Tell me why I shouldn't have you executed for failing me?" Mercia demanded.

A scuttling sound caused Neesa to jump and draw her weapon. A few moments later, a mouse scurried past and the assassin sheathed her sword, letting out a relieved sign.

Asahel slunk back against the wall. He was hidden well amongst the ivy that had infiltrated the palace walls on the upper level and had begun to take over the upper floors.

Rumours had circulated the city about the king's return and upon investigation; Asahel and Helez had discovered that the king was meeting his assassin before returning to the palace. The exiles from the Gibborim had agreed that it was wise for one of them to observe the meeting, whilst the other watched the streets.

Asahel had won the honour of infiltrating the palace, though he had begun to wonder whether Helez wasn't the one with the better assignment. Asahel resisted moving to ease the cramp in his leg that had begun to seize after spend so long in the same position. The more he moved, the more likely Neesa would detect his presence, especially since the assassin was already on edge.

"Well?" The king demanded.

"Sire, I have always served you faithfully and well. You cannot doubt that," Neesa said firmly.

"That is no reason to excuse your current failures," the king said, raising an eyebrow. His muscles burned and the pounding in his head was getting worse as the two spoke. Sound seemed to echo off every wall making it almost impossible for the king to think straight.

"Sire, what can I do to show you that I am still your loyal servant?" Neesa asked, knowing that the longer they spoke, the less clearly the king would think. She was well practised at her craft and had many years in which she had extended her influence over the king that she could exploit.

"Kill them," Mercia gasped as he clutched the side of his head. He felt an explosion of hatred course through his veins as the moon rose, a blood moon, that brought a smile to Neesa's lips.

"Kill who, sire?" she asked as the king dropped to his knees and screamed.

"General Bird and his filthy half-spawn. I want the children dead so their mother will weep and I want General Bird captured before he returns to the city. I want him imprisoned and executed for treason," Mercia yelled, his eyes wild and unfocused.

"I will send out riders to intercept the general. The children, I will deal with personally," Neesa bowed.

"Whilst they live, there are heirs to the throne of the Order and heirs that give General Bird a strong claim to my throne. I will not let my wife, and her lover, conspire to remove me from power and not face retribution," Mercia gasped.

"What about the Lady Mia?" Neesa asked.

"She will come running back when she knows I have her precious brother," Mercia sneered.

"As you wish, your majesty," Neesa smiled and left the king amongst the crumbling walls of the city palace.

Asahel waited a few moments before departing; making sure that Neesa was not lingering anywhere close by. The streets were still empty as he slipped between shadows and made his way to the rooms that he and Helez had found above an abandoned warehouse.

They were not comfortable, but neither man was used to comfort, and they were dry and private. No one had come to these rooms or the warehouse since the two men had been exiled, and until they had a better idea of what was happening on the surface of the city, the rooms would do.

"Did they come?" Helez asked as Asahel crawled through the hatch from the warehouse below.

"Yes, Neesa and the king," Asahel shook slightly as he spoke. It had been cold out in the ruins, but it wasn't the weather that had left Asahel shaking.

"What's wrong?" Helez frowned as he studied the face of his

friend.

"Neesa, she's not just an assassin. She did something to the king," Asahel explained as he sat on one of the wooden chests the men were using for furniture.

"Did something?" Helez raised an eyebrow. "Did she poison him? Hypnotise him?"

"No, the moon, the blood moon, when it rose, the king collapsed, like he had been possessed," Asahel looked at his friend with a worried expression.

"You think she's summoning demons?" Helez asked in a half-mocking tone.

"No," Asahel replied flatly. "I think she's a witch."

Chapter 16

Kasna opened her eyes and for a few minutes was confused about where she was. The inside of the tent seemed like such an alien place to her after spending so many nights under the stars, but the privacy of the tent had been welcome. Kelmar was asleep beside her, the Duke's arms and legs still intertwined with her own.

She felt content to lie there with him, no need to move and dress quickly or wake him to find out what she should do next. Yet she also felt guilty, she had failed to avenge Renta and instead of killing the man that had tortured someone she cared for; she had ended up in his bed.

Kelmar stirred beside her and she felt his lips on her neck, moving down to her shoulder before he whispered to her.

"Good morning."

Kasna rolled over in his arms and kissed him. Instead of the aggressive and urgent way she had kissed him the night before, this had more emotion and less desire.

"Good morning," she replied as their lips broke apart. Kelmar felt like he was being toyed with as the princess gently rolled him out his back so that she was lying on top of him.

He ran his hands over her back and sighed. A few short hours ago, she had wanted him dead, now she was content to simply lie in his arms. As long as he lived, Kelmar was positive that he would never understand women.

"Do you still want to kill me?" he asked as he kissed the top of her head.

"Yes," she replied as her fingers traced circles on his chest. "But I am willing to wait, at least until you can attempt to prove what you said about something else forcing you, controlling you whilst you murdered Renta."

"And how can I prove that?" Kelmar asked with a frown.

"I don't know," Kasna shrugged. "You're the one who has to figure it out."

As his fingers ran over her skin, he could feel the scars that had been left on her back. He had his fair share of scars obtained in battle, when he had been too slow to block or parry, or when a stray arrow had pierced his armour, but the ones that Kasna bore were different.

The duke shuddered slightly as he pushed aside thoughts about how she had received them. Kasna sighed to herself and closed her eyes as she lay in his arms.

"You're so different," she whispered as they lay there.

"To what?" he asked, looking down at her.

"To who you were when you were chasing us. In Roenca, in Abergorlech, even out on the plains, you were cruel, relentless, you seemed to be so soulless," Kasna observed and felt Kelmar shifting uncomfortably beneath her.

"Maybe that is what I am and what you see now is merely an act," his mouth was set in a thin line as he rolled onto his side so that the princess would slide off him.

"It's a possibility," she shrugged as she propped her head up on her hand. "But I don't think so."

"You have no way of knowing what I am really like," he replied with spite, and rose from the bed.

Kasna watched him move across the tent and dress without saying a word. It was clear that there were things about the duke she didn't know, but it was even more apparent that he was struggling against his own inner demons, his duty and the changing reality that war brought.

Kelmar cursed himself as he stepped out into the fresh air. He felt his head clear instantly and smelt the dying embers of the camp fires on the air. He took several deep breaths before beginning a camp inspection so that he could refocus his mind on what he had to do.

The king had made it clear that the princess was needed for something, but he had never been told exactly what it was. He only knew that she had to be delivered to the king alive. There was something in not knowing what Kasna was needed for that made the Regent of Delma uneasy, but he also knew that he had to do what was necessary to allow the kingdom of Delma to survive.

He assumed that the princess was to be used as a bargaining

chip to end the hostility between the army of the Order and the nation of Delma, but now he was not so certain.

Cassandra looked at Tola with a worried expression; the man hadn't been the same since Renta had died. It was understandable, but the Guardian of the Wilds had expected some improvement in his countenance, even if it had only been a mask being placed over his emotions.

He'd watched the woman he loved being murdered, in cold blood, by Duke Kelmar DeLacey. She had died willingly, sacrificed herself without a second thought in order to save the lives of Tola, Mathias, Kia, Kasna, Mia and Joab.

Tola had known when he had seen her kneeling on the ground that she would die, but that had not meant that her death had not left him a hollow shell of a man. He was void of all emotion, save for anger.

Rage was his only driving force, urging him onwards to vengeance against DeLacey, not King Delich and not the kingdom of Delma. It was Kelmar's blood he wanted.

Cassandra knew what hatred like that did to a man, to his heart and soul. How it consumed him and left him empty with nothing to live for, no purpose and completely void of passion.

She had hoped that as time passed, his rage would have eased somewhat, that he would have begun to see his way clear to moving on and forgetting about his revenge, but time had only made things worse.

The Guardian of the Wilds had thought that by getting Tola to see there was more to life than living for vengeance, that she could help him. The two had left Kasnata's camp early without telling a soul where they were going, only that they would be gone for a few days.

Tola didn't know where they were going, nor did he care to ask. His mind was focused on replaying Renta's death. He had lost many friends in battle as well as men under his command, but Renta was the woman that he loved.

They had never married; their relationship had been one of chance more than design. They enjoyed passionate affairs when they were stationed in the same encampment, but when one or the other left for another posting, their relationship came to an end.

They had both thought that by living their lives like this, there wouldn't be pain if one of them died, that the one who was left behind would be able to think back on their time together fondly, but ultimately be able to move forward with their life.

If their positions had been reversed, Tola thought that Renta would have been able to move on with her life, but the hero of the war of the east couldn't. Each time the two had met, he had fallen more in love with the general. She was funny in her own way, strong and clever and her smile was something that he dreamed about when they were apart.

Now the memory of her smile had been replaced by the face of Kelmar.

"We're here," Cassandra said, her voice snapping Tola's attention back to the present.

He looked around. They were in the Chesil Void, an expanse of fine white sand and salt that stretched for miles. There was almost no life in the void and no water. Despite the lack of life, there was an energy to the place that Tola could not explain.

Cassandra had dismounted and was setting up camp. She worked in silence, every so often glancing up at the horizon, as if she expected something to appear from beyond it at any moment.

"What is it?" Tola asked after the fifth time she looked up.

"Nothing," the Guardian said quickly. She shook her head and passed some of the rations she had packed for their journey to Tola.

The two ate in silence. The small fire, that was providing a small amount of warmth, was not large enough to cook on. Cassandra had prepared for their journey well, she knew that there was nothing she could burn in the Chesil Void and had brought enough wood with her to build small fires for seven days. She didn't expect it to take longer than that to find what she was looking for.

The Chesil Void was a focal point for the energies of existence. It was the one place on Celadmore that Cassandra could use the full extent of her power. As one of the four immortals of Celadmore, Cassandra was blessed with power beyond comprehension, but it was not magic.

There was only one form of magic that still existed on Celadmore – blood magic. There had been others, long before Cassandra had been born, but they were now extinct, the only evidence that they had ever existed was contained in the ancient writings that were kept in the library in the palace of Grashindorph.

"You should get some sleep," Cassandra said to Tola. The Roencian blinked a few times but nodded. He hadn't slept properly since Renta had died and when he did, he woke up screaming her name, his blood thirsting for vengeance more than it had before he had gone to sleep.

The Guardian of the Wilds sat and listened to Tola's breathing for a while. She waited until it changed to the slow rhythm that told her that the hero of the war of the east had fallen asleep.

She stood up and wandered away from the fireside. When she had been a child, Kania had told her stories about the world before the four immortals had existed. There were people that had come before those that lived now, civilisations that made those that existed now look little more than mud shacks thrown hurriedly together by comparison. There had been wars, wars that had crossed the face of all realms, wars that had ultimately led to the nothingness of the Chesil Void.

This mixture of salt and sand was what remained of those that had come before. It was a region that most inhabitants of Celadmore avoided; the air was dry due to the power that hung in it and the bitter memories of those that had perished hung in the air.

It was not a comfortable place for most mortals to visit. There were those that found the void had an irresistible draw and those that were in so much of their own pain that the memory of it was comforting. In his current state, Tola would sleep well here.

Cassandra sank to her knees, when she was far enough away from the fire, and plunged her hands into the sand.

"By the blessing of Arala," she whispered.

A breeze lifted the sand from over hands. It was a gentle movement, slight and almost indiscernible. She knelt and prayed. No more than seven days. she thought and smiled to herself.

"Let your wisdom guide us. Let your voice speak clearly. Let my words be yours."

"Your highness, there is a party waiting to see you," Marissa bowed to the queen as she spoke. Kasnata had refused to receive any visitors for the past few days. General Seaton had completely taken over the army of Nosfa, and the commands that the queen issued were not being carried out.

Methanlan had confirmed that they were not being given orders from the queen and that General Seaton seemed to be content to wage his own siege against the city of Delma without the support of the army of the Order.

Since Rathe had departed, Kasnata had found her heart was heavy with worry once more. The Lady Mia seemed to be safe for now, though, which she knew Rathe had wanted more than his own safety.

Kia and Mia had taken to being part of Misna's company with ease, they were not being trained to spy, but could take part in the daily routine of training and camp activity without raising any suspicion.

Misna trusted each of her warriors with far greater secrets than the identity of Kia and Mia, so Kasnata was content in the knowledge that they would not be betrayed, and it would be many months before General Seaton discovered that either of the girls had ever been in the camp. Joab and Mathias had taken to helping around the camp where they could, but there was little for either man to do.

So the two had taken up training with the Eight, teaching the young warriors techniques they would not learn from those amongst the Order.

Kasnata emerged from her tent with a deadpan expression, Marissa at her shoulder. She looked over to where a young woman stood holding a horse and twelve hounds sat looking up at her.

"Nasus? What brings you to my camp?" Kasnata asked with surprise as she looked at the woman of Benadrocca.

"Greetings, Queen of the Order, I come bearing gifts," Nasus smiled as she opened her arms and whistled. The twelve hounds all leapt to their feet and growled, looking around for any enemies.

"Gifts from your father?" Kasnata asked as Nasus walked forwards with the dogs and whistled again.

"Not only from him, but the people of the Free Cities. Word of General Samara's task has begun to spread as the walls to the fortress she is building grow. Her scouts have sent word to the Free Cities of the other places she is considering for settlements and forts, asking for information about the areas. It has been a long time coming, your highness," Nasus smiled and bowed.

"What do you mean? A long time coming?" Kasnata frowned and motioned for Nasus to follow her. The two women walked towards Kasnata's war tent, the hounds following obediently behind.

"The blood moon has risen; the leaders of the great

nations of Celadmore are descending into madness. There is no coincidence here. People talk of the evil of the hearts of men, but there is a greater evil at work here," Nasus spoke in a hushed voice as they entered the war tent.

Marissa had hung back and now waited outside the tent, keeping away any that would pry too closely.

"You are talking of prophecy?" Kasnata gave Nasus a withering look.

"If I were, there would be no call for such derision. I am speaking of history and what we have learned from it. There is a small window where the odds are in your favour, your highness, when your actions will shape what is to come more than any others. You sent out Samara to build, this shows you have hope for the future. Your army has not destroyed Delma, this shows you wish there to be a peaceful end to this terrible war. You have two beautiful babies, this shows your husband's hold over you is failing. There is something out there that is far worse than Valians, assassins and the armies of your assembled enemies and it is to you that the task of defeating it falls."

"You speak in riddles and vague assertions," Kasnata yawned and covered her mouth with her hand.

"I am willing to explain what I know, if you are ready to listen, though I think it is best that you speak to Cassandra about what is unfolding and your role."

"Cassandra is out in the wilds with Tola," Kasnata replied.

"Then it is best if I wait until she returns before I say more. I was sorry to hear of Renta's death. She was a great asset to your people, and a woman who even Haras liked," Nasus said changing the subject.

"Thank you, she is missed," Kasnata replied as she rubbed her eyes.

"Do you have any news of your daughters? They passed through Roenca with Mathias with Neesa and Kelmar pursing them."

Scattergood was the oldest of the children of the Eight. He didn't look it; in fact Merinda and Lucinda both looked far older than he, though they were both three years younger than him. He had always thought of it as some form of curse, to look so much younger than he was, but there were some unexpected advantages.

Scattergood had been named the leader of the Eight, as the oldest of the children, but Queen Kasnata when she had invited them to stay within her camp.

She referred to him not by name, but by title, so when members of the Order came looking to speak with him, to try and send the Eight off on errands they didn't want to do themselves, they always came to Merinda or Lucinda and were caught off guard when he stepped in and refused their requests.

There were so many people amongst the Order that had an inflated sense of their skills. It wasn't hard to understand why, they were led by some of the most gifted warriors on Celadmore and trained more rigorously than most soldiers could ever dream of, but for all their training, there were those who were held back by their lack of natural talent.

These were the individuals who spent their days trying to send the Eight out on trivial missions that they didn't want to conduct themselves, and the same people that talked of nothing but their lives on Anamoore.

Scattergood had been part of one of the tribes of the wilds. They were a proud people, not warriors, but survivors and even the children were trained to kill if they had to, but their strength lay in reading the land, in tracking. It was almost instinctive to each of them and even the best trackers in the Order had been put to shame by their skills.

The village of Ashpa, to the south of Olney, had been their home until the soldiers of Delma had marched and burned their village to the ground. Scattergood had been badly injured as he tried to save people from the buildings they had become trapped inside, but he had only been able to save one, Warner, not yet eight years old and the youngest of the Eight to survive.

They had not been the only ones to escape the flames. Scattergood had convinced them that they needed to leave the ruins of the village, that they needed to walk until they found some help. Merinda had worried that they would run across more soldiers, but the real danger had come from the scavengers.

During their first night, they lost five of their number, carried off into the night by the moorin packs. The terrified ones that remained had huddled together and listened to the screams of their friends filling the night. There had been twenty that had survived the burning of Ashpa, two died from injuries they had sustained during the moorin attack, three more were taken during the second night. The others had managed to fend off the moorin, Scattergood and his brother, Jericho, protecting the smaller children and those who were too week to fight.

One of the smaller children became separated from their number during walking the next day and Jericho went back to look for her, that was the last that any of them had seen of either of them. Scattergood had wanted to go back and find them, but by then he was too weak to move very far and the others were beginning to suffer from lack of food, rest and water.

He knew that has the army of the Order not found them, he

would have died within hours and the others would have all been picked off by the wilds.

It was a debt he knew that could never be repaid, but he would gladly serve the Queen of the Order and those that followed after her to show his gratitude.

Merinda, Lucinda, Warner, Resha, Colm, Vaike, Adino and he were the only survivors. Scattergood hoped that Jericho was still alive and safe, but after having no word for so long, he was starting to lose faith that he would ever see his brother again.

The queen had offered them each the opportunity to train with her warriors, to discover their strengths and weaknesses at a young age and develop them. Scattergood had left it to each of the Eight to decide for themselves what they wanted to do.

He chose to train under General Misna and her Raven warriors, the leader of the Eight had never wanted to be a soldier and fight, but if he could strike from the shadows, track better, gather information, read situations and know how to distract or exploit them for his own gain, then he could still serve.

Not only this, but he would be able to see what news the Order had gathered and if there were any leads as to the whereabouts of his brother.

CHAPTER 17

2432GL 66ᵀᴴ SPREGAN

Shaul had felt jumpy for three days. Long shadows caused him to overact when patrolling the camp of the men of Nosfa and his nervous demeanour was starting to affect the people around him. Harry and Jack had laughed at the shift in Shaul's personality, from being laid back and nonchalant to seeing danger in the embers of the fire, to begin with, but as the days passed and more of the officers were found murdered they started to become more agitated as well.

Methanlan was the only one of the four who managed to keep a level head. He sighed and dismissed the ravings of the men. He'd hoped that his comrade had been putting on an act to distract the other men from the investigation that the Queen Kasnata had ordered, but even when the two were alone, Shaul was still jittery.

Between the shift in Shaul's personality and the bloodlust of General Seaton, Methanlan had begun to wish that this particular assignment was over.

Methanlan's mistrust of General Seaton was founded on more than simply despising his bloodlust. The attitude of Seaton was unnerving, from the way he looked at each of the men that served under him, from the way he focused them with a cold stare when reports were being given.

The slight shifts in his body language that came when he

didn't like what he was hearing told Methanlan that there was a lot that was hidden under the surface of the stoic expression that remained fixed on his face in almost every situation.

The years Methanlan had spent as a spy for his people had taught him to approach men and women like General Seaton with extreme caution. The general didn't seem concerned with the murders taking place either whenever a nervous officer spoke of them. Seaton seemed bored by the subject and did nothing, save for rolling his eyes and waiting for an opportunity to change the subject or dismiss the officers.

Methanlan had tried several times to talk to Shaul about General Seaton, but his friend barely heard a word as he was consumed with jumping at every shadow.

As time had ticked by, Shaul had become convinced that there was dark magic at work, that witches were stalking the camp. The long cold of winter, still unabated, and rumours of a blood moon had him convinced that there was something worse to be feared than war with the people of Delma.

Methanlan had stopped Shaul from telling General Misna his concerns up until now, but with his duties investigating General Seaton, he had less time to keep a watchful eye on his companion.

Despite feeling that the General Misna should be informed, Shaul had no intention of reporting to her without evidence. Misna dealt in gossip and misinformation, but she was the one that created them and had them spread. When her people reported an unfounded rumour and gave hysterical reports, she was less than amused.

When she had been raised to the position of spymaster, she had quickly made examples of those who were not diligent in their work and there were many that had suffered humiliation, embarrassment and even torture for failing her. There were only two that had been sentenced to death for treason against the Order, though it was a sentence that was passed and carried out by the Queen, not by a mere general.

Shaul knew that he needed to prove dark magic was at work, and the only way he could do that was by investigating camp gossip. He enlisted the help of Harry and Jack, under the pretence that the murderer could turn his hand from officers to men of the ranks at any moment, and General Seaton was doing nothing to protect his men.

They could only investigate when they were off duty and when Methanlan was with General Seaton. Shaul didn't want Methanlan to throw they were trying to find evidence to support the hysteria that was slowly gaining momentum in the camp, mostly because he feared that Methanlan would declare it all nothing more than camp fire stories that Shaul was giving credence than they deserved by investigating.

Misna had been investigating the murders in the name of the Queen, but General Seaton was doing all he could to inconvenience the Raven General. Methanlan had tried to be as helpful as he could without being discovered.

Shaul suspected that Misna was making very little headway, though it was not something that the general would ever discuss with the spy.

"You think this is a good idea," Harry asked as the three men stood where Commander Grice's body had been found. This area had been left abandoned by the soldiers of Nosfa, all the men in the camp avoiding it out of fear. This meant that it had remained largely unchanged since the discovery of his body. There had been some fresh snowfalls, so the ground was covered in a light dusting of powder.

The commander's body had been taken back to Nosfa, to his family rather than being buried in a field outside an enemy city.

"I think something strange is going on and we're all in danger," Shaul shrugged. "Officers are doing what officers do best and sitting on their brains."

"Tam, you really think that this could be the work of witches?" Jack asked as he shivered slightly at the thought of them.

"I don't know, but if it is a witch -" Shaul began, but was cut off by Jack sighing.

"Please don't finish that sentence. It's only gonna end with us feelin' guilty and doin' exactly what you want, so might as well just agree and skip the lecture and guilt trip," Jack shook his head as he began looking around for things that didn't belong in the camp and Harry did the same.

Shaul took a deep breath before ducking into the tent of the commander. It hadn't been touched, except for the commander's body having been removed. It was eerily silent in the tent and he had to suppress a shudder.

Shaul stood in the tent where the commander's body had been and tried to remember the scene. The commander had been on his back, his eyes staring up at the sky, his throat cut and arteries cut, blood sluicing the ground and tent.

The blood had long since dried, but there was a dark feeling about the place. Shaul looked at the blood marks and for a split second he was sure he saw some form of pattern, but before he could be certain, Harry came blundering into the tent to get him.

"Tam, Jack's found something," the two men ducked back outside to where Jack was kneeling by a small mound of snow that he had cleared to reveal something underneath.

"What is it?" Shaul asked as they reached Jack.

"A symbol, burned into the ground," Jack shook his head. "It ain't natural."

"Could just be the sight of an old fire pit," Harry shrugged as he knelt beside Jack to examine the scorch marks.

"You think anyone would build a fire here?" Jack demanded.

"It could be a few seasons old," Harry defended his viewpoint.

"It can't be," Shaul said slowly. "We're camped in farmland. These fields are normally used for crops, not animals and no one would camp in fields of crops when there are trees you can shelter in to the west and the city is so close."

"So it is something?" Harry asked with an edge of panic to his voice.

"Highly likely. It looks like a summoning symbol," Shaul tilted his head as he looked at the scorch marks and squinted.

"Oh and now he's a regular expert in magic," Jack said rolling his eyes. Shaul ignored him.

"If it is a summoning symbol, then there should be three more, spaced evenly about the tent. If it's a draining symbol, there will be six," he said as he paced out the distance the symbol was from where the commander had been butchered.

"You want us to dig through more snow? Without spades or shovels?" Jack asked with a raised eyebrow.

"We don't need to dig, the snow is light enough to kick aside in most places," Shaul smiled. The symbol was four strides from the tent. He walked round to the other side and paced out four strides. Sure enough, as Shaul kicked the snow aside, there was another scored symbol that looked identical to the first.

"You find one?" Harry shouted.

"I did," Shaul said sadly. He had his proof that magic was at work, but he needed to know the number of symbols before he knew what kind of magic it was.

Harry moved round the tent so that he was half way between the first symbol and where Shaul was. He moved the snow aside.

"Can you see one?" Jack asked.

"There are two," Harry said standing up and looked at Shaul. The Queterian frowned.

"Clear all the ground," He said firmly. The three men worked through the pain of the cold eating at their fingers and turning them numb until a ring was cleared around the commander's tent.

There were fifteen symbols in total.

"What do fifteen symbols mean?" Harry asked as he tried to get some feeling back into his hands and feet.

"That men should not let their curiosity get the better of them," a voice spoke from behind where the three men stood. Jack and Harry both spun round on the spot, but Shaul remained rooted to the spot. The Queterian spy didn't need to turn round to know who it was that was stood there.

"General Hesla," Shaul said as he took a deep breath. Jack and Harry looked between the general of the Order and Shaul, neither understanding what was happening.

"I see you found some friends," Hesla said with a cruel smile.

"Was it you?" Shaul asked as he turned and drew his sword as he moved.

"You have enough of the pieces to know the answer to that

question," Hesla shrugged.

Shaul looked down and shook his head.

"What's going on, Tam?" Jack asked, looking at him with suspicion.

"They don't know who you are? Well, you and Methanlan are far better at your jobs than I thought," Hesla crowed.

"Go, both of you. Find Sidney; tell him what happened here, what we found," Shaul said urgently. He tried to keep his voice low so that it would be harder for Hesla to hear what he was saying to the two men. Harry nodded, but Jack stood and stared at Shaul. "Go!" Shaul shouted as he ran forward. He lunged for Hesla, who parried his strike easily.

Harry grabbed hold of Jack's arm and dragged him out of the range of fire. The two men ran, neither looking back. They could hear the sound of swords clashing growing more distant behind them.

They ran through the camp, asking people they knew as they passed if they had seen Sidney. It was starting to get dark by the time the men found him, sat by the fire side in their section of the camp.

"Where the hell have you been?" he asked as they two men collapsed by the fire breathing heavily.

"Tam, he's in trouble," Harry said.

"He's not really Tam, that woman, he called her General Hesla, she called him Shaul," Jack said bitterly.

"What happened?" Methanlan asked jumping to his feet. The

colour had drained from his face. He listened intently as Harry told him what they had found and where Shaul was now. Jack said nothing. When Harry had finished, the two men had managed to recover from running through the camp.

"You need to come with me," Methanlan said shortly.

"What? Where?" Harry asked.

"To see the queen," Jack said with disgust. "That's right, isn't it? You're one of them."

"We need to go. Now," Methanlan replied.

Kasnata had spent hours pacing her tent, second guessing herself and what she had decided to do. As long as General Seaton was in her camp as part of the army of Nosfa, her children would not be safe. The assassins that had made attempts on her life had been quiet for too long, which made her nervous.

"You sent for me, highness?" Yoav asked as he entered the war tent.

"I did," Kasnata sighed. "We need to wait for the others before I can begin."

The two sat in silence as they waited. Small talk was the province of cities and countries that considered themselves more civilised than the barbarians of the Order. Kasnata had been schooled in the finer points of polite conversation for the sake of diplomacy, but it was not something that was practised amongst the people of the Order.

There was no fear of silence, no judgement or discomfort in not speaking. In fact, their refusal to speak when it was unnecessary was often a useful tool of intimidation when sat in talks with those that spoke at great length without any need to.

It did not take the Eight long to arrive. Marissa and Quisla were with them.

"I have a special duty to charge you all with," Kasnata sighed sadly as she addressed Yoav and the Eight. "I fear my children are no longer safe here. I want you to take the twins to the fortress Samara is constructing. The nine of you are to do whatever it takes to keep them both safe," the queen had stopped pacing, though Yoav could read the agitation the queen suffered from in the shaking of her hands.

Kasnata had spent so long part from Kasna, Kia and Leinad. The pain of that separation had become etched in the lines on her face as the years had passed. She had been reunited with Kia, but she was no longer a child, she was a woman that had bypassed growing up before her time, and Kasnata regretted it. Yet now, the dark angel was being forced to part from her newborn children before they had even begun to learn to walk and talk.

"Surely it isn't necessary to take them from the camp-" Yoav began, but Quisla cut him off.

"Whilst you are here, there will always be other duties that you are expected to perform. Away from the camp, there is nothing but the prince and princess to protect. There are certain dangers that we must contain and, whilst the twins are in the camp, they will always be at risk. By moving them now, without announcement, we not only remove them from the immediate danger of assassins and murderers in the camp, but we may also confuse our enemies as to their whereabouts. At least long enough to allow you to set up the necessary defences at the fortress," the vulture general said firmly. The Eight remained silent as the generals spoke.

"You're worried about the blood moon," Yoav stated.

"I'm more worried that the murders of the officers in Nosfa's army are a distraction from something greater. Her highness has a war to wage against a city that has dug in, as well as assassins that have not been caught," Marissa said stoutly.

There had been no further discussion amongst the generals about the assassins or about the murders in the camp, but as each day passed and no answers came, tension had begun to grow as those investigating felt the sting of failure and those that were relying on them were growing impatient.

"Quisla has personally arranged for horses for each of you. General Yoav's horse has baskets to carry the twins in. General Quisla will provide you with the location of the fortress when you are mounted and ready to depart. You leave at midnight. Tell no one that you are leaving. General Yoav, I will speak to Abendigo once you have left, he will be in charge of your men in your absence," Kasnata gave the order and dismissed the eleven. Yoav lingered for a moment; he looked at the queen, opened his mouth, but thought better of speaking.

Kasnata sat down beside the crib that contained her children and felt the two babies grip her fingers tightly.

CHAPTER 18

General Kia was sat beside the fire in the centre of the section of the camp that her warriors were billeted in. Her warriors moved in shifts, their training patterns, watches and other camp activities scheduled to perfection. During a siege, there was little that the general had to do, save for attend the queen and investigate whatever Misna passed to her.

She stared into the flames as she thought through the murders of the commanders.

"General!" Methanlan shouted. He was breathless and was flanked by two men dressed in the uniform of Nosfa.

"Methanlan, what is it?" Kia asked standing and moving away from the fireside to where Methanlan was bent double, trying to recover his breath.

"Shaul," he replied, shaking his head.

"What happened?" Kia asked, keeping a cautious eye on the two men of Nosfa.

"He was investigating the murders with Jack and Harry, he's in trouble," Methanlan tried to collect his thoughts as his breathing returned to normal. Jack and Harry were both still struggling to breathe.

"Who are these men?" Kia asked with a slight frown.

"Jack and Harry. They're friends, they came to get help," Methanlan explained.

"Where is Shaul?" she asked.

"Where Commander Grice was murdered," the Queterian spy replied. Kia moved without another word. Methanlan fell into step behind her, and motioned to Jack and Harry to follow.

"I don't bloody believe this," Jack murmured under his breath.

Kia was a woman of action, she hated having to wait for the right moment to do what needed to be done, and the siege of Delma lasting for so long had begun to frustrate her.

The distraction of assassins lurking in the shadows had proven to be a mild diversion for a time, but when no attempts had been made on Kasnata's life in the new camp, the boredom had returned.

The arrival of General Seaton, and the murders of the commanders, had seemed to convenient. I was too easy for it to be General Seaton that was responsible for the murders, but the more that Kia thought about it, the more it made sense that the general was responsible.

Misna was certain that Hesla was a traitor and in league with not only the Valians, but with Nosfa as well. The Raven General had even begun to form a theory that Nosfa had formed an alliance with the Valians to remove Kasnata from power.

When Misna had first suggested it, Kia had laughed, but now, the Hawk General didn't think it was as far-fetched as it had originally seemed.

"Methanlan, find Quisla and Marissa. Bring them. Jack, Harry, you come with me," the Hawk General ordered as they reached the edge of the camp of the Order. "And keep up,"

She could feel a shift in the atmosphere between the camps. She drew her sword as she ran, her eyes fixed ahead of her. Harry glanced at Jack, who nodded. They were barely able to keep up with the pace the general ran at, yet her breathing wasn't even laboured. Both men were glad that they were commanded by the army of the Order and not facing it on the battlefield.

They were used to commanders who barked orders and sat behind the troops that were set into battle, not those that led from the front. To soldiers, the way that the Order waged war made sense, but it was still not civilised.

"Ahh!" Shaul's voice carried across the camp and Kia lengthened her stride. Jack and Harry fell behind as the general hurried to the tent of Commander Grice.

Shaul was lying on the ground, his face was ripped open and his arm was bleeding badly. He still gripped his sword, but it was clear that he was struggling to lift the blade.

General Seaton stood over him, but Hesla was nowhere to be seen. He was bristling with power as he stood there, not a scratch on him.

"And so the cavalry arrives," he said as he looked up at the Hawk General.

"Shaul, can you stand?" Kia asked, her eyes fixed on General Seaton.

"I can stay on my feet. But reaching them is a little beyond me at the moment," Shaul replied as he winced in pain. The injuries to his face meant he would not be able to smile for a long time.

"Harry, Jack, take Shaul to see Payne. Shaul will direct you," the general ordered.

"What about you?" Harry asked.

"Shut up, you fool, woman has told us to do somethin', I'd rather not be here when they start fighting," Jack said pushing past Harry towards Shaul.

"Do you think I will let you have this poor excuse for a warrior back?" General Seaton laughed. "He is barely worth the effort of executing, let alone saving," he crowed. His voice caused a terrible chill to run down the spine of Shaul, Jack and Harry.

Almost lazily, General Seaton raised his blade, intending on bringing it down on Shaul's skull. He took his eyes of the Hawk General for the briefest second and pain exploded in his side.

He staggered sideways, clutching the wound that Kia had inflicted on the man.

"Do you think that a man of Nosfa could countermand the orders of a woman of the Order so easily?" she asked with a note of disgust.

She had been at least eight strides away from General Seaton when she had moved and now was three strides past him.

Neither Harry or Jack had seen her move. The idea of spending any more time amongst the people of the Order than was necessary was now even less appealing than it had been before.

With an arm around each of their necks, the two men lifted Shaul to his feet and moved away from the two generals as quickly as they could.

"I see. You might be worth fighting after all. Though, you should know, I am no man of Nosfa," General Seaton grinned with wide eyes and laughed as Kia parried his first strike.

"Kia!" Quisla shouted as she and Marissa reached the commander's tent.

"The last heir of Valia, I presume," Kia said dryly. Quisla and Marissa had their swords drawn and were slowly advancing on the two.

"How wrong Hesla was, you aren't as stupid as you seem," General Seaton laughed. The bleeding in his side had lessened, the fit of his armour helping to put pressure on the wound.

"Methanlan has gone to Misna," Marissa said quietly as she stepped to the left of Kia.

"Do you think you can fight all three of us?" Quisla asked from Kia's right.

"I know I can fight all three of you, whether I win or not, that is another matter. But if I cannot defeat three lackeys, I have no business taking the throne from the usurper," Seaton spat with venom.

"The bloodline of a traitor has no claim to the throne," Marissa replied hotly.

"Traitor? TRAITOR?" General Seaton roared. "The sovereign ruler of the Order by birth cannot be a traitor; all she did was just and within the law," he barked.

"She was condemned by her father and her grandfather, the father of our people! She was a traitor and you shall never have the throne," Kia snapped as she launched herself towards General Seaton.

The sound of metal clashing rang out repeatedly as the four generals clashed. The three generals of the Order did not take it in turns to attack. Their enemy deserved no quarter. General Seaton fought back with as much skill as the women possessed. He was an enemy that could have bested any in the Order with a blade, save for Yoav, Shamgar, or Avner.

They were not technically brilliant, but instead they were brutal, taking advantage of every weakness that presented itself. A slight flicker of hesitation was punished with deadly force.

General Seaton's fighting style was no different. Even the most gifted of swordsmen would struggle to defeat the general alone.

Harry, Jack and Shaul could hear the sound of steel ringing as they made their way across the camp. Soldiers from Nosfa were moving away from the sound, whereas those of the Order were gathering their weapons and heading towards the source of it.

Shaul felt dizzy as the two men of Nosfa carried him to the healer's tent. When it became apparent that Shaul was unable to direct them, Jack and Harry stopped some of the warriors that were running to battle to ask for directions.

Shaul let his eyes wander around the camp. His eyes fell on where General Hesla was directing her warriors to stand down from fighting. His vision was blurred and his hearing dulled, but Shaul was certain that it was Hesla. She had a peculiar expression on her face.

"Get that man to the infirmary!" General Shamgar yelled as he directed his men towards the fighting. The gruff man was pointing towards Payne's domain and waited impatiently until he was sure that Shaul had been delivered into the healer's care.

He watched the three men disappear inside the tent before he followed his warriors. He didn't know where the other generals were, but the sound of fighting in the camp had stirred his blood. Mathias was the not only one that was billeted amongst the Order of the Bear that was not going to investigate the sound of battle. He stayed behind with nine hundred of the warriors and watched the rest of the camp. The Order of the Hound and the Order of the Wolf were waiting for their commanders to arrive before reacting.

Mathias knew that the Order did not see whatever was causing the noise to be a serious threat, but it concerned him that so many of the generals were absent. His first thoughts flew to Kia and

Mia's safety amongst the troops of General Misna.

The Roencian was on his feet and running to where the girls were billeted with Joab within seconds. General Hesla watched the strange young man with a frown, taking great care not to be noticed as she followed him through the camp.

Shamgar gave a mighty roar as he approached the skirmish. The warriors from the Order of the Bear had formed a ring around the four generals that were fighting, none of them daring to interfere.

"Stand aside," Shamgar bellowed. Kia, Quisla and Marissa all looked at their comrade with icy expressions. General Seaton laughed.

"Why send a woman to do the work of a man?" he asked Shamgar, who shook his head.

"You're a whelp, too much honour in being killed by three generals of the Order. You already have an overinflated ego, so I'll have my men cut you down to size," Shamgar growled. The Order of the Bear slammed their spears down on the ground in response.

Kia, Quisla and Marissa retreated from the circle of men to stand beside Shamgar. They had a few scratches and cuts, but nothing that was life threatening.

General Seaton laughed and threw down his sword as the Order of the Bear raised their spears.

"You think that it will end with me? Fools, all of you! Blinded by your own ignorance."

"Etha aval," Shamgar ordered. General Seaton was still laughing as the spears of thirty men were thrown and pierced his body.

The laughter choked in his throat as blood escaped into his lungs and replaced the air. Before the general's body hit the floor, the thirty men stepped forward and reclaimed their spears for his body.

There was an atmosphere of disappointment over the warriors; General Seaton had given up too quickly. After so many weeks of sitting, waiting to assault the city of Delma, they had been hoping for more of a fight.

"Did Methanlan tell you what they found here? Why the general attacked them?" Kia asked as she knelt over the dead body of General Seaton.

Now that he lay still, he was an attractive man and he had been exceptionally talented with a blade. Such a shame, Kia thought, such good genes wasted.

"I'll report to the Queen, she should know what happened here," Marissa sighed. The blood of the general was seeping into ground.

"He said there were odd symbols on the ground, like summoning symbols, but too many of them for the magic he knows of," Quisla explained as Marissa disappeared back to their camp.

"How many symbols?" Kia asked sharply, leaping to her feet.

"Fifteen," Quisla said with a flicker of confusion behind her eyes. Shamgar watched Kia carefully, his men were already moving back to the camp, General Seaton's body being left where it was for the crows.

Kia ran to look at the symbols in the cleared ring around the tent.

"What is it?" Shamgar asked.

"Fifteen symbols, murders, the last heir of Valia," the Hawk General was shaking as the severity of the situation dawn on her.

She turned back to the body of General Seaton and watched the blood draining from his body into the snow. The symbols behind her began to glow.

"Blood magic," Shamgar growled.

"We need the Abbott," the colour had drained from Kia's face.

"I'll ride out and find Cassandra. She'll need to know too," Shamgar sighed.

The sky had already begun to darken.

"A blood moon rises and madness is unleashed," Quisla said in a quiet voice as the dusky orange moon that rose against the darkening sky turned deep crimson.

"Men of the Bear!" Shamgar shouted. "Secure the camp of Nosfa," twenty-nine of the men responded to the general's order, whilst the last man acted as a runner to fetch the other members of the unit.

CHAPTER 19

Mia and Princess Kia were sat under a stretch of canvas that ran down the centre of General Misna's area of the camp. It was not under the wooden structures that were erected over the tents; instead it was swept free of snowfall each day and used as a congregation area.

The two women were wrapped in large furs to keep out the cold. Mia was reminded of the winters in Afdanic, when her mother would sit on the balcony, overlooking the city, in her own furs, which Mia would snuggle into as she sat on her lap.

Kia had never needed a fur of any description; the cold had not been a problem in Grashindorph or at the fortress of Abergorlech. She knew what snow was from the stories that her mother had told her of the campaigns that were waged in the name of King Mercia Nosfa. But she hadn't seen it for herself until she and Kasna had fled from the fortress.

It was strange not having her sister there. She felt guilty that Kasna had been taken so that she would be spared. The guilt had driven her to work harder in her training with the Abbott so that no one would have to give their life for hers.

She didn't think that her sister was dead, but she didn't want to think about what Kasna was going through in the hands of the enemy.

Spending time with Mia had helped distract her though. The young lady of Afdanic had been very nervous about talking to the princess of Nosfa and the Order.

When she had been confronted with Kia aged by several years in the space of several days, Mia had been terrified, but as she had watched Kia and spent more time in her company, it became clear that the princess had not changed her personality despite her rapid development.

Joab had taken to lurking in the shadows, rather than being at Mia's side. The shadow always preferred being around lots of people, it helped him go unnoticed, though it did make trying to protect Mia all the harder.

Whilst the Lady of Afdanic was with Princess Kia, she was safe enough, especially when the women were sat at the heart of the Raven General's section of the camp.

Mia had wanted to learn to fight now that she was in the camp of the Order, she didn't want to feel helpless and useless. But after several attempts at trying to teach her how to fight with a sword, it became clear that Mia was not suited to combat, not even when it came to defending herself.

She was raised as a lady of the court and that was the sphere that she would excel in. Kia envied Mia that. She had wanted to be with her mother for so long, dreamed of what it would be like to be part of the Order instead of a prisoner of her father, that the reality of it couldn't compare.

Though she had been a prisoner, she had been left to run wild with her sister. Here, in the camp of the Order, there was discipline. There was a strict routine in the camp – not just for those that stood watch, but for every member of the camp. Training, cooking, maintaining the camp, reporting information, sending out patrols; there was much more to military life than Kia had realised, especially when it came to digging new latrines and filling in the old ones.

It was different from training with the Abbott as well, but Kia found that as hard as life was hiding amongst Misna's troops, she was enjoying it.

"Thank goodness," Mathias interrupted the giggling and conversation between the two girls.

"Mathias, is everything all right?" Kia asked as she stood up. She had travelled with Mathias across half of Celadmore, and he had risked his own life to see Kasna and herself safely to Tulna.

"There was a disturbance in the camp. I wanted to make sure you were both safe," the Roencian was out of breath and clearly relieved to see that the women were unharmed.

"We're safe," Mia smiled. "Joab is watching over us," the young lady glanced shyly over to where the shadow was lurking. Joab was not paying attention to what they were saying. Instead, his eyes were fixed on the row of tents that marked the boundary of Misna's domain in the camp.

"Come out," Kia shouted, her eyes fixed on the same spot that Joab was watching.

"Well, well, what a fiery young thing you've turned into," General Hesla grinned as she strolled out from between the tents.

"Mia, stay back," Joab warned as the shadow moved from his favourite hiding place to stand between the general and his ward.

"There are many secrets in this camp; love affairs, murder, assassins, but this, this is one of the better secrets that Misna has kept to herself," Hesla mused to herself. "Who would have thought that both the Lady Mia Bird and Princess Kia would be hiding in the camp of the queen, right under everyone's noses. I can't begin to tell you -"

"Then don't," General Misna's voice cut across General Hesla's. The Raven General stood a short distance away, watching Hesla intently.

"Misna, I knew that you were good at keeping secrets, but this, I have to marvel at your skills. A true master of deception," Hesla gave Misna a nasty smile.

Kia was watching Hesla with wary eyes, her hand resting on the hilt of her sword. She could sense Mathias standing close by, his body taunt, like a coiled spring.

The sky darkened above them and Mia felt a cold chill run down the length of her spine.

"The last heir of Valia is dead, Hesla," Misna said, her eyes not moving to look at the sky.

"I see you have discovered much in your digging," Hesla smiled to herself and snorted. "But if you had learned everything, you would not see the death of General Seaton as a victory," the Eagle General closed her eyes as the blood moon began to rise in the sky behind her. The wind, which had begun as a slight breeze, was growing in power. Misna frowned,

"I see. Sacrificing the commanders was not enough; you needed the blood of Valia," Misna grunted.

"The blood of the usurper would have sufficed, but after a few attempts to assassinate her caused such a stir in the camp, I knew that trying to use her blood would be pointless," Hesla shrugged with a smirk.

"You brought Mercia here? So that he could bring General Seaton, bring the blood you needed?" General Amalia asked from behind Hesla's shoulder. The Kestrel General had appeared silently, Hesla was surrounded on three sides, but she didn't appear to be concerned.

"The king is a man that is governed by baser passions. Though it is beyond me as to why, he still desired the usurper. Telling him that his own general had betrayed him with his wife was enough to draw him here," Hesla explained. She was glad that she no longer had to hide and her joy rang in her voice.

"And you did all this for power?"

"Power? No," Hesla laughed. "Contrary to what you may all believe about my people, we are not obsessed with power. We want what is rightfully ours and will do whatever we can to possess it,"

"Then why the murders? Why the blood moon?" Mathias asked. Mia was shaking and pressing herself against Joab, not knowing what was going on.

"You Roencians, so proud of your skills as assassins, but you really are little more than tools. You don't have the ability to think for yourselves. You're slaves to the Abbott, nothing more," Hesla spat in Mathias' direction. "If he cared about anything, then I would suggest he'd be proud of what a good little lap dog you are," Hesla sneered, "but as it is, you are just pitiful wretches that are little more than dirt under our feet."

"Dirt under your feet?" Mathias asked with a raised eyebrow. "And what is it that makes Valians so superior? Your failure to win a civil war? Or your continued failure to remove the rightful rulers of the Order from the throne?" he asked in an offhand voice.

"You have done all this for the throne? Do you think anyone of the Order would follow you? Those that disapproved of the queen left long ago and she has only grown in strength," Amalia said in a disgusted tone.

"They will either follow our rule or die," Hesla said with finality.

"Then the blood moon is just about power," Misna said, shaking her head with disappointment.

"I told you, we don't care about power," Hesla growled.

"Then it is the madness," Joab said in a quiet voice. "The blood moon unleashes madness amongst those with afflicted minds. You are unleashing chaos as well as increasing your power," the shadow scowled and wrapped his arms around Mia, moving her out of Hesla's eye line.

"You know a lot for a Roencian puppet," Hesla sneered at Joab.

"Hesla, former general to her royal highness, Queen Kasnata Nosfa, you are to stand down to face the justice of the Order for treason," Misna said formerly.

"I would rather die," Hesla drew her blade and lunged towards where Joab shielded Mia.

Misna and Amalia reacted a fraction of a second after Hesla moved, but it was Kia that intercepted the general.

The princess knocked aside Hesla's blade with case.

"Attacking an unarmed opponent is the act of a coward," Kia scolded Hesla. Mathias had moved and was now stood beside Joab, the two men completely obscuring Mia from Hesla's view.

"You think you can beat me princess?" Hesla laughed cruelly. Misna and Amalia were stood a few feet from where Kia now faced Hesla. The two generals were content for the princess to deal with the traitor, as was her right as the third in line for the throne, after her sister and brother.

"I should be no match for you. After all, I'm simply a puppet of the Abbott as well," Kia smiled. She felt confident in her abilities. She wasn't a snivelling child playing at war. She wasn't a girl running for life, relying on strangers to protect her. She wasn't a young woman that needed someone else to take her place and save her life. She was a princess of the Order, a warrior trained by immortals. She had sacrificed for her training, more so than any other warrior.

"You think she is ready for this?" Amalia asked under her breath. Misna nodded slightly. She had been able to study Kia in the training sessions she had been involved in and how she carried herself.

"It is her right to face Hesla, regardless of whether she is ready," Misna replied in equally hushed tones.

The men and women that served under General Misna were being drawn to the sight of General Hesla fighting the princess.

Most watched silently, but there were a small number who commented in hushed voices, offering opinions on stances, footwork and anticipation of the other's moves.

Kia was far less experienced in battle than Hesla, but in a one-on-one duel, the years she had spent training under the Abbott had proven to level the playing field between the general and princess.

Hesla had not expected much from the magically-aged princess. She had expected that her first attack would have been enough to dispatch the princess, and then she could have pressed her attack against Joab, Mathias, and the Lady Mia.

Instead, Kia had easily blocked the strike and responded with her own; Hesla had stumbled back, caught off-guard by the riposte.

The surprise had not lasted long. Hesla was an excellent swordsman and her years of training far outstripped Kia's. Hesla was natural gifted with a sword, whereas Kia had trained as an archer. In a contest with swords, she would always be at a disadvantage.

Misna watched the princess carefully; the general was impressed by how well the she managed to meet each of Hesla's strikes. But the Raven General knew that Hesla was toying with the princess.

There was little that she could do though. The honour of the princess would be compromised if the general intervened. Kia had challenged Hesla and whether she defeated the traitorous general was down to the princess and the princess alone.

Kia was getting tired; the longer she fought the harder it was to raise her sword. Her mind felt foggy and Hesla seemed to have a limitless supply of energy. More than once, Kia contemplated surrendering, but a voice somewhere in her mind told her that to surrender would mean death.

Before her was a traitor, a woman that she had volunteered to punish. She couldn't surrender, she couldn't lose, but she couldn't see a way in which she could win.

"Hesla, throw down your sword!" Kasnata ordered. She appeared with Marissa and Avner at her side. Kia didn't look over to where her mother stood; she kept her vision focused on Hesla. The advice of the Abbott rang in her ears. *When you face an enemy, you must never take your eyes off them. No matter how defeated they may appear. Unless their head is severed from their body, never shift your focus from them.*

Hesla snorted and ignored the queen. Instead she lunged for Kia. The princess jumped back, trying to put some distance between herself and the general. She cast aside her sword and reached for her bow. She drew back the string and fired three arrows in quick succession. The first arrow was deflected by Hesla's sword. The second caught the general in the leg, grazing her and the third struck Hesla in the side. The general roared and rushed towards the princess in a blind rage. She was blinded by anger at being wounded by the princess and didn't notice those moving around her.

Hesla drew back her blade to take slice across Kia's neck.

"I said, throw down your sword," Kasnata spoke coldly as she stood between Kia and Hesla. The queen looked down at the general with disgust. She had caught the strike intended for Kia with the edge of her blade.

Those that had assembled to watch Kia and Hesla duel had now drawn their swords, bows and spears.

"No," Hesla replied. Without a moment's hesitation, Kasnata knocked the general's blade aside and sliced Hesla's hand from her wrist. The Valian screamed in pain as her sword clattered to the ground.

"Misna, you know what to do," Kasnata said grimly. The Raven General nodded and signalled for a handful of her warriors to take Hesla away. "Are you all right?" Kasnata asked as she turned her attention to her daughter.

"Yes, mother. Thank you," Kia said glumly.

"You did well. I am proud you could fight against her for as long as you did," Kasnata said warmly as Kia retrieved her sword.

"But I still needed to be saved," Kia shook her head.

"Everyone needs saving sometimes. Come, all of you, there is much that needs to be discussed," Kasnata spoke and motioned for Mia, Mathias, Joab, Marissa and Amalia to follow as she led Kia away from Misna and Hesla. The queen knew what Misna would do to the former general, and it was a sight that Mia and Kia did not need to see.

The people of Grashindorph screamed and wept. The soldiers that remained to guard the city had been turned against the people. Innocent people were dragged from the homes in the middle of the day as well as the night.

Those that were taken without a fight were not seen again, those that tried to resist were boarded up in their homes with their families and the buildings set alight, so that all that was within them was tuned to ash.

Helez and Asahel could do nothing to help the people of Grashindorph. They watched in silence from the rooftops, and followed those that were arrested. They knew where those accused of treachery were being held, but with only two of them, they could not attempt to rescue them all.

So the two men waited, gathering what information they could, praying that the Gibborim would soon be able to move against the king and end the madness.

"Idiots. I am surrounded by idiots," Payne grumbled as he worked. Shaul had been closer to death than he would have liked to admit when he had been brought to the healer. There were no other injuries to heal, but the severity of Shaul's wounds had taken a considerable amount of his skill to heal.

Healing was the only area that the Order still practised blood magic. The healer drew upon his own blood and the blood of the wounded party in order to heal wounds. The more severe the injury, the more taxing it was on the healer. If the injured party had lost too much of their own blood, there was nothing that any healer of the Order could do.

The Order had five healers, and Payne was the strongest of them. The other four were his subordinates and only used their skills after battles. The rest of the time, healing was now left in the hands of Payne.

"His actions were brave," Kasnata said with a tired tone to her voice.

"His actions nearly got him killed," Payne snorted.

"Well then, what a good thing that you were here," Kasnata replied. "How are you feeling?" she asked, turning to Shaul.

The Queterian was unable to sit up, but he was awake. Jack and Harry were sitting at his bedside. Harry had stayed out of concern for the man he considered a friend, but Jack had wanted answers.

Princess Kia, Joab, Avner, Mathias, Mia, Amalia, Marissa, Quisla and Methanlan were sitting in the healer's tent. General Kia had been sent to deal with the summoning runes in the camp of Nosfa and to try to maintain some semblance of order amongst the terrified soldiers.

"Much better, your highness. Where is General Shamgar?" Shaul asked as he tried to roll onto his side.

"Don't move, you fool, you'll open all your wounds again,"

Payne scolded him. The healer had threatened to tie the Queterian to the bed if he wouldn't lie still.

"He is needed elsewhere," Kasnata replied with a shrug. "General Seaton was the last heir of Valia," she said, shaking her head.

"So it would seem," Quisla was sitting in a corner, her lips resting on her peaked fingertips.

"Harry, Jack, what effect will this have on the soldiers of Nosfa?" Marissa asked, turning to the two men. Jack shifted uncomfortably, but Harry was happy to respond.

"Most of the commanders are dead, none of the lower officers are respected enough by the men; we'll all sit in the camp and refuse to do anything - until we get a new general," Harry said as Jack elbowed him in the ribs.

"I see," Kasnata frowned. "Will they listen to General Kia?"

"They'll be scared of her and the warriors she has with her, but fear of a barbarian won't inspire any of them to action," Harry caught Jack's elbow before he could jab his ribs a second time.

"Then we have some time to deal with the more pressing issues," Amalia spoke through pursed lips.

"Hesla and Seaton have been dealt with, so what remains is who was behind them," Mathias mused.

"Do you believe that General Seaton was the last heir?" Amalia asked, turning to her queen.

"No. The last heir wouldn't sacrifice themselves in such a manner, General Seaton may have had the blood of Valia, and able to wield blood magic, but he wasn't the one in charge. Someone else is pulling the strings, and whoever that is, that is the true heir of Valia," Kasnata said firmly. "Harry, Jack, you can return to your camp."

The two men looked at each other before Jack spoke,

"Your highness, we want to know what is going on. Our lives were in danger today, our friends turn out to be your spies, our general murdered the commanders in our camp and then tried to kill us. We are supposed to be fighting Delma and all of you seem pre-occupied by something else. We want to know what is happening."

Mathias and Joab stared at the two men of Nosfa, no one they had ever known spoke to a crowned head of Celadmore in that manner.

"It's not your concern," Marissa said flatly. "You're soldiers. You follow orders. Your queen has dismissed you," she said coldly.

"Peace, Marissa," Methanlan said. The general glared at the spy. "I will answer the questions that I can," Methanlan stood and led Harry and Jack from the healer's tent.

"Insolent whelp," Marissa cursed under her breath.

"Do we know of any other Valians in the camp?" Princess Kia asked.

"That is Misna's domain. Those that she knows of, she will deal with and whatever information she can gather from Hesla, she will tell us what we need to know," Amalia shrugged.

"Have we had any word from Nosfa?" Kasnata asked.

"None," Quisla sighed. "However, a messenger from Delma arrived."

"What did they have to say?" Kia asked as she moved to sit beside Shaul. As the Queterian couldn't sit up, he couldn't drink. Instead, someone had to dip a cloth in water and squeeze droplets out of it into his open mouth.

Payne didn't have time to constantly nurse the Queterian so Kia had volunteered to take care of Shaul.

"They have issued an ultimatum. We leave or they will attack the camp," Quisla replied.

"We've heard nothing from them and their first attempt at contact is threatening us. They are desperate. Morale in the city must be low and they have no one to lead their troops with the prince dead and the duke absent from the city," Amalia said dismissively.

"Do we have any word from our scouts as to where Kelmar is?" Kasnata asked.

"None, there have been sightings of parties that might be Kelmar and his men, but nothing to help us find the princess, your highness," Marissa replied.

"Very well. Now we have removed General Seaton and General Hesla, there is no need to hide Mia and Kia with General Misna," the queen said, "Kia, you will train with Amalia and Marissa and when they are satisfied with your skills, you will be named Eagle General in place of Hesla. Until then, Misna will be in command of the Eagle division. Mia, you are not of the Order, so you may stay in the camp or Joab and Mathias can take you somewhere else where you will be safe,"

"I would like to stay here," Mia said in a quiet voice.

"Very well, whilst you are in the camp, you are under my protection. Marissa will find you somewhere appropriate to have as your quarters. Mathias and Joab, I assume that the two of you will act as her protectors?"

"Yes, your highness," the two men said in unison.

"Are you finished? I have work to do and you are all in my way," Payne said grumpily.

Kasnata's spirits were higher than they had been in weeks. The removal of General Seaton and General Hesla had dispelled the atmosphere that had hung over the camp. The men of Nosfa were proving difficult, but General Kia was more than equal to the challenge of setting the camp to rights.

There wasn't much for the queen to do, now that the internal threats had been dealt with. She had her scouts searching for her daughter; Yoav and the Eight had departed with her babies to take them to safety, and she had spies dispatched to watch over Rathe. Though this all weighed heavily on her mind, the only thing she could do was wait.

The Abbott's gift to her had gone almost unused, but now there was time for her to practice with it. The black staff was dangerous, that much was apparent to Kasnata. The moment she had first held it, she had felt the power contained within the staff stirring power in her blood.

Avner accompanied the queen out of the camp to a clearing in the nearby forest. The general didn't like the idea of the queen being on her own outside of the camp. Shamgar came with them as far as the treeline, but then took his leave. He was being called elsewhere, he couldn't explain by what, but the call haunted his dreams and pulled at his mind whilst he was awake. He had already volunteered to inform Cassandra of what had happened with General Seaton and Kasnata had agreed, but he hadn't mentioned the dreams to anyone.

Avner had brought some of the war dogs to guard the perimeter, but it was too dangerous to have them in the area where the queen would be practising.

"It summons fire," Avner had explained to Amalia, when she had objected. "Having too many people there will put them at risk and place a burden on the queen's shoulders that will only distract her from mastering the staff."

"How long will you be away from the camp?" Amalia asked.

"However long it takes for her to control the power of the staff. I don't think it will take more than a few weeks, but I would not expect her to return until the end of Antompne. She will be perfectly safe," Avner assured Amalia.

The bodyguard had begrudgingly agreed.

Avner had set a small camp for them half a mile from where the queen would be training so that they would be able to return there at the end of each session.

Kasnata had spent the time that Avner was setting the camp ensuring that there was enough space in the clearing for her to practice. She had created several targets to aim at and made sure that there was nothing nesting in the undergrowth that surrounded the area.

Avner was glad of the excuse to be out of the camp. With both Yoav and Shamgar absent from camp, he was feeling a little surplus to requirement. As a general, he had nothing to do during a siege. His men knew what their responsibilities were in the camp, they were more than capable of organising their own training and since General Seaton and Hesla had been dealt with, there was no immediate threat to the queen that demanded his attention.

There was only the slow dredge of time until Misna had all the information that was needed to end the siege and take the city.

Avner wasn't entirely convinced that the Raven General

wasn't intentionally drawing out the siege to gather more intelligence from other quarters without arousing suspicion. She was certainly shrewd enough to do that, however, she was famous throughout the Order for despising the cold. Even with Benaiah's cleverly crafted shelters, Misna had been heard grumbling about the weather under her breath and how warm the hearth was back in her tower of Anamoore Castle.

To Avner, it felt like such a long time had passed since her had last been in the castle, surrounded by the young war hounds that were too inexperienced to head into battle.

Riding out to the clearing with the queen was similar to all the hunting trips that they had taken together when Kasnata had only been a child, still protected by her parents from the realities of ruling the Order.

When he had finished setting the camp, Avner had walked slowly through the trees where Kasnata was training. The Dog of War tried to move silently and settled himself amongst the foliage, away from the targets that Kasnata was aiming at.

There was a grim determination set on the queen's face as she tried time and again to hit the targets. After a half an hour, there was sweat streaming down her face, her breathing was laboured and she looked close to collapse, yet she had still to hit any of her targets.

"You should rest now, your highness," Avner said from amongst the undergrowth. "There is time enough. We should go to the camp, when you've recovered, you can try again."

Kasnata nodded, not having the energy to speak. Avner stood and walked to the queen's side. He helped her to her feet and acted as her crutch, gently taking her back to the camp.

This routine was repeated over and over again for four days. Each day, Kasnata was more exhausted than the previous day and it was clear that to Avner that if she continued on this path, she would be dead before she had come close to understanding how to control the staff properly.

The blood magic that the staff employed was clearly powerful, possibly too powerful to be wielded by anyone, yet the Abbott had given it to Kasnata, and he seemed certain that she would be able to use it.

So Avner sat and watched, on the 6th day, she hit her first target. It was another two days before she repeated her success, but it gave Avner an opportunity to encourage the queen to rest for a few days before she continued her training.

By the end of three weeks, the queen was able to hit three out of five targets. By the end of six weeks, she could hit all five.

Avner and Kasnata stayed at the forest camp, letting the queen train for as long as possible. It wasn't until the end of Sagma/Sumar that the queen and Avner returned to the camp of the siege to hear Genera Kia report on the state of the camp of Nosfa.

CHAPTER 20

After seven days of sitting in the Chesil Void, Cassandra had gained clarity, but she still had no answers to her questions. As a being of power, she was drawn to places of power. In those places, she could still her mind and see what she needed to do much more easily.

Her mind worked differently to her brother's. The Abbott would do what he felt was necessary, often without needing any reasoning or information that would tell him why he what he was doing was needed.

Cassandra had to have reasons. She was a spontaneous creature in many respects; she was dangerous in a fight, more dangerous than the Abbott is some ways as her temper was somewhat less restrained. But when it came to taking action, she needed time to process what was to be done and would do nothing without the answers to the questions she had.

The Chesil Void had not given her the answers, so she had broken camp and taken Tola to the east. They moved quickly; Cassandra didn't want to linger too long in any of the civilised lands. Though there were no battles being fought in the south, war was not absent.

There were enemies of Nosfa, the Order, and Tulna in the south, as well as allies in Benadrocca. Cassandra didn't want to spend any longer than she had to in the south. If she had been travelling alone, it would have taken less than two days for her to reach her destination, however with Tola as her companion, it took closer to four weeks.

They had to cross the Chesil Void and then head towards the Ballo Sea. There was nowhere to cross the sea on the western or southern shores, so Cassandra and Tola had to travel to the northern shore and find a ship to carry them to the fortress that stood on Ballo Island.

On the outskirts of Stoke-sub-Hamdon, Cassandra and Tola made camp. It was too late to journey into the village and find beds for the night at one of the inns and those that owned ships would either be too drunk to speak to them or long since gone to sleep.

The Ballo Sea was a dangerous place in the day time, there were creatures living in the water that were older and far more dangerous than any of the immortals. Those who lived on the shores of the sea knew better than to travel across it after dusk.

"It seems I came at the right time," Shamgar greeted Cassandra and Tola as he rode into the camp.

"General, what brings you out this far?" Cassandra replied as she stoked the fire with a longer piece of firewood.

"Dreams that need answers. I am not surprised to find you here, Kasna Mashala," Shamgar said as he dismounted and joined Cassandra and Tola by the fire.

"The Ballo Fortress holds many secrets" Cassandra replied. "Do you think your answers lie within?"

"I think my answers will be the same as the ones that you are looking for," Shamgar shrugged.

"Then you'll join us?" Tola grunted.

"In the pursuit of knowledge, no one should travel alone," Shamgar replied.

Cassandra grinned and shifted round the fire to give Shamgar space to sit. The general removed his sword from his back and stabbed it into the ground beside where he chose to sit.

"What did you find in the void?" Shamgar asked as he pulled some dried meat from the satchel he carried on his scabbard. The belt of the scabbard hung in a diagonal across his chest; the sheath lay across his back and stuck out from behind his shoulder and his hip.

Cassandra had always found the weapon that Shamgar carried to be rather comical in appearance. When the general had been a boy, he had always overextended himself. He was not a small man in stature, but his father had been almost twice the size of Shamgar in build and reputation. His father cast a long shadow that had followed Cave Dweller for much of his life; so the general had done all he could to surpass his father.

His sword was a foot longer than the broadsword that Jethro had carried and though his father had been a hero in his time, he had never been a general.

Cassandra remembered Jethro as man that was kind to a fault, a man that had loved his son regardless of what other said or what Shamgar had achieved. He would have been as proud of his son if Shamgar had remained a warrior and not risen to rank of general.

To Shamgar, he remembered his father as a man that he could never surpass. But Cassandra knew that the paths that both men walked were different. Jethro had died in his bed, his heart not strong enough to support his ample frame or his legendary appetite, he had seen a few skirmishes and fought beside King Jadow and Queen Tsmara in the border wars, but he had never known the conflicts that Shamgar had to endure.

Jethro had never known what it was like to command men, to send them to their deaths and feel the weight of each of his decisions to the extent that Shamgar did. Cave Dweller had forged friendships that had helped him to find his own path in the midst of war and now he was content, but his sword served as a constant reminder to the general of who his father was and what he had been to his people.

"Silence," Cassandra replied.

"It's becoming harder to hear?" Shamgar asked with a frown as he gazed at the fire.

"It is," Cassandra sighed. "There has been too much noise in the world for centuries, but now, it is more difficult than it has even been before."

"The Abbott doesn't seem concerned," Tola interjected.

"He has a different way of seeing the world. He feels like he should do things and feelings are easier to discern that words are to hear. I listen and not even a whisper comes," Cassandra replied.

"Then we go to the guardians?" Shamgar asked

"We go to the guardians," Cassandra said grimly. "It is they who summoned you, I am sure."

"Why would they summon me?" Shamgar frowned.

"I don't know, but both of you should be wary of them, they have their own agenda that benefits the guardians before it benefits the realm," Cassandra said seriously.

"Aren't they guardians like you are?" Tola asked.

"No, they are mortals, chosen by the Goddess to protect the realm. We are born of the Goddess, immortals who act to see her will done."

"So why do we need to go see the guardians?" Tola asked in frustration. He hadn't wanted to accompany Cassandra on her journey across the realm.

"Because I need to be sure that they are not the ones interfering or plotting to use the wars amongst the nine kingdoms for their own gain."

Shamgar yawned and rose from where he sat and started to wander away from the light it cast.

"What is it?" Tola asked, leaping to his feet and drawing his sword.

"Can't you hear it?" Shamgar asked as he walked further away.

"Hear what?" Tola demanded as he followed.

"It sounds like a child crying," Shamgar replied. Cassandra stayed beside the fire and felt a ripple of apprehension travel down her spine.

As they moved away from the fire, Tola could hear the crying too. They two men walked for a few hundred metres and found a small boy curled in a ball by the foot of a rock. He was covered in wounds; his clothes were almost completely shredded and around him lay the bodies of twelve moorin. The creatures lay dead, not a sign of any outward injury on their corpses.

"What happened here?" Tola asked, without expecting an answer, his eyes were wide as Shamgar knelt down beside the boy and spoke reassuringly to him. The general scooped the boy up into his arms and carried him back to the fire.

"Put him down, Shamgar," Cassandra ordered from the edge of the circle of light that the fire cast. Her face was covered in shadow, but her tone of voice was clear. Shamgar hesitated for a moment, but did as Cassandra instructed. "Stand back."

Tola and Shamgar glanced at one another, but retreated a few paces.

"Tesnash iten baslorn teq unin faschneil?" Cassandra asked in a terrifying voice. It was a language that neither Tola nor Shamgar had ever heard before. "Detelish!" Cassandra shouted when the boy didn't respond.

The ground shook as she spoke; there was an ancient power in her words that seemed to resonate with the ground below their feet.

"Gernalin. Hocleesh oni," the boy replied in a voice that sounded much deeper than any voice a child should have. "Bastilnon techine rasturnesh,"

"He is the one that called to you, Shamgar," Cassandra said turning to the general. "He is yours to do with as you wish," the Guardian of the Wilds said flatly and turned back to the fire. "We go to the fortress at first light. Get some sleep."

Kelmar had been on his guard around Kasna, he had her guarded continually so that she could not make her way back into his bed.

Kasna had not reacted to Kelmar's change in attitude, but had felt the sting of rejection every time he avoided making eye contact with her.

Kelmar's men were well practised at living off the land and scouting the wilds for danger. Each night they camped, Kasna felt safe whilst these men protected her, and even more so since the men had begun gossiping about the relationship between Kelmar and the prisoner. No man amongst their number would dare to lay a finger on her whilst they believed she belonged to Kelmar.

The princess had been given her own horse, so that Kelmar didn't have to put himself through the torture of her body against his as they travelled.

"Sir, there are bandit signs ahead," a scout reported. Kelmar had sent his men ahead to see what lay between the camp and the river before they had departed.

"Then we should journey further to the north, we can camp at the pillars, there is a good line of sight on all sides," Kelmar ordered, and the men had broken camp. The scouts rode ahead of the soldiers, Kelmar adjusting their path based on the information that they relayed back to him.

It was close to sunset when the pillars appeared on the horizon and the imposing silhouette of the Spire. The company had halted and Kelmar had asked for scouts to ride forward to investigate, but none of his men were brave enough.

"I'll go," Kasna snorted, slightly disgusted at how cowardly the men of Delma were.

"No, you're a prisoner; you don't scout ahead for my men," Kelmar sneered.

"Then you'll have to accompany me," Kasna smiled. Kelmar scowled,

"Fine, men, hold here until we return. Make camp to the east if we don't return before sunset," Kelmar ordered and nudged his mount forward, with Kasna following close behind.

The two approached the Spire at a trot. The building looked forbidding, and a strange energy radiated from it. The horses seemed to be unaffected by it and eagerly trotted towards it. There was nowhere for the horses to be tethered outside the Spire, but the animals seemed content to paw at the snow in search of the grass that was hidden beneath rather than bolt into the night.

"Dismount, we need to see what is inside," Kelmar said gruffly as he swung himself gently to the ground.

The two moved slowly towards the two giant doors that swung slowly open as they climbed the steps. In front of them was a single room that caused Kasna to shiver slightly with fear.

The princess shrank to Kelmar's side and seized his hand with hers. Kelmar squeezed her hand reassuringly as they moved into the room. It was dark and evil looking; the stone of the walls was so dark that light seemed to be drawn into it.

"Welcome," the voice of the Abbott rang off the walls as he stepped from the shadows, caused Kasna to jump and Kelmar to take the princess into his arms.

"You," Kasna sounded relieved as Kelmar released her and the Abbott smiled at the two of them.

"I must admit, I did not expect that it would be the two of you that came here," the Abbott said with an airy tone and pointed towards the centre of the room.

There was a pedestal with a long slim knife lying across it and at the base of it a large round basin that was shallow but etched with runes stood at the centre of the room.

Behind the pedestal was a vast altar that had a variety of different artefacts from the nine nations of Celadmore displayed upon it.

"What is going on?" Kelmar frowned. He looked between the Abbott and the princess, unsure of what to do.

"Duke Kelmar DeLacey, Regent of Delma, you were charged by King Delich to save your people, correct?" the Abbott asked formerly as he moved to pick up the knife.

"That's right," Kelmar replied slowly.

"Your people are threatened by madness, you have felt it creeping up on you, but there are those within your country, especially in the capital, who have succumbed completely to the madness," the Abbott continued as he walked towards Kelmar with the knife.

"How do you know that?" Kelmar asked, fear rising in his chest.

"You were sent to capture the princesses in order to bring an end to the war that you believe is responsible for the madness of your people, but I am here to offer you a way to save your people and end the war now," the Abbott ignored the question as he presented the knife to Kelmar.

Kelmar reached out and took the knife without thinking. He felt the same fog of madness beginning to descend that had filled his mind in Abergorlech, and when Renta had thwarted his plans.

Kasna felt Kelmar's grip on her hand tighten so that she couldn't let go.

"What's happening?" she demanded of the Abbott, but he wasn't listening to her. Instead he beckoned for Kelmar to follow him and the Regent obeyed, dragging Kasna with him. The three approached the pedestal and without thinking, Kelmar let go of Kasna's hand and grabbed her by the hair instead. He pushed her forward so that she was bent over the pedestal, her head and neck hanging over the rune bowl.

"You can save your people now, in this instant, all you have to do is spill the blood of the goddess. Slit the throat of the princess and allow the rune bowl to fill. Your people will be free of their madness and you will be able to return home to your king with pride," the Abbott explained. Kelmar's eyes had glazed over, as though he were listening to something other than the Abbott.

"Please, Kelmar, don't do this!" Kasna screamed as she felt his grip on her hair tighten and the tip of the blade being brought to her throat. Kasna began to cry and grabbed hold of Kelmar's wrist with both her hands, trying to pull the blade away from her.

"If I do this, she'll die," Kelmar said slowly, his eyes coming back into focus.

"She will, but your people will be safe and you will have done your duty," the Abbott assured him.

"No," Kelmar said dropping the knife and releasing the princess. Kasna staggered back from the pedestal and collapsed on the floor sobbing. Kelmar moved to her side and wrapped his arms around her. "I'm sorry," he whispered as she leant against him and cried.

The room around them began to change, the black stone melted away, changing to crystal. The single room transformed into a foyer that led to countless other rooms and floors.

"How interesting," the Abbott sounded pleasantly surprised. "I did wonder what it was all in aid of."

"You!" Kasna shouted at the Abbott as she recovered herself. "What were you thinking? You tried to have me killed!"

"I am sorry, princess, but it was necessary. Your grace, let me assure you, the madness you have felt will not be ended by spilling her blood. If anything it will be worsened. In fact, when she is with you, the madness will be kept at bay," the Abbott looked at the two with curiosity. "How odd."

"What is this place?" Kelmar asked as he stood and helped Kasna to her feet.

"This is the Spire. It is a curious place, it changes to provide for the needs of the realm and clearly you both needed to be tested in this way. For what reason I couldn't tell you, but with this transformation to its normal state, it would seem that you have passed," the Abbott smiled.

"You trained me, promised I would be reunited with my mother, convinced me you would protect me," Kasna fumed. "You were going to let him kill me!"

"Your highness, you were not in any danger. The Spire would not have allowed your blood to be spilt on its hallowed grounds," the Abbott replied in a comforting tone.

"Hallowed ground?" Kelmar asked with a sceptical tone.

"This is the Spire; it exists between realities, a floating entity that belongs to no realm. It is filled with the presence of the Goddess and those that reside here have dedicated their lives to her service," the Abbott explained. "If the doors were to close whilst you were inside, there is no guarantee that when you opened them again that you would see the plains of Celadmore before you," he continued with a grin. "Though in these times, that might be no bad thing."

"So what was the purpose of that ridiculous exercise?" Kasna demanded. "This whole building transformed into a grotesque ritual chamber just to frighten us?"

"Peace, princess, peace," the Abbott held up his hands as he tried to quiet Kasna's rage. "I cannot tell you why for certain, only that you were supposed to come here. The will of Arala cannot be denied in this place. I can only speculate, but I believe the reason was twofold." A smiled played at the corner of his mouth as he looked at the duke and the princess.

"Twofold?" the Regent of Delma asked as he slipped his arm around Kasna's waist, the princess turning ever so slightly as he did so that she could lean against him.

"The first, I would suggest, is self-evident. An alliance of marriage between Delma, Nosfa and the Order would bring a swift end to this war, disrupting the plans of those that seek to extend it for their own gain. The two of you, it seems, have grown close on your travels, perhaps even feel something more than an attraction between you, but recent events had bred a level of distrust between you. This was keeping you both from embracing how you felt, but now -" the Abbott allowed his voice to trail off and shrugged.

"You think the Goddess cares whether we trust each other?" Kasna asked as she frowned.

"There is no greater sign of the power of above than in trust and in love," the Abbott replied simply.

"What is the second reason?" Kelmar asked.

"Ah, the second reason," the Abbott clapped his hands together and rubbed them with glee. "The second is simpler than the first, after all love and trust are never simple. The second reason was to test you," the Abbott pointed at the duke as he spoke.

"Me?" the regent replied.

"Yes. There are darker days ahead of you both, ahead of us all. Before this war is over, you will both have to make hard decisions, some that will make you unpopular, even hated. You were given the opportunity to sacrifice the life of the woman that you love in order to bring an end to the suffering of thousands. Everything that you have been brought up to believe told you that it was the right thing to do, though it would break your heart and leave you a shell of a man, your duty demanded it. Yet, you cast it aside so you would not be the one to murder her," the Abbott spoke in a quiet voice.

"This was a test to see whether I would kill Kasna out of duty?" Kelmar's calm countenance was disintegrating as felt the same indignant rage that had gripped Kasna rising in his own chest.

"It would seem that way. But before you lose your temper, please think about why the test was necessary. You kidnapped the princess from Tulna, took her because she was willing to sacrifice her own freedom for that of her sister. You were sent to capture the princesses by your king, who did not give you any explanation as to why he wanted them. There is something wrong in Delma, something that has been growing in power and corrupting those with influence in the kingdom, something that has allowed the blood moon to rise. It is not just Delma either, in Grashindorph, the same danger lurks, though so far it is only the king who has been affected."

"What is your point?" Kasna asked.

"My point? My point is, princess, that when surrounded by the people of Delma, in a place where duty is held as the most sacred aspect of life, Kelmar has been ordered to do, and has done far worse things, for the sake of his kingdom than slitting the throat of a woman he has bedded without hesitation or even the smallest of doubts. But since Renta's death there have been doubts growing in his mind, a feeling in the pit of his stomach that tells him something is wrong. This test has shown that he is more than a slave to his duty," the Abbott replied. Kasna looked up at Kelmar; his eyes were fixed on the Abbott, though his face was set in a passive mask.

"Do you know what King Delich has planned?" the duke asked.

"Yes," the Abbott said shortly. "And I know what he does to those that refuse him."

Kelmar nodded grimly.

"What if I let her go?" he asked, removing his arm from around the princess.

"It would make no difference. Both of you are called to Delma, you both have a part to play in bringing an end to the madness and today has shown, Kelmar, that you are equal to your task," the Abbott smiled.

Chapter 21

2432GL 17th Antompne

The fortress to the west of Roenca was still under construction, but General Samara had put her time and resources to good use.

There were a few settlements that she had sent consignments of warriors to found, it would take a few years to make them sustainable, but once the settlements were ready, more fortresses and even cities could be built. When Samara first set out, she had only a glimmer of what Kasnata had intended with these settlements and fortresses.

After weeks of finding locations and beginning construction, Samara was beginning to understand the grandeur of what Kasnata was plotting.

It was an empire, an empire that would stretch across Celadmore; it had the power to unite the people of the nations and of the Free Cities. It was the way to bring about an end to war. It was a plan for the future. The unity of nations wouldn't happen in their lifetime, but there was hope for the generations to come.

The gates of the fortress had been finished and the inner wall was done. There was a ditch being dug between the inner and outer wall, and the foundations had been laid for a wall of stone to form the outer wall, whilst the inner wall was a wood palisade.

It was secure enough to allow construction to continue, but it was not yet a fortress that could stand against any army on Celadmore. It was more than capable of withstanding raiding parties or bandits, though none had come yet.

The people of Nosfa seemed to be unaware of the fortress' existence. It seemed to Samara that only those in the Free Cities and those in the Order that knew of the general's mission knew of the settlements and fortresses that were appearing across the face of Celadmore.

Haras and Nasus had been providing Samara with resources on a daily basis, there seemed to be an unlimited supply of wood, stood and labourers that would stream to the fortress from Roenca. There was lime and mortar in plentiful supply as well. Samara suspected that the daughters of Epoch had called for aid from the other Free Cities and that they were responding with what they could spare.

The people of the Free Cities had not been left untouched by war. They had suffered as much as those in the kingdoms that were engaged in war. Refugees spilled into the Free Cities seeking aid, but few offered it. They had chosen to live apart from the rule of the kingdoms and were excluded from trading with the settlements that formed countries such as Nosfa and Delma. So the Free Cities traded with the Order and with each other.

Most had no pity for the refugees. There were those in the

Free Cities that could remember their homes being burned by the people that now cried out to them for help. They had watched their children being taken from them, their crops destroyed and the laughter in the eyes of those that enjoyed the destruction. The people of the Free Cities had grown cold towards those of the nine kingdoms and had no interest in helping them.

The Free Cities saw the Anaguras and Queterians as their only hope of seeing order restored to Celadmore, bringing an end to the waves of refugees and an end to the persecution of the people of the Free Cities.

For this reason, they were more than happy to give what they had to see the settlements and fortresses built for Kasnata, especially if it meant that there would be a military presence close to their cities that would intervene on their behalf.

Samara had received no word from the camp of Kasnata since Nasus had returned.

"Riders to the east!" the lookout cried. Samara had positioned a small number of her warriors on the walls of the fortress to protect those who worked to build the rest of the fortress.

"How many?" the general called. She was in one of the ditches, digging a trench that large wooden pikes would be mounted in. Should anyone breach the outer wall, they would have to cross not only water but stakes that would easily impale those that fell from the battlements.

"Nine," the reply came back. Samara frowned. Nine was too small for a raiding party or bandit attack, but it was also too large for a scouting party.

The general scrambled out of the ditch and climbed the narrow, unstable ladder to the battlements. She approached the lookout as she tried to wipe the mud from her hands and her face.

"Where are they?" Samara asked as the lookout point to the edge of the treeline.

"They're moving quickly," the lookout confirmed. "Do you want the alarm raised?"

"No, find me two riders, I'll go out and meet them. If I am not back before the sun sets, raise the alarm," Samara ordered. The lookout nodded and moved down the ladder with a practised, but frightening, speed.

Samara followed at a slower pace. By the time she had reached the makeshift corral, which lay just inside the gate, the two riders and three horses were ready. The lookout saluted and started back to his post on the wall.

The general mounted and set off through the gate at a brisk trot, the two riders following close behind. They couldn't move at a faster pace through the trees in the forest around the fortress, but Samara also knew that the riders approaching would be reduced to the same speed.

They had been riding for a few minutes when Samara

signalled they should halt.

"Go back and raise the alarm," the general ordered.

"What is it?" one of the riders asked, her horse skittering sideways.

"There is something here that shouldn't be," Samara replied. "Go now." She drew her Cedema Coxan and shortened her reins.

The two riders turned back and Samara closed her eyes so that she could focus on the sounds around her. There were no birds or scurrying animals in the undergrowth, but the wind rustled through the branches around her. She had grown used to the cold and the snow that had permanently settled on the ground, she had learnt to ignore the presence of the blood moon and its deepening hue, but no life in the forest was a warning sign that she had been trained to take as seriously as an army bearing down on her.

She sat and waited for any sign of where the danger lurked. There was nothing. She was acutely aware that the nine riders were approaching, but she was certain that this was something else.

The sound of the alarm at the fortress filtered through the forest to her and there was still no sign of what was lurking. Samara opened her eyes and urged her horse to walk on, towards the incoming riders, her sword still drawn.

"Lower you sword, Sprite, we're not enemies," Yoav's voice rang out. Samara looked to her right and saw the general sat with the riders of the Eight and the twin babies of Kasnata and Rathe.

"There is something else here, Wolfsblood," Samara replied. "If you are here with what I think you are carrying, then I should think that it is you that it is hunting."

"How far from the fortress?" Yoav asked, his tone of voice changing instantly.

"A few minutes at most. I don't know what it is, I can't hear it moving,"

"Will we be safe at the fortress?" Scattergood asked.

"There are walls and a gate, the alarm has been sounded, we will be safer there than here," Samara sighed.

"How many do you think there are of – whatever it is?" Warner asked.

"There can be only one," Scattergood said decisively.

"If there were more, it wouldn't be working so hard to disguise its presence," Yoav agreed.

"Follow me," Samara ordered and skirted to left of where she had come from, "It is a longer route back, but it should put some distance between us and it," she whispered.

Yoav and the Eight followed. Yoav was encircled by the eight riders and Samara rode slightly ahead of them. If they were attacked, their formation would allow Yoav to flee with the children whilst the other riders held off whatever stalked them.

They rode in silence, each alert to the slightest change in the forest about them, but no attack came. They reached the fortress unharmed. The gate swung open allowing the generals and the Eight into the courtyard and was hurriedly slammed and bolted behind them.

Samara abandoned her horse and ran to the wall. Yoav took the children to one of the small structures that lay in the centre of the fortress. It was surrounded by a palisade wall that had a small moat dug around it and seemed the safest place in the fortress.

"Yoav, what is going on?" Haras asked as the general entered the building. The Benadroccian woman didn't seem surprised to see Yoav or the royal babies.

"I don't know. Something is out there," Yoav said gruffly as he lay the two babies down on the bed that sat in the corner of the room.

"Something is always out there," Haras snorted. She sighed heavily and looked at the babies. "Go deal with whatever it is, I'll stay with the children and keep them safe," she said wearily.

"You're a soft-hearted wench at heart, Haras," Yoav grinned at the young woman as she swung from the general. The leader of the Order of the Wolf easily dodged the blow and ducked out of the structure, Haras shouting abuse after him.

The light of the day was bleeding out of the sky at a faster rate than Samara thought was natural. The blood moon hung in the sky, as red as fresh split blood and three times larger than the normal moon of the season.

"I'm here for the children."

Samara felt her blood run cold as she heard the voice of Neesa echo off the walls of the fortress.

"They are not yours to take," Samara replied. All light, save for the horrendous glow of the blood moon, fled. Torches were extinguished around the fortress in a single blast of icy air and the gate of the fortress exploded into splinters.

Samara leapt from the wall and rushed to the hole where the gate had been. The Eight were stood, their weapons drawn, ready to face the assassin. Yoav was stood a little way in front of them, his eyes hardened, his sword held out to his right, his armour lay in a pile to his left so that he was clothed only in his wolf pelt and hessian trousers.

Neesa stepped over the pile of splinters that she had created. She moved as if she owned the fortress and the land that it sat upon.

"I'm here for the children," she said more firmly.

"No, you're here to die," Yoav growled. Neesa laughed.

"You think you can kill me?" she asked with contempt. "You are nothing more than an ant waiting to be crushed, once I have destroyed you, and all the other ants that are stood in my way, I will crush those tiny children that you think are so precious. Then I will take your pretty little queen and crush the life out of her body for all to see. I'll do it slowly, breaking one little bone at a time so that she is still alive when I drain the blood from her body."

"Your threats are empty, witch," Samara snarled.

"You dare to call me that?" Neesa asked, her eyes narrowed at Samara and her nostrils flared.

"You think you deserve a more impressive title?" the general replied.

"I am more powerful than any creature that has ever walked the plains of Celadmore. I have created this!" Neesa threw her arm out and pointed at the blood moon. "I have taken the nation of Nosfa for my own and have dictated where your precious queen should go and who she should fight for decades and once I have Delma, I will be able to take on the Goddess herself," Neesa crowed.

"You are nothing more than a woman drunk on a power she can barely control," Yoav said dismissively.

"Barely control?" Neesa scoffed. She held out her arm towards Yoav. "Move," Yoav was flung across the courtyard and rolled over several times in the snow and dirt before he staggered back to his feet.

"Barely control," Yoav laughed. "I expected something far more impressive from the last heir of Valia. But instead, there is you. How disappointing."

Rathe had spent weeks travelling to Grashindorph. By the

time he reached the city, he was tired and caked in ice that had matted into his fur cloak.

He looked more like a peasant than a noble. He rode towards the palace and noticed how quiet the streets of the city were. He knew that the people were scared of their king, but it seemed that they feared each other as well.

A few faces appeared at windows as he passed and disappeared almost instantly. The bars and inns were all closed and the markets that had once traded until the early hours of the morning were closed, shut up more tightly than any vault.

The uneasy feeling that Rathe had in the pit of his stomach was getting worse by the second. He reached the steps to the courthouse that he had been directed to and dismounted. The moment his feet touched the ground, soldiers poured from every direction, throwing the general to the ground, they clamped irons around his wrists and ankles.

"General Rathe Bird, by order of the King, Mercia Nosfa VI, you are hereby arrested for the crime of high treason. You are sentenced to hang for your crimes on a date that is to be determined. For committing high treason, you are hereby stripped of all rank and title and your lands are forfeited to the crown."

Rathe was hauled to his feet and brought face to face with the Knight-Marshal of Grashindorph. Rathe glared at the man. The Knight-Marshal punched the general in the stomach, but it didn't break Rathe's stare.

"Take him to the dungeons. Send word to the barbarian queen. Tell her, her spy is to die."

On the roof of the courtyard, Helez and Asahel watched the scene silently. The Knight-Marshal looked about the streets before retiring to his bed, but he was of no interest to the two men.

Instead, they followed the contingent of soldiers that surrounded the general. He was marched through the streets to the gallows and the cells that were built into the wall of the city so that the prisoners could be seen by the people and abused before they were executed.

Not all prisoners that were to hang were placed in these cells, they were used for prisoners that had taken a stand against the king or had enjoyed some popularity amongst the people before they had crossed the king. Mercia wanted to ensure that the people wouldn't rise against him and the idea that they may find themselves in such a position was one of his most powerful weapons of fear.

The door to the cell was dragged open, Rathe was flung into the small, dank room, and the door was slammed shut behind him. The soldiers jeered and spat at the general as he struggled to get back to his feet.

When Rathe didn't react, the soldiers grew bored quickly and left to return to the barracks.

"High treason? Seems serious," Helez spoke as he and Asahel

dropped silently down to the ground, one on either side of the cell door.

"Hanged. Had to be serious," Asahel replied.

"Seems to be a lot of it going around," Helez said sourly.

"So, what do you think he did?" Asahel asked, glancing over at Helez. Rathe had managed to pull himself to his feet and was leaning against the back wall of the cell.

"Could have been anything. Rumour has it though, he was plotting revolution," Helez glanced over his shoulder at the general to judge his reaction. Rathe's face was hidden by shadow, but his body language told Helez, he wasn't interested in their conversation.

"No, he doesn't look capable of it. Too much of a lap dog, must have been something else," Asahel said dismissively.

"There is another rumour," Helez said as he looked down at his hands.

"Oh?"

"Rumour has it he bedded the queen, chose her over the king and even fathered some children that could take the throne from the king." Both Asahel and Helez were watching Rathe and saw the general shift his weight and clench his fists.

"No wonder the king isn't very happy with him. A loyal general doing that, well that's something out of fairytale, not reality. What would his father think?" Asahel turned as Rathe tried to lunge at the bars, but because his feet were still chained, the general fell forward onto his face.

"I think you hit a nerve," Helez observed.

"Whatever I have done, you have no right to talk about my father. You didn't know him," Rathe spat and pushed himself back to his knees.

"Didn't? Your father is Lord Haston Bird, isn't he?" Helez asked with a frown.

"He was," Rathe growled.

"Didn't? Was? You use a lot of past tense for a man that is still alive," Asahel said as he crouched so that he could look Rathe in the eyes.

"My father is dead, he has been dead for a long time now. The king had him killed," Rathe said as he stared at the ground in front of him.

"General," Asahel spoke softly.

"What?" Rathe scowled as he looked up at Asahel.

"He's not dead. He's with the Gibborim. He's fighting against the king with the help of a lot of others that the king tried to have killed," Asahel watched relief flood over Rathe at the news, but it was soon replaced with despair.

"Is what the rumours say true?" Helez asked. "Are you the lover of the queen of the Order? Do you have children that could take Mercia's throne?"

"It is," Rathe said sadly.

"If you were freed, would you fight against the king for their sake?" Helez stepped forward and grabbed hold of the cell bars.

"Yes," Rathe replied firmly.

"Then we can't let you hang," Asahel said standing up. "You'll have to languish for a little while, prison breaks take time to arrange, just be ready when to run."

Helez and Asahel scrambled back up the breastwork of the wall and disappeared from Rathe's sight. The general stayed kneeling in the cell and laughed to himself.

"Be ready to run," he said shaking his head, swinging his legs around so he could stare at the bounds around his wrists and ankles.

The people of Delma were suffering under the siege. There was a shortage of food in the city, not only because of the army preventing traders from entering the city, but the winter unleashed by the blood moon meant that nothing could be grown in the gardens and window boxes of the city, let alone the outlying farms.

The water that flowed into the city had been dammed up by the Order of the Wolf and the wells in the city were beginning to run dry, if nothing was done, there would be no water in the city within a few weeks. The people in the poorer quarters of the city had begun to dig down further in an effort to find more water. Those that lived in the richer quarters sent their servants to bang on the doors of the palace, demanding that the king take action.

But the biggest danger to the city was not the shortage of food or water, but the disease that was spreading within the walls. This was all causing the morale of the people to plummet and every day, more and more people were discussing surrendering the city to the Order.

The king and queen had sealed themselves away in the palace; they were awaiting the return of Duke Kelmar DeLacey with their prize. Prince Jayden had been all but forgotten. There had been no grand funeral in the city when his body was brought home, he was simply taken to the crypt below the castle and his body sealed inside a stone casket.

General Avner sat and watched the city; it was easy to read the signs of growing despair. Avner hated sieges. It wasn't that he preferred to fight his enemies, but sieges hurt people, more importantly, they hurt the innocent.

The military tactic was a good one, but when faced with a leader that would rather see his people die than surrender, it seemed like a needless waste of life.

This siege was one that Avner found particularly distasteful as it was his daughter that was refusing to surrender and inflicting suffering on the people she was supposed to protect.

"It won't last much longer," Kasnata assured Avner. The general had spent much of the time since they had returned to camp brooding over the state of the city.

"If it does, there will not be anyone left alive in the city," Avner grunted.

"I want you to go to the city and ask for their surrender. You can set whatever terms you think are fair," Kasnata said. The generals that remained in the camp had reported to her over several days and the queen had decided, given the state of the army of Nosfa and the actions of the Valians, that it was time to bring an end to the siege.

"You won't assault the city?" Avner had always thought that the queen would burn down the gates and take the city, street by street, the army of Nosfa being thrown in as fodder so that the warriors of the Order could effectively remove any opposition.

"If there is no need to, then why waste the lives of our people? Ask for their surrender. If they refuse to give it, come back and go back to the city tomorrow and ask again."

"How long do you want me to do this for?" Avner asked.

"Until they surrender," Kasnata said firmly.

It didn't take long for Cassandra to haggle with the local fishermen. She agreed to loan a boat from one of the fishermen for the day and gave him four times his monthly income for the privilege.

Tola had watched the men of Stoke-sub-Hamdon eyeing the travellers with suspicion until Cassandra had started negotiating the suspicion had quickly been replaced by greed. It was understandable. Stoke-sub-Hamdon was not a rich village. It was not one of the Free Cities. It was a place that was famed for fishing, one of the few places that you could get Ballo Salmon from, because of this, there were several skirmishes that had been fought over the village by varying kingdoms.

The village had changed hands so many times, Tola wasn't sure who it currently belonged to. There were soldiers posted in the town, but he didn't recognise their livery.

For people living in those conditions, it wasn't surprising that they would be eager to make a large amount of money off the few travellers that passed through there.

When the negotiations had concluded, and they had paid three times what Tola thought the boat was worth, Cassandra took command of the vessel and sailed it easily to the island. It was clear to Tola and Shamgar that the Guardian of the Wilds was adept on the water and familiar with the waters around the Ballo Fortress.

The boy sat in the boat and simply stared at the fortress as they approached. He hadn't said a word since his exchange with

Cassandra, but each time he had wanted something, he had tugged at Shamgar's clothes and pointed.

The small fishing boat crunched on the shore of the island that the fortress sat on and Cassandra leapt out. The water came up to her shoulders.

"Stay in the boat until it's halfway up the beach," the Guardian of the Wilds warned.

She disappeared beneath the surface and the boat lurched upwards; the keel grinding against the sandy stones that made by the beach, then stopped. Cassandra's head bobbed above the water; her eyes fixed on the water to the east of the boat.

"Hold on," she barked before disappearing again. Tola and Shamgar gripped the sides of the fishing boat as it lurched sideways, threatening to capsize. The boy was not holding on and came dangerously close to falling out of the boat.

A tail flicked above the waves and disappeared. The boat was rammed again, harder than the first time. Shamgar grabbed for the boy and managed to draw him into a bear hug before he could fall out of the boat. The general clung to the boy with one arm and the boat with the other.

Tola glanced over the side and saw six shapes moving around beneath the water. He couldn't make out what they were. One seemed to break away from the pack and headed towards the boat.

Tola and Shamgar braced for another hit, but instead they

were showered with water. A monstrous creature hung over them. It looked to be made from crystal or rock that glistened in the light; it would have looked beautiful if it weren't for the glaring yellow eyes, twelve of them, pitted across the front and sides of its head. It opened its maw and revealed six rows of teeth that looked as though they were made from broken glass and were just as sharp.

It screeched; a high pitched noise that split the ear drums of the three in the boat. Tola didn't take his eyes of the creature. He reached for his sword and was ready to fight off the beast when a second and third appeared out of the water; then a fourth and fifth.

They were surrounded on all sides and the boat had slipped back into the water so that they couldn't escape to the beach.

"Ebrana tonculo. Hebreshin ashan dos ebrano,"

The water around the boat began to swell. Tola looked for the source of the magic and saw Cassandra stood on the shore. She was covered in scratches and bites, but they were healing quickly. The stones and sand on the beach were being forced away from her by the power she emitting and the water was becoming more violent with every passing second.

"Peace, Cassandra," a woman's voice came from the wall of the fortress above. The five monsters disappeared beneath the water and the boat gently moved up onto the beach. "You should have sent word that you were coming; we would have made sure you had safe passage," the woman continued.

Tola and Shamgar climbed out of the boat, the boy still in Shamgar's arm.

"What have you created?" Cassandra demanded of the woman.

"Created? Us? These are the creatures that live in these waters," the woman replied calmly

"No, those creatures were created; they are not natural, not of this world," Cassandra said hotly. "What are you scheming now, Lavinia?"

Neither Tola nor Shamgar had ever heard the Guardian of the Wilds speak to anyone in the way she addressed the woman on the battlements.

"We do only what we are duty bound to do, as you do," Lavinia observed as she left the battlements and appeared on the beach a few minutes later.

"What we do is nothing alike," Cassandra spat.

"Then why did you come here?" Lavinia asked.

"I want to know what you are doing, and I think I now have my answer," Cassandra sneered.

"Is that so," Lavinia said testily.

The two women stared at each other with an intense hatred. The boy was struggling in Shamgar's arm, so the general put the boy down. As soon as his feet touched the sand, Lavinia began screaming in pain.

"That cannot be here," she stammered through the pain that was swamping her mind.

"Helor kesan belna teran toron," the boy pointed at Lavinia as he spoke.

"He says you brought him here, with those monsters," Cassandra translated.

"It's a lie," Lavinia said desperately.

"He also says you tried to kill him," Cassandra narrowed her eyes at the woman.

"We are the guardians of Celadmore. We do what we must to—"

"Enough of your lies. Shamgar, pick up the boy," Cassandra instructed. The pain in Lavinia's mind ceased as soon as the boy was picked up.

"Kill it!" she screamed. The five creatures rose out of the ocean again.

"I think not," Cassandra gave Lavinia a withering look and raised both her hands.

"In the name of the Goddess, to dust return."

In an instant the creatures dissolved into sand that stood in five pillars on the edge of the ocean. There was no blinding light; no rolling thunder or foul weather, there had no even been a wave of power that had accompanied her words. Cassandra had simply spoken and the creatures were no more.

"Come, there is nothing for us here. We go to Asuna," Cassandra said beckoning to Shamgar and Tola to follow her. Shamgar placed the boy into the boat first and climbed in after, followed by Tola. Cassandra pushed the boat out into the open water and hauled herself over the side once it was afloat.

As the boat pulled away from the island, two women appeared on the shore beside Lavinia.

"Is something wrong?" one of the two women asked.

"No, Lacenta, everything will be fine," Lavinia replied as she dusted off the sand and stone as she got back to her feet.

"You think we should go to the mainland?" the second woman frowned.

"Yes, Muse, it seems that the Abbott and Cassandra are occupied elsewhere and the queen of the Order is in need of our guidance," Lavinia said, turning back to the Ballo Fortress. "Make the preparations; we'll be gone for quite some time."

"What about the boy?" Lacenta asked.

"There will be time enough to deal with him, we'll leave at sundown. It shouldn't take more than a few weeks to reach her camp."

Runners from the Gibborim had brought word that the people that Hermia had evacuated were safe and settled. Haston, Hermia, Layla and Jephthah had moved into one of the upper tunnels that the soldiers had already cleared. They could still hear the men Mercia had sent into the undercity. Some of the soldiers had become separated from their patrols and were now lost in the tunnels. Men were dispatched to look for them, but they never came back.

This meant that the undercity had become chaotic. The soldiers had been in the tunnels for nearly two seasons, and those that had become lost were now close to starving.

For all the soldiers' searching, no signs of the Gibborim had been found. They had come close to discovering where the four were hiding on a couple of occasions, but had passed by the grates that had led to their many cubby holes.

After Layla and Jephthah had failed to retrieve Prince Leinad from the palace, Haston had insisted that they remain hidden, making no further inroads into the city, but as time had passed and no repercussions had been felt, Hermia was adamant that they make their next move.

"Layla, Jephthah, I want you to go into the city and find leaders. If we are to start a full-scale rebellion, we need the people to be with us," Hermia said with certainty.

"The people are divided, they are scared, they have been for years," Haston tried to talk Hermia out of taking direct action.

"Then we need to unite them. Find people that will be a help to our cause. See what news there is of the attempt to kidnap Leinad and anything else that may be of interest."

The Shadow and Shield nodded their acceptance of Hermia's orders and left Haston and Hermia to wait in the dark and listen to the dying cries of the men that the king has sent to their deaths.

Chapter 22

Kasnata was in bed when the messenger arrived. He was greeted by Mathias and shown into the war tent to wait for Kasnata. The message he had to deliver was a sealed dispatch that was to be given to the queen and no one else.

Misna and Amalia were woken to accompany the queen to receive the messenger. Mathias stood by the entrance to the tent to make sure that no one interrupted.

The messenger presented Kasnata with the missive and left without waiting to be dismissed. He was on his horse and leaving the camp before Kasnata had finished reading the message, eager to be far from any retribution she might feel the need to mete out.

Kasnata broke the seal and read the message slowly. She turned pale as she read and dropped the paper as she finished the message. She drew in her breath slowly and sank into her makeshift throne.

Misna stooped to pick up the message and read it quickly.

"I'll fetch Mia," she whispered and left Amalia to stand with the queen whilst Kasnata recovered from shock.

Misna returned with Mia and Joab in tow, and invited Mathias to join them. Amalia left to take up Mathias' position outside the tent.

"Mia, the king has arrested your brother. He has been charged with high treason. He is to be hanged at the convenience of the king.

I'm sorry," Kasnata said quietly.

"What are you going to do about it?" Mia wasn't crying. She was calm as she spoke, but her hands were shaking violently. Joab was standing beside her, his arm firmly wrapped around her waist, holding the Lady of Afdanic steady and keeping her from collapsing.

"There is nothing I can do," Kasnata said in a hopeless voice. The queen had tears in her eyes; she knew that Rathe's death sentence was her doing, and that her husband had placed her in an impossible position. Misna was standing between the queen and the others. She was watching Mia carefully and her hand twitched over the hilt of her sword as Mia tried to step towards the queen. Joab was watching Misna and restrained Mia as he saw the Raven General's hand move.

"What do you mean, there's nothing you can do?" Mia demanded. "Of course there is! You have an army that marches on your orders. You can take the city and free my brother!" Mia screeched. Her calm composure had dissolved, and she was now openly weeping.

"She can't," Mathias said softly. Mia turned and glared at Mathias. "The moment that Mercia hears that Kasnata and her army are moving on Grashindorph, he will execute not only your brother, but Prince Leinad as well. He will have them killed and their bodies left outside the city gates as a welcome to her highness. To march on Grashindorph would kill your brother and the queen's son,"

"But someone has to do something" Mia cried. Joab slowly drew the lady to his chest, where she sobbed into his shoulder. "Please."

"If there was anything that could be done, I would do it," Kasnata assured Mia. "We have to rely on your brother's ability to survive."

"There is nothing else that can be done tonight; I suggest you return to your beds. I will see what information I can discover and report in the morning," Misna said, indicating that Mathias, Mia and Joab should depart.

The three left the war tent, Joab had picked up Mia and carried her back to her quarters, Mathias walking a few steps behind them.

Mia was silent as Joab carried her, her face was buried in his chest and her hands clung to his neck. Joab took her to her quarters and gently laid the lady down in her bed. He knelt beside her and stroked her hair.

"If the king kills my brother, I'll be all alone," Mia whispered to Joab.

"You won't be alone," Joab smiled at her. "I'm here," he soothed. Mia reached up and stroked Joab's cheek with her fingers. Joab caught her hand and lightly kissed it. "Rest, my lady. I'll be here when you open your eyes," Joab assured her.

Mia returned Joab's smile.

"Thank you," she breathed and kissed the Shadow. Joab kissed her back and leant his head against Mia's when the two broke apart. "Would you do anything that I asked?" Mia said quietly.

"Of course," Joab replied.

"Then I want you and Mathias to come with me to Grashindorph. I want to rescue my brother," Mia said firmly.

"If that is what you really want to do, then I will go with you. But sleep first, see if that is what you still want to do it the morning," Joab urged. It didn't take Mia long to fall asleep, her soft breathing was a relief to Joab.

"Do you think we can rescue him?" Mathias asked as Joab turned to face the assassin.

"No, but if she wants us to try, then I will try," Joab sighed.

"You should get some sleep too. You've barely slept since you started protecting her," Mathias gave his friend a wry smile.

"Is it that obvious?" Joab said with a slight laugh.

"Only to those that are paying even the smallest attention to you," Mathias grinned. "I'll stand watch over you both tonight."

The cell that Rathe was held in was bitterly cold. There was a stone wall along the back that was part of the outer wall of the city.

The other three walls were formed of iron bars that had stone pillars at the corners. This meant that the snow and biting wind blew through his cell and there was nowhere for the general to shield himself from the elements.

Weeks had passed since Helez and Asahel had offered to free him, and Rathe had seen neither hide nor hair of the two men since the first night of his incarceration.

Every day people walked passed his cell and threw insults and waste into the cell. Some people threw rotting food, others brought their chamber pots to empty at him, the first few days had been unpleasant, but after a week of living in squalor, the smell no longer bothered the general.

He knew that the king was not only trying to break his spirit, but trying to crush any thought of rebellion in the minds of his people.

He ignored the jeers and taunts that people jabbed him with; instead he focused on thoughts that brought him comfort. He had two beautiful children with a woman he loved, all of whom were safe, his sister was safe from the king in the camp of his lover and his father was alive. He would hang, but the people he loved were safe from the reach of the king.

As he sat in his cell, his thoughts drifted back to the day that he was dispatched as the general of Mercia's forces in Kasnata's army. He remembered the young boy in the castle and was struck by how much the boy looked like Kasnata.

"Is it true?" a voice asked Rathe. The general looked through the bars and saw the boy from the castle stood with his head pressed against the metal.

"Is what true?" Rathe asked.

"Are you a traitor?" the boy asked. His hair was the same colour as Kasnata's and his eyes were the same shape, if a different colour.

"It depends on who you ask," Rathe shrugged.

"What did you do?" the boy asked.

"I fell in love," Rathe sighed and leaned his head back against the stone.

"My mother told me that love was a dangerous thing," the boy said sadly, looking at the ground.

"She's right. As dangerous as she is, but just as worthy of the risk," Rathe replied.

"You know my mother?" the boy looked up at Rathe with surprise.

"You are the son of the king?" Rathe asked. The boy nodded. "Then I know your mother. I fell in love with her. That is why I am here."

"Then she will come and rescue you," the boy said firmly.

"She won't, Leinad," Rathe smiled at the boy.

"She will! If you love her, she will not let you die for it," Leinad said defiantly.

"No, she won't, she loves you more. If she came to rescue me, your life would be in danger, and she wouldn't risk you dying just to save me," Rathe said warmly.

"Your highness! Step away from that dangerous prisoner!" the Knight-Marshal shouted as he walked into the square. Leinad turned around and stuck his tongue out at the Knight-Marshal before running off through the crowd. "What were you saying to him, traitor?"

"He asked if the charges were true," Rathe replied with contempt.

"And what did you say?" the Knight-Marshal growled.

"I told him they were," Rathe narrowed his eyes.

"You may be sentenced to hang, but that doesn't mean that I can't deal out daily punishments against you," the Knight-Marshal warned. Rathe folded his arms and closed his eyes.

"Hey!" the Knight-Marshal banged on the bars. "I'm talking to you!"

Rathe ignored the man. The Knight-Marshal reached for the keys on his belt and unlocked the door of the cell.

Screaming erupted in the square and people ran in all directions, soldiers were trying to fight through the panicked people to the sight of the disturbance. Smoke was rising from one of the abandoned market stalls and fire had started to lick at the buildings that stood around it.

The Knight-Marshal turned from Rathe's cell to try and help the soldiers contain the fire, but as he turned, he found he was face-to-face with Helez.

"You're the man who killed my sister," Helez growled and stabbed the Knight-Marshal in the stomach. The Knight-Marshal collapsed to the ground, blood covering the dirty snow.

Asahel grabbed the keys from the Knight-Marshal as Helez swung open the cell door. Asahel darted into the cell and unlocked Rathe's shackles.

"You might need these," Asahel said as he handed Rathe his sword and the other belongings that had been taken from him when he was arrested.

"Hurry up, the fire's going out," Helez warned. Asahel helped Rathe to his feet and the three men disappeared amongst the crowd.

A shout went up that the prisoner had escaped, and the Knight-Marshal was dead, but Helez and Asahel had already made their escape with the general.

Despite the protestations of Misna and Mathias, Mia was determined to rescue her brother. Joab and Mathias prepared their horses for the journey and the three set out before most of Kasnata's camp had arisen.

Misna had watched the party leave, a sinking feeling in her stomach.

"Do you think they'll be all right?" Kasnata asked, joining Misna on the outskirts of the camp.

"You knew she was going?" Misna asked, a little surprised at the queen's appearance.

"She's like her brother. I couldn't help him, but she can try to. I didn't need Mathias reporting to me to know that she was planning a rescue," Kasnata smiled.

"He came to me in the early hours. I didn't want to wake you after the news of Rathe's capture," Misna smiled.

"You tried to talk her out of it?"

"I did, but she was resolute. There was nothing I could say that she would listen to," Misna shrugged.

"So, do you think they'll be all right?" Kasnata repeated her question.

"I don't know," Misna sighed. "There are too many things that I don't have information about. I hope they will be successful, but–"

"But they are a Shadow, an assassin and a lady that hasn't been raised as a warrior," Kasnata finished Misna's sentence for her. "I agree. Do you have agents you can send to follow them?"

"No, they are all engaged at present," Misna shook her head.

"Then we must pray," Kasnata said firmly.

Mathias rode ahead of Mia and Joab, scouting the trail to the city. Joab and the Roencian had packed the horses with supplies for three weeks travelling in the cold, though the Shadow was certain the journey would take longer.

Mia wanted to get to Grashindorph as quickly as possible, refusing to set camp until it was almost dark and forcing Mathias and Joab to rise and pack the camp before the sun had risen.

They made quick time across the plains of Celadmore; they reached the outskirts of the city of Triban only a week after leaving Kasnata's camp. Mia was bone tired and Joab insisted they rest for a day in the city, and try to find some extra supplies.

Triban was one of the cities of Zenix, and had managed to avoid being ravaged by the war of the nine kingdoms. It had once been one of the Free Cities and still enjoyed a level of autonomy that the other cities of the nine kingdoms didn't. It had become a centre for refugees to pass through and trade in, and as such, the three travellers went unnoticed and unquestioned as they entered the city.

Joab found them accommodation at one of the nicer inns in the merchants' quarter. Mathias had suggested they stay in the weavers' district, but Joab had been concerned that Mia would attract too much attention. The merchants' quarter was much safer for Mia and the rooms at the inn were much more comfortable than any that they would find in the weavers' district.

Their horses were stabled at the inn, and the stable boys seemed to know their trade, so Mathias had no objection leaving them to their craft.

They ate in their room, a meal of salted beef stew, bread and some poor wine, but it was a welcome hot meal that was better than anything they had eaten since leave the war camp.

There were only two beds in the room, Joab had offered to take the floor, but Mia had insisted that they share a bed and Mathias take the other. No watch was set either; there was nothing about the city or the inn that raised the suspicions of Joab or Mathias. They bolted the door and barred the windows and settled down to sleep.

The sound of raised voices woke Joab in the early hours of the morning. He slipped out of Mia's arms and slipped out of the door to the landing to see what the noise was.

There was someone hammering on the door of the inn. The innkeeper had risen from his bed and was walking to the door with a candle to light the way when Joab appeared in the shadows of the landing.

"Hold your horses," the innkeeper yawned as he pulled back the bolts on the door. "People are trying to sleep upstairs—"

The innkeeper opened the door and a blade was slipped between his ribs. The candle was taken out of his hand as the man collapsed to the ground.

"Search all the rooms. Find the Lady Mia, kill everyone else," the Baron of Fintry ordered as he stepped into the inn carrying the candle.

Joab slipped back into the room and woke Mathias and Mia.

"Take her out of the window, get to the horses and run," Joab told Mathias as he and Mia quickly dressed.

"No, I won't go without you," Mia insisted. Joab clamped his hand over her mouth and the sound of feet pounding on the stairs could be heard.

"They've come to take you back to Grashindorph, you have to go. I'll be fine, but you need to get out," Joab whispered. He took his hand off Mia's mouth and she kissed him.

"I'm not running away," Mia said wrapping her arms around Joab's neck.

"You have to. Mathias take her."

Mathias put his arm around Mia's waist and lifted her off her feet. Joab removed her arms from around him as the door was kicked open.

The Shadow leapt back, only narrowly avoiding the sword of the first soldier through the door.

"I've found her!" the soldier yelled. Within seconds the room was filled with soldiers. The window was still barred, leaving the three trapped in the room. Mathias put Mia down and she clung tightly to Joab, who made sure that Mia was hidden behind him.

The Baron of Fintry was the last to enter the room. "You and you, go make sure everyone else is dead in this place, I don't want word getting back to the barbarian whore that we've got Mia until we've reached Grashindorph."

Two soldiers left the room and Mia shuddered as she listened to doors being kicked open and the sounds of people's protests being cut short.

"Well, well, Joab. Kidnapping nobles is a serious offence. The king has been baying for your blood since Mia disappeared. My lady, it is quite safe, you can return home to Grashindorph with us and escape the clutches of these rough men," the Baron of Fintry said as he set down the candlestick and removed his gloves.

"No, I won't go back," Mia said, her eyes screwed up as she hid behind Joab.

"Now, now, little girl, it may sound like I am giving you a choice, but you don't have one. You're coming back with me. Either you come quietly and you'll be treated nicely, or you can resist and things will get – unpleasant," the Baron said in a tired voice.

"You're not taking her," Joab growled. Mathias grabbed hold of Mia and pulled her away from Joab as the Shadow launched himself at the soldiers. He moved without warning and three soldiers were dead before the others had reacted. The Baron looked unimpressed as Joab killed one man after another,

"Do you think I would come with so few men?" the Baron

asked. Footsteps outside heralded the arrival of a second detachment of soldiers.

Mia screamed as the second detachment seized hold of Joab and forced him to his knees in front of the Baron.

"No, don't, let him go!" Mia tried to scramble free of Mathias' grasp.

"Joab, for kidnapping the Lady Mia and disobeying the king's orders, I have been authorised by his majesty, King Mercia Nosfa VI, to execute you," the Baron said with a measure of glee.

"The revolution is coming, Baron. You may think that your ambition and loyalty to the king will protect you, but you will be punished for what you have done in the name of duty and loyalty," Joab spat.

"And you are going to die for the same," the Baron said with a false smile. The Baron drew his blade and stabbed Joab in the chest. Joab coughed and choked as blood filled his lungs.

"NOOOOOOOO!" Mia screamed as Joab was thrown to the floor by the soldiers. "Joab! No, don't die," she cried and broke free of Mathias' arms.

The lady rushed to Joab's side, the Shadow was collapsed in a ball, struggling to breathe as Mia sobbed over him.

"Arrest him," the Baron pointed at Mathias. "I want him questioned on his part in all this."

The soldiers clamped Mathias' wrists in irons as the Baron

threw a sack over Mia's head and cords were brought forward to tie it around her.

Mia struggled and tried desperately to stay beside Joab, but the soldiers simply picked her up and carried her from the inn. Joab could do nothing but watch as Mia was carried from the room and Mathias was marched out after her.

"I'm sorry, old friend," Mathias whispered as he passed. Joab closed his eyes and listened to Mia's screams, knowing that he died trying to protect the woman that he loved and that loved him in return.

Kelmar waited until nightfall before he chose to approach the city of Delma. The camp of Kasnata was spread over such a wide area that the duke was worried they would be spotted if he tried to reach the city without the cover of darkness.

The men that had been with him had vanished whilst Kasna and Kelmar were in the Spire, so now the two travelled alone. Kasna's horse had become lame just outside the city of Calathia, so now the two rode on Kelmar's horse.

"If you want to go to your mother, I won't stop you," Kelmar said. The two were lying in the long grass that lay to the north of the camp, waiting for the night to set in.

"What would happen to you if you arrived back without your men and without me?" Kasna asked. Her head was resting on Kelmar's chest as he stared up at the sky.

"I'd be all right," Kelmar shrugged.

"Liar," Kasna shot back.

"I still won't stop you, if that's what you want," Kelmar said, tilting Kasna's chin up and gently kissing her.

"You could leave Delma and join my mother's army," Kasna smiled.

"No, not after what I did to Renta. No one would trust me and there are those that would kill me the first chance they got," Kelmar said, shaking his head.

"Then we go to Delma," Kasna said simply. Kelmar wrapped his arms around her and held her tightly.

"I won't let the king harm you," he assured her.

"I've made my choice, my love, whatever happens, I won't regret it."

The two lapsed into silence and drifted off to sleep. The day slipped by and the drop in temperature brought on by the crisp night air woke the pair. Kelmar sent his horse towards the city at a gallop, a decoy for those that were watching the city.

He took Kasna by the hand and led her further to the north, where the entrances to the mines beneath Delma were located. The mines had long since been abandoned, so the entrances were well concealed.

Kelmar navigated his way through the mineshafts that led to trapdoors in the basement of the Pick and Axe, a public house in the industrial quarter of the city.

The publican jumped with fright as the trapdoor was flung open and Kelmar leapt up through it, followed by a woman that looked like the queen laying siege to the city.

Trumpets sounded throughout the city and cheers went up from the people as Kelmar walked through the streets, leading the princess to the palace.

The doors to the palace were flung open and the king and queen appeared at the entrance to it. The king's face was drawn, and he looked to be ten years older than he had been the night that he had come to Kelmar in the Shango Desert.

"Finally, you have returned to us, and you bring such a prize with you. Duke Kelmar DeLacey, Regent of Delma, you have excelled yourself," the queen greeted Kelmar as she descended the palace steps to examine the princess.

"A fine prize indeed," the king said gruffly and walked back into the palace. "Have our army prepared," the king added as an afterthought.

"Of course, your majesty," Kelmar bowed.

"Have her taken to the dungeons," the queen ordered.

"Your highness, if I may," Kelmar stepped between the guards that moved to arrest Kasna and the princess.

"Yes, Regent?"

"If it pleases your majesty, I would claim her as my reward for my duty," Kelmar said quietly.

The queen smiled and nodded,

"Very well, take her to the Regent's quarters and have her prepared for him," the queen ordered. Kelmar watched as Kasna was marched up the steps to the palace and shuddered at what would have happened to her if she had been taken to the dungeons instead of his quarters.

"Sir, the men are awaiting your orders," a lieutenant saluted Kelmar, who turned his attention back to his duty and went to inspect the soldiers.

Mia was not returned to Grashindorph as a noble, but as a prisoner. She was flung into the dungeons, chained to the walls and left to regret running away from the king.

Mathias was tortured for hours by the Baron of Fintry, but the assassin refused to give him any information. The pain was unbearable, but Mathias was glad that it was the Baron conducting the interrogation, not Neesa.

Each day he was whipped and marched through the streets of Grashindorph before being returned to be tortured by the Baron. He was denied sleep and food, given only half a cup of water a day, but still Mathias did not break.

"What do you want me to do with him, your majesty?" the Baron asked Mercia.

"Have a bag placed over his head, his body stripped and placed in the cell that the general was in. We'll tell the people we have recaptured the escaped traitor and hang that man instead," Mercia ordered. "Where is the woman?"

"If you follow me, your majesty," the Baron led the way through the maze of corridors that led down to the dungeons and unlocked the cell that Mia was chained in.

Mercia marched into the cell and slapped Mia across the face with the back of his hand. Mia yelped as she hung helplessly on the wall of the cell.

"You ungrateful bitch," he snarled. "First your brother is a traitor, then you take up with your bodyguard. Your lover is dead for his crimes, and your brother will soon hang for his," the king leaned in and spat down Mia's ear. The girl shuddered and wished she had died with Joab.

"What is going to happen to me?" she breathed.

Mercia grabbed her by the chin and wrenched her face

towards his.

"You are going to be my wife. You are going to sire an army of sons for me and play the faithful wife. You will never disobey me; you will never take another lover. I will have my sons so that I can be free of the influence of barbarians on my bloodline. My descendants will be of pure royal blood. I will sire wives for those sons with the daughters of other nobles and create the most powerful dynasty to ever grace the face of Celadmore," Mercia spoke inches from Mia's face and aggressively kissed her when he had finished.

Mia bit the lip of the king in an effort to stop his unwanted advances, but the act of violence only made the king more aggressive. Mia felt her body being crushed between the king and wall. She gasped for air. The king moved his lips down to her neck and bit hard, his teeth breaking the skin and causing her to cry out in pain. He ripped her clothes from her body and ran his hands over it.

Mia closed her eyes and cried as the king forced himself on her. Her lover was dead and Mathias was being tortured, all because she had run away. Run away only to end up back in the hands of the man she had so desperately wanted to escape from.

"What if I refuse to be your wife?" she sobbed when the king was done.

"You will stay here in this dungeon and my men will ravage you until you are unable to breathe. I will then send you to the worst brothel in the city where you will be abused by some of the roughest men to ever be born in this land, and you will die a painful death. Your body will be thrown in the gutter to be eaten by the dogs and you will be forgotten by everyone."

Mia closed her eyes, not sure which fate was worse.

"I am announcing our betrothal at sunrise. You will stay here until our wedding day," Mercia said as he left the cell, leaving Mia naked and hanging on the wall.

"Are you satisfied?" the Baron asked as the king made his way out of the dungeon.

"Send Lieutenant Thomas Regus down there. I want him to show her what fate will await her if she decides to refuse me," the king replied.

Mathias didn't know where he was or what was happening; only that it was cold. He had a bag thrown over his head, a chain clamped around his neck as well as round his wrists and ankles and was dragged out into the city.

He knew he had to survive, escape somehow and find out where Mia was, but he had no plan or allies in the city.

"You would have thought they'd change the locks," a voice tutted somewhere close to where Mathias was sat. He heard a metal door being heaved open and the footsteps of a few men approaching.

"They're soldiers. They aren't paid to think," a familiar voice replied.

"Rathe?" Mathias asked reaching out to where the voice had come from. He felt a warm hand grasp his.

"Keep your voice down, Mathias," Rathe replied. Mathias heard a key grinding in locks as the chains were removed from his wrists, ankles and neck. The bag was gently pulled off his head and a cloak was draped around his shoulders.

"You escaped?!" Mathias couldn't hide his surprise.

"Thanks to Helez and Asahel, yes. What are you doing here?" Rathe asked as he picked up Mathias and carried him from the cell.

"You don't need to carry me," Mathias sighed.

"You've lost a lot of blood and you're much thinner than the last time I saw you, carrying you is safer until you've got some strength back," Helez countered as he led the way through the dark streets of Grashindorph.

"Who are these two?" Mathias asked.

"Exiles from the Gibborim, enemies of the king, former Shields of Queen Hermia, allies to the house of Bird and all round good guys," Asahel said with a grin.

"You haven't told me why you are in the city," Rathe said as they rounded a corner and slipped silently up a rickety staircase.

"Mia, she wanted to come and rescue you. Kasnata couldn't

come; it would have signed your death warrant and Leinad's," Mathias explained as Rathe set him down on the floor of the loft. Asahel brought over a small amount of water.

"I know," Rathe said with a smile.

"Mia said she wouldn't let you die, she asked Joab and I to come with her," Mathias continued. "We got to Triban and took a room at the inn, but the Baron of Fintry came in the night."

"What happened? Where are Mia and Joab?" Rathe frowned.

"Joab is dead. Fintry executed him in front of us. He put Mia in a sack. I don't know where they took her," Mathias said helplessly.

"Here, eat this," Helez said, handing some small, hard biscuits to Mathias.

"She'll have been taken to the king," Asahel said sadly. "And Joab is dead? I'll send word to Layla; she'll want to know so the Gibborim can honour him."

"What does the king want with Mia? Do either of you know?" Rathe asked Helez and Asahel, as Asahel gave another small cup of water to Mathias.

"Not specifically. He has taken the daughters of many nobles as his mistresses, but he's never invested so much time or effort in reclaiming one that went missing like he was with Mia," Helez frowned and chewed his bottom lip.

"We need to find out, and we'll need somewhere better to hide. After two prisoners escaping, they will be searching the city much more thoroughly, trying to find us," Rathe said firmly.

"Do you have anywhere in mind?" Asahel asked.

"The tower of the church in the merchants' district. The king would never set foot in a place that honours the Goddess his wife worships and the soldiers would be too terrified to search it too carefully just in case the barbarian queen should appear and smite them for their sacrilege," Rathe smiled.

"Let Mathias rest for a few hours, then we'll move, I'll make sure we leave no sign that we were here," Helez grinned.

"I'll go out on the streets in the morning and see if there are any rumours of the Lady Mia that could be helpful," Asahel nodded.

Mathias sat and watched as the three men worked around him, gathering the few things that were in the loft. It was mostly weaponry that they tied into skins so they could be easily carried on their backs. Food was stuffed into satchels and water skins were collected from around the room.

The assassin found that his eyelids were growing heavy and soon drifted off the sleep, only to woken too soon to dress and move from the loft to the church tower.

Kelmar's horse had made it to the city without being stopped by the army of Nosfa or the Order. The beast was tired from trekking across Celadmore and so the king's destrier was saddled for Kelmar to ride.

The men were half-starved, their morale low and they were desperate for clean water, but seeing the duke back in the city with the princess of the Order had given them hope.

They would follow Kelmar without question, no matter how hungry and thirsty they were. Kelmar had split the forces into four divisions, three of them were to follow him and the forth was to break the dam, under the command of Colonel Deena Mae. Mae was a capable officer, and one of the few women to serve in the army.

She had been born to a noble house, but named barren by the royal physician, so was not permitted to marry. Deena had been Kelmar's childhood sweetheart, but the two had drifted apart when it was clear that they would never be able to wed. Deena had decided to serve her country in the military. Only women that were barren were permitted to fight or spy for their country. Those that could bear children were too valuable to lose in warfare.

It was an archaic policy that dated back to a time when plague had ravaged the city, effecting women of childbearing age more than any other demographic. The king had declared that the lives of women that could bear children were too precious to be thrown away in fighting or in other dangerous professions.

It was a law that had never been repealed, even now when

there were more women than men in the kingdom.

Deena had applied herself to her duty and proven not only to be one of the best commanders in the army, but a staunch ally to Kelmar.

The duke knew he could rely on Deena to break the dam and restore water to the city. Deena had chosen six men to go with her to the dam; the others were to remain in the city and supervise the citizens in storing as much water as they could in barrels and other containers. It would not take the Order long to block the supply of water once the army retreated back behind the walls.

Kelmar mounted the king's horse and drew his sword. The horns on the walls of the city didn't sound as the gates of Delma were thrown open. Kelmar led the army out in the early hours to attack the camp of Nosfa.

The men of Nosfa were still sleeping as the army launched its assault. Men were trampled underfoot as the men of Delma unleashed their fear and frustrations on their sleeping enemies.

Kelmar felt disloyal to Kasna as he led his men against the forces of her mother. He had placed himself in a difficult position, but he knew that in order to keep Kasna safe, he had to follow the king's orders, for now.

"The camp is under attack!"

The shout went up and the men further in began to stir to action, but without commanders, the men of Delma were slaughtering them.

Kelmar felt his blood stirring as he cut through men on either side; it was not the same thrill that came from battle, but something different, chilling, almost like a madness threatening to take control of him.

Harry and Jack were not asleep. They had been sat round the fire talking, Harry trying to convince Jack that Shaul and Methanlan had not betrayed their friendship, but rather saved their lives, but Jack still disagreed. They were arguing when the cry went up.

Chaos was everywhere as men fought in small pockets against a pincer movement that threatened to overwhelm the whole camp.

"Form up!"

The sound of two women shouting in unison brought a surge of hope to the army of Nosfa.

"Hawk division one!"

"Eagle division three!"

"Forward!"

Jack and Harry stared as Princess Kia of Nosfa and the Order and General Kia of the Order led two divisions of warriors forward. Methanlan and Shaul were riding beside the generals.

"Men of Delma, reform the ranks!" Kelmar shouted as he saw the approaching forces of the Order.

The men of Nosfa ran from the men of Delma to form their own lines behind the two divisions of the Order. Jack and Harry fell into line as well.

"Halt!" The two Kias ordered. The divisions stood as one and slammed their spears on the frozen ground. The light of the blood moon made the bloody scene in the camp of Nosfa look even more horrific than it was.

"Kelmar!" Princess Kia roared. "Where is my sister?"

"She is in the city, as my prisoner," Kelmar replied. He meant to sound reassuring, but Kia knew nothing of the duke's change of heart, only that he had taken her sister from her whilst threatening her life.

"Eagle division three! Destroy them!" she ordered. The men and women of her division cheered and threw their spears at the Delmarian lines.

"Hawk division one! Advance!" the Hawk General ordered. The men of Delma nervously held their line. The anger they felt at being subject to the siege was ebbing away as they were faced with the slowly advancing warriors.

"Eagle division three! Men of Nosfa! Forward," the princess ordered.

"Hold the line!" Kelmar barked as some of the men started to back away.

A few heartbeats went by, the roar of the men of Nosfa mixing with the battle cries of the Order, and then the sickening crunch of two lines colliding.

Princess Kia fought her way to Kelmar and rode at the duke with her full fury. She intended to spear his horse and then leap upon him on the ground, slicing his guts open and leaving him to slowly bleed to death, but Kelmar was ready for her.

"You would have been better shooting me with a bow," Kelmar grinned as he parried Kia's sword.

"How dare you!" Kia screamed and rained down blow after blow on the regent.

"You hate me this much for taking you sister?" Kelmar asked. He was not fighting back; merely block each of Kia's blows.

"I will see you dead for taking her from me!" Kia replied. "For murdering Renta, for destroying our home."

"From what your sister tells me of your treatment there, it was not much of a home to lament losing," Kelmar replied.

"You are not allowed to talk about my sister!" Kia yelled.

"I'm sorry about Renta. I can't explain or excuse what I did to her, and I know I will have to pay for my actions, but when this is done. If he still lives and I am still breathing I will gladly submit to whatever punishment Tola wishes to deal out," Kelmar said calmly.

Kia was thrown by Kelmar's words and almost lost her balance in the saddle as she stopped mid-blow.

"I can't return your sister to you, but as long as I am alive, she will be safe, even in Delma. I have sworn to protect her, and I do not go back on my word," Kelmar said, coming in so close that Kia could not use her sword. The princess stared at Kelmar.

"I don't trust you," she replied.

"I can understand that. But I love your sister. Whether you believe me or not, I will not see her harmed," Kelmar reined away from Kia to ride out to the flanks, where men were trying to run from battle.

Shaul's blade caught a strike that was aimed at the princess.

"Careful, your highness, don't get too distracted. It's not a safe place to sit and think," he smiled as he pushed aside the blade and kicked the soldier in the face.

"Yes, I'm sorry," Kia replied, shaking her head and re-engaging the enemy.

Jack and Harry fought side by side, the initial appearance of the Order had given the men of Nosfa the morale boost and the discipline that they needed to fight back against the assault from Delma.

Methanlan was not far from the two men, though he was sure that Jack hated him, the Queterian was making sure that the two men were not being overwhelmed by the men of Delma.

"Press the attack!" General Kia ordered.

The men of Nosfa and the warriors of the Order pushed forward, forcing the men of Delma back.

"Launch spears!" Kelmar ordered. The spears that the Eagle division had thrown were being picked up by the men of Delma.

Those that still had fine points were thrown back at their owners.

Jack blinked and ducked as a spear came dangerously close to his head.

"That was a close one, eh, Harry?" he breathed and looked at where Harry had been standing, but Jack couldn't see his friend. He looked over at where Methanlan was sitting on his horse, staring at something slightly behind where Jack stood.

He turned slowly, already knowing what he would see. Harry lay pinned to the ground. One of the spears had caught him in the chest, throwing him backwards. He was still alive.

Jack rushed to his friend's side and Methanlan kicked his horse over to the two men.

"Do something!" Jack demanded as Methanlan dismounted. The Queterian snapped the shaft of the spear.

"Help me get him on my horse; we'll get him to Payne," Methanlan said, and the two men gently lifted Harry onto the back of Methanlan's mount.

"Hold on, Harry. You'll be fine," Methanlan led his horse back to the camp of the Order, Jack running alongside, holding Harry in the saddle.

"Payne! I have a casualty," Methanlan shouted as he carried Harry into the tent. Payne took one look at Harry and shook his head.

"Heal him!" Jack shouted.

"You don't understand; it's not that simple," Payne said gently.

"I have seen you heal worse," Methanlan replied. "If you need blood, use mine. All I'm asking is that you try."

Payne closed his eyes and nodded.

"That bed. You, if you stay, you stay quiet," he said gruffly to Jack. Jack nodded meekly and grasped Harry's hand.

"You're going to be okay," he assured his friend.

Shaul watched Methanlan leaving the battlefield with Harry and Jack. He had seen that kind of injury before and knew that it was probably too late, even for Payne to heal him. Shaul couldn't help Harry, but he could protect the princess. He fought at her side, covering every opening that she left.

She was not lacking in skill, only experience, and Shaul was determined that she would live to reap the benefits of it. General Kia was keeping the line organised as Princess Kia led it forward.

"Sir! Colonel Mae sends her compliments, the dam is broken," a messenger reported to Kelmar.

"Excellent. Men, retreat by numbers 7, 3 and 5!" Kelmar ordered.

Horns on the battlements sounded as the men of Delma slowly retreated towards the city, Colonel Deena Mae's detachment joining with Kelmar's as they re-entered the city.

"Do not pursue them!" General Kia ordered and the line halted at the edge of the camp of Nosfa. There were many bodies that had to be buried and the camp had to be almost completely rebuilt.

The men of Nosfa were crying over their fallen comrades and picking up the pieces of their belongings that had been destroyed in the raid.

"Eagle division three, offer what assistance you can. If the men reject it, don't force your help on them," Princess Kia ordered and Shaul nodded his thanks to the princess.

"You fought well today," he said as they dismounted and moved through the camp together.

"Thank you, I know that I have a lot to learn still. I also know you saved my life more than once today. So thank you for that," Kia smiled at Shaul.

"It's my duty to protect a general of the Order as well as my princess," Shaul bowed ever so slightly to Kia. The princess smiled.

"Please, don't do that. No one has ever bowed to me before, I'm not sure that I want them to start now, especially not you," she said as she knelt down beside a man crying over three bodies.

Shaul watched as she talked to the man, who nodded and mumbled replies without even looking at her. When he finally did look up at the princess, he fell face down in the mud, bowing to her.

Kia looked at Shaul helplessly. The Queterian laughed and came to help the princess with the grieving man.

General Kia ordered her division to carry the wounded to

Payne. When she was sure that all the wounded had been retrieved, she went to the healer's tent.

Methanlan was sat with Jack at Harry's bedside. The man was white as a sheet, Jack gripping his hand tightly.

"Will he live?" the Hawk General asked Payne as he moved between patients.

"No, he has minutes to live at best. Methanlan gave him more time to say his goodbyes, but his injuries were too severe, too much damage to repair when his spirit is so weak," Payne said sadly.

The general nodded and watched as Harry lapsed into unconsciousness, his breathing shallow. Jack clung desperately to his friend's hand with both of his, shaking it, trying to wake up his friend. Harry's chest stopped moving and Jack repeated his name, over and over again, breaking down into tears.

Methanlan clasped his hand on Jack's shoulder as he collapsed to the ground sobbing. General Kia closed her eyes and said a silent prayer to Arala for Harry's soul.

"So much death," Kasnata said as she appeared beside the general.

"Kelmar led the assault. It was a distraction to break the dam," General Kia reported.

"Abendigo and his men are already working to rebuild it. The water they will have gathered may give them a few weeks of water, or perhaps a few months, but it will not be enough for them to outlast us,"

Kasnata assured her general.

"Yes, your highness, if I may, I'll help see to the wounded," General Kia bowed, and moved to help Payne. Kasnata walked over to where Jack sobbed and knelt down beside him.

"Your friend was a very brave man. You both did a great deal to help save the lives of all the men of Nosfa. I don't think I ever thanked you for that," Kasnata said softly.

"We're soldiers, Majesty, we don't need thanks," Jack said gruffly between sobs.

"Because you don't need them, doesn't mean you don't deserve them," Kasnata replied with a smile. "You may not want the friendship of the Order, but it is yours if you desire it. Methanlan will help you with Harry's body and you may ask any favour you like of me. You, Jack, will always be welcome amongst our people," the queen rose without waiting for a response and went to see the extent of the damage to the camp of Nosfa.

Kelmar didn't stop to be congratulated by the people that surged on to the streets, cheering at the water they were now collecting. His heart was pounding in his ears and the feeling in his blood; that same feeling that had driven him to murder Renta, was clawing at his mind.

He charged through the corridors of the palace to his quarters. He threw open the doors and found four women surrounding Kasna. One was pulling at her hair, trying to cut it, another was trying to pull her clothes from her, whilst the other two were dragging her towards the bath they had drawn for her.

"GET OUT!" Kelmar bellowed. The four women shrieked in fear and ran from the rooms, shutting the doors behind them.

Kelmar was trying to fight his way out of his armour, his movements frantic and his breathing laboured.

"Kelmar," Kasna's voice sounded in his ear. She was beside him in an instant. He felt her fingers unbuckling his armour and removing it from him; he collapsed into her arms and felt the feeling subside as she held him. "I'm here," she soothed as she held him, one hand stroking his hair, the other wrapped around his back.

"The battle, the feeling, it was worse than ever before," Kelmar breathed. "I had to stop fighting, ride the lines to escape it. I couldn't risk it."

"Couldn't risk what?" Kasna asked as Kelmar rocked back onto his knees, Kasna's hands on either side of his face.

"Killing your sister," Kelmar said, staring at the ground. "She hates me with a passion, she was determined to kill me, but I didn't fight back, I couldn't."

"Because of me?" Kasna asked. Kelmar nodded, and Kasna

kissed him.

"I told her that you were safe, that I would protect you, that I love you," Kelmar sighed as he pulled the princess into his arms.

"She wouldn't believe you. I'm not sure I believe it," Kasna laughed. Relief filled Kelmar as the clawing vanished. "You're covered in blood and dirt," Kasna said as she kissed Kelmar's cheek.

"Then I will not let the bath those harpies prepared for you go to waste," Kelmar said as he let Kasna stand and draw him to his feet. "You know, you aren't exactly clean after riding across the wilds," Kelmar teased.

"Is the bath big enough for two?" Kasna asked, leading Kelmar to where the pool was sunk into the floor.

"It's big enough for four," Kelmar replied with a slight laugh.

"I don't want to know how you know that," Kasna said with a raised eyebrow. Kelmar watched as she undressed, her eyes fixed on him as she did so, and slipped into the hot water. The duke removed the rest of his clothing and followed her.

Kelmar lay back in the water, resting his head on the side, letting the warmth of the water wash over him. He felt Kasna's hands on his chest as the princess straddled him.

Kelmar looked up at the princess with a quizzical expression.

"Have you ever fought in a battle?" Kelmar asked as he ran his hands over her hips.

"No, aside from the skirmishes with you," Kasna shrugged.

"They are not pleasant affairs," Kelmar sighed and closed his eyes as Kasna leaned forward and kissed his neck.

"Then what I do should be a distraction from it for you," she replied teasingly. "After all, I am your prize of war."

Kelmar pushed the princess back so that she was sitting upright.

"You heard that?" he asked with an angry tone in his voice.

"Yes," Kasna replied with a stony expression.

"You weren't meant to hear that," Kelmar breathed out with frustration.

"Because if I know how you think of me, I won't co-operate?" Kasna asked with an unimpressed expression.

"No, because it wasn't true. I had to say something to the queen to keep you from being held in the dungeons. The only thing Adina would agree to was you as a prize," Kelmar said defensively. "You are not my prize. I love you, I would die for you, I retreated from battle to keep from hurting you," he spoke rapidly, his fingers digging into the princess' waist. Kasna weighed her words before she spoke.

She reached for one of the cloths that lay in a pile beside soaps and creams around the edge of the pool. She dipped the cloth in the water and rubbed one of the soaps into it. She gently lifted Kelmar's head and used the cloth to softly remove the dirt and blood from his face, neck and ears. Kelmar closed his eyes and sighed with pleasure.

"I am your prize, or at least for tonight I am your reward. You didn't kill my sister and I have no other way to thank you than that," Kasna said as she removed the last of the dirt and kissed Kelmar. The duke sat up and pulled back from Kasna.

"I only want you if you want me," Kelmar said crossly. "You are not a prize or a reward for gallant behaviour."

Kasna sat in the water and smiled at him with a smug satisfaction.

"You are a cruel woman," he scowled at her.

"I love you," she replied. "I want you, and I am glad that you didn't die today."

Kelmar dunked Kasna under the water.

"That's for testing me," he said as Kasna threw the cloth at him.

"Clean your own face next time," she replied, sticking out her tongue at him. Kelmar reached for the soap and rubbed it into the cloth. He grabbed hold of Kasna and pulled her over so he could pin her against the side of the bath.

"Your turn," he said with a smile.

Outside the door, Queen Adina stood listening to the two talking. She frowned and clicked her tongue against her teeth.

Having Kasna in the city was dangerous, but it wouldn't be for too long. She would monitor the influence the young woman had over the duke and decide on whether direct action would be necessary.

Loved <u>Princess of Broken Dreams</u>? Get the next book in the series now!

An empress isolated. War rages on in an eternal winter under a blood moon created by dark magic. Can she bring an end to two wars, dark magic, and save those she loves from being lost to the darkness or will her final sacrifice be the greatest of all?

<u>Empress of New Beginnings is book 3 in Guardians of Light Saga. Buy it now!</u>

Thank you for reading Princess of Broken Dreams. I hope you enjoyed it! Want to read more about the adventures of the Kasnata before she became queen? Read the prequel trilogy for free by becoming part of my Ream Community! Click here to learn more.

Want to help a reader out? Review are crucial when it comes to helping readers choose their next book and you can help them by leaving just a few sentences about this book as a review. It doesn't have to be anything fancy, just what you liked about the book and who you think might like to read it. Leave a review for Princess of Broken Dreams here.

If you don't have time to leave a review or don't feel confident writing one, recommending a book to your family, friends and co-workers can help them choose their next book, so feel free to spread the word.

About the Author

I am a New Zealand resident, wife of a wonderful kiwi and we have two lovely cats. Fantasy has always been one of my favourite genres and something I have always loved writing in.

When I am not writing I love to spend time working in my garden and spending time lost in the worlds of other authors.

TikTok: https://www.tiktok.com/@miaheraldhillauthor

Website: https://reamstories.com/guardiansoflight

<u>Acknowledgements</u>

To my wonderful VA, Vicky, you have been such a great help and really are worth your weight in gold. For everything you do, thank you!

To my husband, thank you for being a constant source of love and support.

To you, my reader, thank you for taking the time to read this book, I hope you enjoyed it! Without you buying and reading my work, I would not have a career.